Edward moved quietly, hoping to surprise the intruder.

The sight that met his eyes as he pushed open the door was not what he expected at all. Standing in front of the fire was a young woman in the process of undressing. Edward swallowed. She had already shed her dress and petticoat and was now clad in just her chemise and stockings. Both items of clothing were soaked with rainwater, and the chemise clung to her body in a scandalous fashion, revealing much more than it was designed to.

As he watched, her chemise slipped from one shoulder, revealing the creamy white skin beneath. The young woman then bent down and started to unroll her stockings, sighing with pleasure as she peeled the wet material from her legs.

Edward knew he had already been watching for far too long to be considered a gentleman. Long-forgotten emotions were beginning to stir in his body and, as he watched the mystery woman arch her back and let her head drop backward, Edward felt a surge of desire.

Author Note

In my job as a doctor I am lucky enough to be a part of many people's lives. Sometimes it is my role to comfort them when they receive bad news, sometimes it is to celebrate when it is good. Often people just want to talk, to discuss the highs and lows of their lives and figure out ways to make it through the tough times. Over the past few years I have seen many suffer sad bereavements, lose the very people they got up for each and every morning, and I have marveled at their resilience and fortitude. Despite these devastating losses, these people struggle on, and after a period of time things do start to get easier.

Nevertheless I think the old adage "time heals" is only partially true. I believe that it is what you do with that time that helps the healing process, and this was a theme I wanted to explore in *Heiress on the Run*. Edward's bereavement is still fresh and raw while he locks himself away brooding; it is only as he begins to accept that there must be a future for him that he can truly begin to heal. In writing Edward's character I sometimes wondered if I had given him too much to bear, but I kept reminding myself of the real-life examples that show people can endure and can flourish again no matter what.

LAURA MARTIN

—

Heiress on the Run

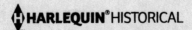

Recycling programs
for this product may
not exist in your area.

ISBN-13: 978-0-373-36948-5

Heiress on the Run

Copyright © 2017 by Laura Martin

This edition published by arrangement with Harlequin Books S.A.

For questions and comments about the quality of this book, please contact us at CustomerService@Harlequin.com.

Printed in U.S.A.

Laura Martin writes historical romances with an adventurous undercurrent. When not writing, she spends her time working as a doctor in Cambridgeshire, England, where she lives with her husband. In her spare moments, Laura loves to lose herself in a book and has been known to read cover to cover in a single day when the story is particularly gripping. She also loves to travel, especially visiting historical sites and far-flung shores.

Books by Laura Martin

Harlequin Historical

The Governess Tales
Governess to the Sheikh

The Eastway Cousins
An Earl in Want of a Wife
Heiress on the Run

Stand-Alone Novels

The Pirate Hunter
Secrets Behind Locked Doors
Under a Desert Moon

Visit the Author Profile page at Harlequin.com.

For Nic,
for all those marathon make-believe sessions.
One day I'll forgive you for Jasmine's head.

And for Luke and Jack,
you make all my dreams come true.

Chapter One

Amelia ran through the trees, ignoring the branches that whipped at her face and the brambles that caught at her skirts. She was exhausted, her lungs felt as though they were on fire and the muscles in her legs protested with every stride, but still she kept running. Risking a glance over her shoulder, Amelia stumbled, her ankle twisting dangerously to one side, but she caught herself and managed to stay on her feet.

A loud clap of thunder sounded overhead and seconds later the sky lit up with a fork of brilliant white lightning. Amelia felt exposed in the bright light, despite the camouflage of the trees, and was glad when the world returned to darkness again. Now the rain started in earnest, big droplets of water that pounded against Amelia's skin and soaked her within minutes. Her dress hung heavily against her, rubbing like sandpaper with every movement, and for once she wished she was wearing something more practical, less pretty, something that might keep her a little warm in this awful climate.

Pausing for a moment to catch her breath, Amelia listened carefully. She'd been walking over these God-forsaken Downs for the past two days, unsure where to go, where would be safe and offer her sanctuary. It had been bad enough when it was just cold and windy, but now, with the storm raging overhead, Amelia wondered whether she might die out here on these hills.

At least the village was far behind her now, the village that she had hoped might give her shelter for the cold night. That had been a bad idea. The first person that had caught a glimpse of her bloodstained dress and windswept hair had backed away, calling for her to keep her distance, and alerting the entire population to her arrival. She'd fled quickly, sparing a glance for the warm glow coming from the roadside inn, and continued her dash over the sodden hills.

Amelia was convinced the villagers would have sent people to follow her. Her face was probably on posters by now, her crime known far beyond the seaside resort of Brighton where it had been committed. She let out a small sob, wondering where everything had gone so wrong, and allowed herself a moment of self-pity. This was not how her life was supposed to be. Four days ago she'd had everything to look forward to: a new life in England, a reunion with the man she loved and a Season in London, whirling through ballrooms and sparkling in pretty new dresses. She had imagined being complimented and courted, not condemned and chased.

Straightening up, Amelia noticed a low wall on her left and a little further on a set of wrought-iron gates, easy to miss as they were so overgrown with curls of ivy and creepers. It only took her a second to decide what to do. Her feet were hurting, her entire body shivering and she hadn't slept for two days. The gates looked as though they belonged to an abandoned estate. If she was lucky there might be a barn or outbuilding still standing, somewhere to provide her shelter from the elements and to rest.

Cautiously she pushed open the gates and slipped through. As Amelia walked up the driveway a sense of unease began to uncurl inside her. The place had a ghostly feel to it and, if she wasn't so desperate to stop for the night, she might have turned back to look for alternative shelter.

The house was magnificent, in a dark and Gothic sort of way. Gargoyles loomed from precipices and the windows all tapered to elegant arched points. Statues and carvings decorated the spaces around the windows and doors, and towards the back of the house Amelia could see two imposing towers climbing up into the sky.

The estate was abandoned, Amelia could see that straight away. The house had an empty, disused feel about it even from this distance and the east side was blackened by fire damage. She wondered how long ago it had been abandoned and whether there might still be a soft bed to rest on inside.

Cautiously Amelia approached the front door and pushed it open, surprised to find it swung inwards without a creak or protest, revealing an empty hallway.

'Hello?' she called out before stepping over the threshold. 'Is anyone here?'

She waited for a second and then, hearing only the howling of the wind outside, she chided herself for the unease that prevented her from pushing the door closed behind her.

After another minute of silence she shut the door and stepped further into the hall. She had to wait for a moment until her vision had adjusted to the darkness before she could see anything properly. Summoning her courage, she walked down the hall, selected a door and pushed it open.

Amelia could see the room beyond must have once been a drawing room, or maybe a sitting room. A com-

fortable-looking armchair tempted her to take a step inside and once she was in the room she could make out the
other contents. Most of the furniture had been covered
over with white sheets, designed to keep the thick dust at
bay, and on the floor was a heavy, luxurious rug covering the floorboards.

Her eyes skimmed over the details of the room and
came to rest on the large fireplace set into one of the walls.
A spark of hope flared inside her as she saw the basket of
wood sitting beside it and visions of a roaring fire, warming her frozen limbs and drying her sopping toes, sprang
into her mind. She almost cried with relief when she saw
the tinderbox sitting on top of the mantelpiece. Finally her
luck was beginning to change.

The practicalities of starting a fire were much more difficult than Amelia had first envisioned. She'd seen fires
laid before—even in India they had needed fires in the
kitchen and sometimes in monsoon season a fire would
be lit to help dry out the clothes—but she'd never actually
taken much notice of what the servants were doing. Hesitantly she piled some wood in the grate, ensuring there
were some small pieces at the top, and then she set to work
on the tinder box.

Fifteen minutes later and she was just about ready to
throw the infuriating little box across the room. Her fingers
were aching from trying to strike up a spark into the tinder
and she had begun to shiver almost uncontrollably, which
didn't help with the delicate manoeuvres needed. With a
growl of frustration she struck the steel against the flint
one last time and almost cried with relief as a few sparks
flew out and ignited the tinder. Carefully she fanned the
flames, blowing softly, then touched the sulphur match
to ignite it, before lighting the taper. With delicate move-

ments Amelia knelt down in front of the fireplace and set about coaxing the wood to begin burning, feeling an unparalleled sense of satisfaction as slowly the wood began to blacken and the flames danced brightly in the grate.

Amelia almost flopped to the floor in exhaustion. The last few days had taken their toll on her not only physically but emotionally, and all she wanted to do was curl up and sleep, but she knew she would be at risk of a fever if she didn't get herself out of her wet clothes. With tired fingers she fumbled at the fastenings of her dress, wriggling and stretching to undo the buttons at the back. Finally she felt the heavy material drop to the floor and she was left standing in her long chemise and petticoat, with her mud-covered stockings on her legs.

She let out a gasp of horror as she looked down. The blood that had stained her dress had soaked all the way through to her undergarments and there were hideous pink patches covering her chemise and petticoats. Amelia felt momentarily sick and had to reach out to the mantelpiece to steady herself. For a few seconds she was back in Captain McNair's study, brandishing the letter opener that had slipped so easily into his soft flesh. Amelia heard a sob escape her lips at the thought of what she'd done, at the image of his bright red blood seeping through his shirt and the knowledge that she had committed the ultimate sin. For two days she had been running, desperate to get away from that cursed room, and she hadn't stopped long enough to allow herself to think. Until now. Here, with the heat of the fire finally warming her skin, Amelia knew her life would never be the same again.

Edward woke with a start. He had always been a light sleeper and any noise, even an animal call from half a mile away, was enough to rouse him from his dreams. For a moment he lay still, not moving a single muscle, but it only took a few seconds for him to be sure: there was someone in the house. He could hear them moving around downstairs, soft footsteps and the swish of material. Within seconds he was on his feet and felt a low growl issuing from his throat at the thought of an interloper in his domain. The cool night air hit his body, making him shiver, and a surge of irritation welled up inside him.

Swiftly he strode across the room, threw on a dressing gown and grabbed the poker from the fireplace in the place of a more conventional weapon. Despite his years of living alone Edward was confident of his ability to defeat any intruder even if they were armed. He wasn't a violent person and much preferred his books and his sketches, but at just over six foot tall he had a commanding presence.

Edward moved quietly, hoping to surprise the intruder before they had a chance to find a weapon of their own, making his way down the main staircase and pausing outside the sitting room.

The sight that met his eyes as he pushed open the door was not what he expected at all. Standing in front of the fire was a young woman in the process of undressing. Edward swallowed. She had already shed her dress and petticoat and was now clad in just her chemise and stockings. Both items of clothing were soaked with rainwater and the chemise clung to her body in a scandalous fashion, revealing much more than it was designed to.

As he watched her chemise slipped from one shoulder, revealing the creamy white skin beneath. The young woman then bent down and started to unroll her stockings, sighing with pleasure as she peeled the wet material from her legs.

Edward knew he had already been watching for far too long to be considered a gentleman, but later he would tell himself it was the shock of finding a half-naked woman in his sitting room. Long-forgotten emotions were beginning to stir in his body and as he watched the mystery woman arch her back and let her head drop backwards Edward felt a surge of desire. He wanted to scoop her into his arms, peel the remainder of her wet clothes from her body and lay her down in front of the fire.

Immediately Edward felt guilty for the thoughts. He loved his wife, missed her every day, but it was a long time since he'd had any human contact.

Just as he made to clear his throat he paused and frowned. He hadn't taken much notice of the state of the woman's clothes before, more surprised at her degree of undress than what she was actually wearing, but he now noticed the pink stains on her chemise and on the discarded dress that was draped over a chair. If he wasn't very much mistaken she was covered in blood and it didn't look as though it was her own.

Edward cleared his throat. The young woman turned round, her eyes widened and she screamed. It was an ear-piercing sound that bore right through Edward's skull and irritated him immensely.

'Will you be *quiet*?' he bellowed.

Immediately the young woman clamped her lips together. She started to back away from him, fear etched on her face, and Edward sighed. He wished he was back upstairs in bed instead of dealing with this melodrama.

He wanted to order this young woman out of his house, push her and her problems out of the door and forget she had ever been there.

'What are you doing here?' he asked, grimacing as the words came out more as a growl than a question.

'Please don't hurt me,' she stuttered.

'I'm not going to hurt you,' he said, in the friendliest

voice he could muster. He tried to smile, but the baring of
his teeth just seemed to make her cower away more and
whimper with terror.

Abruptly he pressed his lips together and took a couple of short steps across the room. He needed this young
woman to be conscious and coherent if he was to have any
chance of getting his solitude back as soon as possible. As
he approached she backed away and Edward saw her sway
slightly on her feet. For a terrible moment he thought she
might faint, leaving him to deal with an even bigger problem, but at the last moment she seemed to rally.

'What are you doing here?' Edward repeated, more
softly this time. He tried to remember how he'd inter-
acted with people in the days when he'd run a successful
and thriving estate and slowly opened his hands, palms
outwards to show he wasn't a threat, and made eye contact with the shivering young woman.

As he looked into her eyes he saw her relax just a little and Edward felt a spark of curiosity about the woman
standing in front of him. Now he was closer he could see
what a state she was in—not only was her chemise covered
in blood, but her entire body was caked in mud and grime.
Her legs had a myriad of scratches and bruises on them
and he had to wonder what trouble she was running from.

'I needed a place to rest for the night, somewhere to
shelter from the storm,' she said quietly.

Instinctively Edward knew there was so much more to it
than that. A well-bred young lady did not wander the hills
of Sussex all by herself covered in blood and soaked to the
bone. He opened his mouth to press her further and then
thought better of it. Whatever drama this young woman
was mixed up in, whatever it was she was running from,
he didn't want to know. He wanted his house back to himself and he wanted her gone.

'I thought the house was empty,' she continued after a few seconds. As she spoke her teeth chattered together and gave her voice a juddering quality.

'It just looks empty,' he said a little gruffly. 'You should go home.'

Quickly her frightened eyes darted to meet his and he saw a flash of desperation in them.

'I can't go home.'

'Then a friend, a family member. There will be some-one to take you in.'

His heart sank as she shook her head. Part of him was whispering she wasn't his problem, to usher her out into the night and forget she'd ever even been here.

'You could stay at the inn in the village.'

The look of panic that crossed her face momentarily piqued his interest, but he refused to be drawn in and quickly moved on.

'No,' she said firmly.

'What's your name?' he asked.

'Amelia.'

'Well, Amelia, you can't stay here.' He tried to say the words softly, but they came out as a harsh bark, almost an order. He watched as she recoiled from him as though she'd been slapped and felt a flash of guilt at the despair that permeated every inch of her body.

Silence followed as Edward waited for her response. As the seconds ticked by he could see her entire body shaking. The blood had drained from her face and suddenly Edward realised her eyes had become unfocused. If he wasn't much mistaken his intruder was close to collapsing.

With quick, purposeful strides Edward crossed the space between them, took hold of Amelia's shoulders and lowered her into a chair. He told himself he didn't want to have to deal with a head injury on top of everything else, but Edward knew his humanity was buried some-where inside him and chose moments like this to rear up and make him act like a decent person. As he touched the bare skin of her arms he was surprised at just how cold they were. He was no medical man, but Edward could see if Amelia didn't get warm and dry soon she would be in real danger of catching a chill, or worse. He remembered the time he and his late wife had got caught out in a storm on the edge of the estate—by the time they reached the house both were drenched to the bone, but whereas Edward had shaken the cold off Jane had been lain up with a fever for a week.

'You can't stay here,' Edward repeated quietly, almost to himself. In reality he knew if he sent Amelia back out into the storm in this state then she probably would die.

With a growl of frustration Edward hurled a cushion from the sofa towards the fire. It smacked into the mantel-piece with a loud thud before falling to the floor. He didn't want to be put in this position, held hostage by his own conscience. He wanted to return to bed in a house only he inhabited and not feel guilty about it.

Amelia looked at him with her large, dark eyes and Edward knew there was nothing else to be done.

'One night,' he said eventually. 'You can stay for one night. But you leave first thing in the morning.'

The relief on Amelia's face should have pleased him, years ago it would have. Edward could remember being the type of person that cared about others, that would go out of his way to help someone in distress, but that part of him seemed to have withered and died along with so many other characteristics. Once he had been kind and caring, but now all he could think about was how he didn't want this young woman in his house.

'What's your name?' Amelia asked, her voice not much more than a hoarse whisper.

'Edward. Sir Edward Gray.'

'Thank you, Edward.'

Next to him Amelia shuddered violently and Edward made a conscious effort to shift his full attention to her, pushing his own concerns to the back of his mind. A warm bed and a good night's sleep would be all Amelia needed to recover. If he sacrificed a little of his treasured privacy now he could send her on her way tomorrow with a clear conscience.

'We need to get you warm.'

Amelia looked at the paltry fire struggling to burn in the grate and shuffled a little nearer.

'Properly warm,' Edward said with meaning.

He hesitated for a few seconds. The last woman he'd touched was his wife, and she'd been dead for three long years. He couldn't even remember the last time he'd shaken someone's hand or laid a hand on someone's shoulder.

Quickly, before he could overthink things any further, he stood and carefully scooped Amelia into his arms. She let out a murmur of protest, but her heart wasn't in it. Already Edward could see the cold was affecting her brain, slowing her thought processes and making her sluggish.

He carried her through the house, up the stairs and into the West Wing where he kept his rooms. After the fire three years ago Edward had closed up most of the house, choosing to live his half-existence in the comfortable rooms of the West Wing rather than venture into the grander family rooms. The West Wing was warm and cosy, he'd had a fire burning in his bedroom grate earlier that evening and the embers would still be glowing.

'I feel so cold,' Amelia whispered, her body shuddering in his arms.

'You'll warm up in no time,' Edward said and for the first time in years he felt a sense of purpose. He would not let this young woman die. Even though he didn't know her or what she'd done he would offer her a warm bed and a safe place to rest.

Edward kicked open the door to his bedroom and set Amelia down in his armchair, pulling the heavy seat closer to the fire. He wondered if he had done enough now. With a glance at the door he weighed up his options: he could either leave Amelia here to fend for herself and retreat to the safety of the rest of the deserted house, or he could ensure she would not die from the cold in what remained of the night.

Now she was up here in his bedroom Edward had to suppress the trepidation that was creeping through his entire body. He had shut himself away from the world to avoid exactly these sort of interactions. After the fire he hadn't wanted anyone to venture into the house, into the space he had shared with his family. This was their private domain and he had tried to keep the memories alive by not allowing anyone else in.

Tonight, with Amelia shivering in the armchair his late wife used to sit in, Edward felt as though he'd already somehow desecrated those memories.

'You need to get out of those wet clothes,' Edward barked, knowing he was taking his displeasure out on Amelia, but unable to temper his tone. As he spoke they both glanced down to the almost-transparent chemise and Amelia shifted in embarrassment.

'I'll give you a nightshirt to wear. It'll be far too big, but at least it will be warm and dry.'

Edward crossed to his chest of drawers and selected a nightshirt, shaking out the creases as he returned to Amelia's side. Living alone, with no servants to surprise, Edward normally slept naked, but he had a nightshirt from the days the house had been bustling and full of life.

In the chair Amelia hadn't moved and Edward had to pause before he could see the gentle rise and fall of her chest.

'Will you be able to undress yourself?' Edward asked.

The image of him having to peel the wet chemise from her body, lifting it inch by inch to reveal the silky skin underneath, had imprinted itself in Edward's brain. He swallowed, closed his eyes, and rallied. He had been without a woman's touch for a long time, but that was no excuse for the entirely inappropriate thought.

He didn't wait for her reply, instead throwing the nightshirt down on the empty armchair by the fire and striding out of the room.

Once outside Edward rested his forehead against the cool stone wall and tried to quash the contempt he was feeling towards himself. For three years he had consoled himself by promising to always remain true to his late wife, and the first time he was tested, the first time a pretty young woman stepped into his world, he allowed his imagination to run wild.

He waited a few minutes, then knocked on the door. When he didn't get a reply he hesitated before opening the door and stepping back into the room.

Amelia had managed to finish undressing herself and don the nightshirt Edward had found for her. The blood-stained chemise was hanging over a chair. Now it wasn't plastered to her body Edward could see just how much blood there was.

'What happened?' he asked sharply, pointing at the bloodstains.

Amelia turned and looked at him with vacant eyes and just shook her head.

Part of Edward wanted to drop the topic. What did it matter to him how she had got to be covered in blood and running through a storm? She'd be gone tomorrow, out of his life never to return.

'Tell me or you can leave,' Edward said firmly.

The frightened eyes that looked back at him were almost enough to make him regret the threat.

'I was attacked,' Amelia said.

'You're hurt?'

She shook her head. 'I fought back.'

For now that would have to be sufficient. Edward knew enough about human nature to be sure Amelia wasn't a threat. He didn't want to be drawn in to whatever trouble she was in, so he let the matter drop.

'Get to bed,' he said. 'I'll see you in the morning.'

He turned and began to walk towards the door, pausing only when he realised Amelia had not even made an attempt to move.

'You'll be warmer in bed,' he said more softly.

She nodded her head, a minuscule movement which seemed all she was able to do. Edward waited for a few more seconds, just to see if she would move, before realising she was just too exhausted to take the few steps to the bed. Cursing under his breath, Edward strode back to her side and without asking permission he swept her up in his arms, carried her over to the bed and deposited her underneath the covers. The encounter must have only lasted ten seconds and throughout Edward gritted his teeth and concentrated on not becoming aware of the contours of Amelia's body in his arms.

Efficiently he pulled the sheet and blanket up to Amelia's chin, stood back and nodded in satisfaction. For a man who had barely spoken to anyone for three years he was rather pleased with his hospitality.

Amelia's teeth began chattering and he could see her body spasming under the covers. Gently he leant over and touched her cheek. Her skin was still icy cold and had that worrying clammy feel to it. Edward hesitated. He wanted to leave, to retreat to another part of the house and sit out the night, waiting for the moment he could send Amelia on her way. He glanced down at Amelia again. Her lips had an unhealthy blue tinge and there were deep black rings surrounding her eyes.

Edward didn't want Amelia here in his bed or in his house, but now she was he wasn't going to let her die. He couldn't have another death on his conscience. He knew the best way to warm a freezing body, but it felt wrong. Amelia let out a pained moan, her whole body convulsing, and Edward heard her begin to sob.

'You're going to be all right,' he said as he slipped into the bed behind Amelia and looped his arm around her.

Through the covers he felt her stiffen as he made contact with her body. He wondered if she would throw him out, demand he leave her alone despite her desperate need for warmth. After a few seconds of indecision Edward felt her relax a little and bury her body closer to his, luxuriating in his warmth.

It was an unfamiliar sensation, having a young woman's body pressed up against his own, and Edward found he kept having to remind himself exactly why he was doing this. He would take no enjoyment out of this situation, but despite his determination he found himself gripping Amelia just a little tighter. For years he had denied himself any human contact. Only now he was lying with a strange woman curled up against him in bed did he realise quite how much he'd missed another's touch.

Chapter Two

Amelia awoke slowly, revelling in the warmth of her bed and the comforting presence beside her. For just a few moments she was back in India, lying beside her cousin Lizzie, and her life was easy and pampered. Her eyes fluttered open and as she stared at the unfamiliar ceiling the events of the past few days came crashing back.

Warily Amelia turned her head and almost jumped from the bed with shock. Lying beside her, an arm flung casually across her waist, was the man who had rescued her from the cold, wet night and given her shelter. Forcing herself to remain calm, Amelia tried to piece together what had happened the previous night. She remembered seeking refuge from the storm and nearly dying from fright when Edward had surprised her as she'd undressed in front of the fire. After that her recollection of events was patchy at best. She had a vague feeling he had carried her through the house, but she couldn't remember how she had got out of the rest of her wet clothes or just what had happened to mean they ended up sharing the same bed.

Risking another glance at the man beside her, Amelia studied his face. He looked youthful and innocent whilst he slept, the frown she remembered from the previous night smoothed over as he relaxed in his sleep. He had a shock of dark hair, too long to be fashionable, and strong, manly features. Edward was the complete opposite of McNair, who was lithe and slender and beautiful.

Choking back a sob, Amelia remembered the events of three days ago and had to close her eyes as a wave of nausea overcame her. She'd killed someone. Never again would she wake up and not be a murderer. She might be a fugitive, running from the law, but McNair, beautiful, vibrant McNair, was dead and it was all her fault. Amelia could feel her hands shaking as she remembered McNair's gasp of surprise as the letter opener slid into his flesh and how after that one movement she had frozen, unable to let go, unable to pull away.

Beside her Edward stirred and Amelia rallied, pulling the bedcovers up to her chin.

It wasn't my fault. She repeated it to herself, forcing the disturbing images and memories from her mind.

She watched as the man beside her slowly emerged from his sleep. Amelia had never woken to a man in her bed before and it was fascinating to see how he stretched and wriggled before finally opening his eyes.

Edward's body froze and his eyes shot wide open the moment he saw her.

'Good,' he said gruffly. 'You're still alive.'

Amelia bristled. She wasn't sure what the etiquette was in this situation, but she rather thought he should greet her with something more poetic, more reassuring.

Without any further communication Edward swung his legs out of the bed and stood, gathering the dressing gown he'd slept in around himself. Amelia caught a glimpse of muscular legs and strong forearms before he was halfway across the room.

'What happened last night?'

Edward turned to face her.

'I remember you finding me in the drawing room, but not much else.'

He shrugged. 'You were cold. I put you to bed.'

A man of few words it would seem.

'And how did you end up in bed with me?' Amelia asked frostily. Two could play at that game.

Edward had the decency to colour a little, but otherwise he seemed unperturbed.

'You were shivering despite the fire and the blankets. I didn't want you to die so I added my body heat.'

He made it sound so detached, so clinical. Without another word he crossed to the door and opened it.

'Thank you,' Amelia said softly.

Edward turned around, gave a short nod, then left. Amelia stared open mouthed after him. Despite all her flirtations she was an innocent, but even so she knew a man of good breeding did not just run out on a woman he'd spent the night in the same bed with. She felt the irritation at being so easily dismissed build inside her and it was a welcome distraction from the guilt and despair she'd subjected herself to over the last few days.

With a huff she got out of bed, gathering the loose material of the nightshirt around her body and letting her bare feet sink into the plush woven rug. Slowly she started to explore the room, running her fingers over the well-made if slight tatty furniture and examining the paintings on the wall. As she came to the large desk set at one end of the room she paused, her eyes settling on the numerous pieces of paper scattered across it. Eyes stared up at her from beautifully rendered sketches, drawing after drawing depicting people as they really were, not the stylised creations you often saw in professional portraits.

'I've brought you some clothes,' Edward's voice came

from near the door. For a tall, powerful man he moved surprisingly quietly.

Amelia jumped back guiltily. She hadn't done anything wrong, the sketches had been lying on the desk, not locked away in a drawer, but still she sensed she'd trespassed on something very private and personal.

'Thank you,' she said, crossing the room and taking the clothes from Edward's arms.

'I will be downstairs in the kitchen. Once you're dressed join me. It's at the back of the house.'

'I'm sorry…' Amelia started to say, but Edward had already gone, closing the door behind him with a resounding thud.

Laying the clothes out on the bed Amelia was surprised to find the styles modern and the garments in good condition. She wondered why this strange, solitary man had women's clothes stored in the house. She couldn't picture him with a mistress squirrelled away somewhere— maybe a wife, someone mousy and quiet, but evidently not around any more.

Everything was too big on Amelia's petite form, but the clothes were clean and dry, and vitally not covered in blood. She badly wanted a bath, a long soak in a deep tub to clean all the grime from her body and soothe her aching muscles, but she sensed she was as likely to get that as the possibility of a man walking on the moon. So instead she scrutinised herself in the small mirror hung on one wall and tidied herself up the best she could.

Grimacing as she noticed the slight swelling to one side of her face, Amelia touched her cheek gently. She could still feel McNair's fist crunching against her delicate bones and quickly she squeezed her eyes shut to stop the memory of what happened next flashing before her eyes.

With great effort Amelia opened her eyes and tried out

a breezy smile. She needed Edward to let her stay here in this strange, half-derelict house, at least for a few days. McNair's death would have been discovered by now and someone would be hot on her trail. Even though Amelia knew she had committed an awful crime, she didn't want to hang for it. She felt remorse and regret, but truly it *had* been in self-defence. Nevertheless she had fled the scene and, as a young woman with no husband and her father many thousands of miles away in India, Amelia wasn't so naive to think she would get off lightly. No, the best course of action would be to hide away somewhere until her trail had gone cold and then find a way to fund her passage back to India. Her father would be irate, but he loved her and would make sure she was safe.

No one would think to look for her here in this house inhabited only by a reclusive bachelor. She just had to persuade Edward to let her stay for a few days, maybe a week. She wished she had something to offer, some practical skill that would make her indispensable, but her upbringing had consisted of painting watercolours, playing the piano and dreaming of a more exciting life.

Straightening her back, Amelia raised her chin and took a deep breath. She was Amelia Eastway. She'd never struggled to get men to do her bidding. Although she rather suspected she had never come across a man quite like Edward before.

Edward clattered around in the kitchen, his mood blackening with every second he couldn't find the bread Mrs Henshaw had left him the day before. For three years he had lived undisturbed in his private refuge. Only Mrs Henshaw, his old housekeeper who had retired to a cottage in the village, came to visit him nowadays, bringing fresh food every few days and keeping the house from falling into complete disrepair.

Now his refuge had been invaded by an impish and vivacious young woman who had already started going through his private possessions. Granted the sketches had just been left lying on his desk, but when he'd first got into bed the night before he hadn't expected to start the morning with a stranger in his bedroom.

He needed her gone, Edward decided as he located the loaf of bread and cut two thick slices. His reaction to her was uncomfortable and he knew it was more than a desire for a return of his privacy that drove that reaction. This morning as he'd woken to a warm, soft body in his bed he'd felt a primal stirring deep inside him. It was absurd and now Edward was even more determined to hasten Amelia's departure from his house.

'Do you live completely on your own?' Amelia asked as she swept into the room. For such a petite little thing she had a way of commanding your attention. A breezy smile was affixed to her lips and Edward wondered again what pain she was trying to hide.

'Completely. My old housekeeper visits twice a week to deliver some food and other essentials.'

'You don't go down to the village?'

Edward shook his head, trying to ignore her incredulous expression. He had ventured out in the painful months after the fire, but the looks filled with pity and the expressions of concern had soon put a stop to his trips to the village.

'I have everything I need here,' he said brusquely, trying to discourage her from asking any more questions.

Amelia wrinkled her nose and looked around.

'Don't you get lonely?' she asked. 'Or bored?'

'No. Not everyone likes chattering away incessantly.'

Amelia looked at him as if she expected him to elaborate further.

He had his sketches and his books, he still kept an eye on the running of the estate, although he had a reliable steward who did most of the work for him. As for loneliness, it was a welcome penance for the guilt he felt for surviving the fire.

'Maybe you would like a little company?' Amelia asked, with a quick glance at his expression.

Edward's first instinct was to march Amelia straight out the front door that instant, but then he paused. She'd survived the night and was back on her feet, there was nothing to hinder her departure today so he could afford to be a little more courteous.

'I can be very good company,' Amelia said.

She might think herself a woman of the world, this little minx, but he could tell straight away that she was innocent in many of her ways.

'Company?' he asked, raising an eyebrow.

Immediately he saw the colour start to rise in her cheeks and her bottom lip drop slightly.

'Not like…that is to say…'

'I know we shared a bed last night, but I am not that sort of gentleman,' Edward said.

'I wasn't suggesting…'

'I'm teasing you,' he said, knowing his serious expression didn't quite tally with his words. Maybe he should stick to his more sombre demeanour.

'Oh. Of course.'

Amelia drummed her fingers on the table as she struggled to regain her composure and Edward took the opportunity to study her properly. She was pretty, there was no denying it. Petite and slender with large brown eyes and soft blonde hair. The sort of young woman who would cause a stir when making her debut in society. His keen artist's eye also caught details others might not notice: the nervous energy that stopped her from standing still for more than two seconds, the little pucker in the skin between her eyebrows that appeared when she was thinking and the way she sucked her bottom lip into her mouth as she decided what to say next.

She was nervous, Edward realised, more nervous than the circumstances should warrant. True, she was in a strange house with a reclusive man, but she'd survived the night unmolested—most young women would solely be concerned with how to leave with their reputations intact. Edward didn't think it was her reputation she was worried about, there was something much bigger going on in Amelia's life.

He thought back to the blood-covered clothes and the panicked state she had been in when he'd first found her almost collapsed in his sitting room. Last night she'd said she had been attacked and had fought back, but Edward sensed there was more to the story than that. For a few seconds he deliberated, wondering if he should delve deeper, find out exactly what sort of trouble Amelia was in, but he knew that would just prolong the time until he could usher her out of his life so he kept his mouth shut.

'Maybe I could stay for a few days?' Amelia suggested, looking up at him hopefully.

For all her beauty and feminine wiles, Edward could read her easily. She might think she was an enigmatic young siren, but every emotion was written across her face just as soon as she experienced it.

'No.'

'No?'

'No,' Edward repeated. It would be a bad idea. A terrible idea.

'You can't just say no. Why not?'

He guessed she was an only child. There was a sense of entitlement about her that suggested she had been spoiled most of her life.

'I can. It's my house.' Edward grimaced and then relented. He was not a child and he would give her a proper answer. 'I live alone. I like living alone, and in a few hours I will go back to living alone.'

Her face fell and he tried to soften the blow.

'Besides, your reputation would be in tatters if you stayed here with me unchaperoned.'

'What reputation?' Amelia murmured under her breath. 'I don't care,' she said louder. 'I could tidy the place up a bit,' Amelia suggested.

'Do you have much experience at domestic chores?'

Amelia bit her bottom lip again. Edward felt the pulse of his blood around his body as his eyes flickered to her lips. 'No,' he said much more brusquely than he had intended, 'I didn't think you did.'

'I could cook you a decent meal at least.'

Edward looked down to the two roughly cut chunks of bread and sighed.

'I'm sorry, Amelia, but the answer is still no. After breakfast I will take you down to the village and you can catch the stagecoach to London.'

'I don't have any money.'

'I'll pay.'

'What if I don't want to go to London?'

'Then you can get off at one of the stops beforehand.'

She fell silent, but Edward could see the cogs turning inside her head as she tried to think of another excuse not to leave. He wondered why she wanted to stay so badly and what it was she had been running from the night before. Just as he opened his mouth to ask, he once again caught himself and silently shook his head. It wasn't his place to get involved. Later, when Amelia was safely on the stagecoach to London, he could brood over his life-style decisions, but the fact was right now he didn't want to delve deeper into Amelia's problems and if that made him unsociable that was fine by him.

Chapter Three

Amelia fidgeted as Edward placed a thick coat over her shoulders. She didn't want to leave. Somehow this strange half-derelict house felt safe, and once she was out in the real world again she knew it was only a matter of time before the consequences of her deeds caught up with her.

'Maybe I could stay for lunch?' Amelia suggested.

'I don't have any food in the house.'

The man was infuriating. Every suggestion she came up with he shot down with that calm tone of voice and unshakeable demeanour.

'I think I left something upstairs.' Amelia was beginning to panic now. The outside world was looming closer and she didn't know if she could cope with another indeterminate period on the run.

'You didn't bring anything with you.'

Amelia scrabbled for something, anything she might have left behind, just to buy herself a few more minutes. She needed to think of a reason to stay, something that would convince Edward it would be in everyone's best interests.

'Please,' she said quietly, 'I can't go out there.'

This quiet plea made Edward pause and for a moment Amelia thought he might relent.

'Why not?' he asked.

Amelia swallowed and bit her lip. She couldn't exactly tell him the truth. Admitting she was a murderer would only speed her departure from the house, not prolong her stay.

With wide eyes Amelia felt the desperation and despair all come crashing together and knew she had everything to lose. If Edward insisted she leave, she had no doubt whoever it was that was chasing her would catch up with her within a day or two. She couldn't sustain her progress any longer, she was exhausted and her feet covered in blisters. Here she had a chance at avoiding the hangman's noose and she realised she would do anything for it.

Straightening her back and lifting her chin, Amelia looked Edward directly in the eye and smiled shyly at him.

'If I stay we could get to know one another better,' she said, trailing a finger up his arm.

Edward stood completely still, his eyes following the progress of her finger. The heat began to rise in Amelia's cheeks, but she knew she had to give this her best shot. Humiliation and ruin was nothing compared to being found guilty of murder.

'I promise I'm very good company.' She didn't even really know what that meant, but she'd overheard some of the less virtuous women use the phrase at a regimental party a few years ago.

Edward took her hand, removed it from his arm and let go, allowing it to drop back to her side. His face was stony and devoid of expression and his movements almost stiff. Amelia felt the flood of shame wash over her. In a way it would have been better if he'd laughed, at least then she would have known he wasn't disgusted by her proposition.

'It must get lonely, living here all by yourself,' Amelia said, giving it one last try. She was desperate and she knew she sounded desperate, but she didn't care. Self-preservation was at the top of her list of priorities, she would have time for embarrassment and regret when she was safe.

'Come on, otherwise we will miss the stagecoach.' Edward said, ignoring her last few comments. He didn't sound angry or disgusted, just tired and worn down, and for a moment Amelia wondered why he was so keen to get rid of her.

Amelia dawdled a little longer, wasting as much time as possible fiddling with the laces on the boots he'd found her and adjusting the bodice of her dress.

Eventually Edward sighed, gripped her arm and led her firmly out of the front door.

It was a cool day, clear and crisp after the storm of the night before. Amelia huddled into the cloak draped around her shoulders and reluctantly allowed Edward to lead her down the sweeping driveway.

'I could tidy up your garden,' Amelia said without much hope as they passed another overgrown flowerbed.

'I like it this way.'

'No, you don't.' No one could. The garden had potential, great potential, and Amelia could see a few years ago it would have looked much different. Someone had lovingly planned and planted, landscaped and tended, but it had fallen into ruin along with the rest of the house.

Edward shrugged again, that infuriating movement he seemed to favour when she challenged him about anything, and continued his steady pace down the driveway. Amelia glanced back at the house and found her heart sinking. Every step they took resulted in her being further away from the place that she'd hoped would be her sanctuary for a few days. She felt like turning and running back inside, slamming the door and locking it shut.

'The village is only twenty minutes away,' Edward

said as they reached the wrought-iron gates Amelia had squeezed through the night before. 'If you don't walk at the pace of a lethargic snail,' he added under his breath as she lagged behind, dragging her feet.

She watched as he tore some of the overgrown vegetation from the bars of the gates, frowning thoughtfully as he did so. Amelia wondered if he saw the house and gardens as she did, with all the cracks and faults, or if when he looked around he saw the place as it used to be.

As Edward pushed open the gates Amelia felt an icy stab of panic jolt through her body. Inside the estate grounds she felt peculiarly safe and now she was being asked to step over the threshold. Out here, in the wider world, who knew what awaited her.

As if sensing her reticence to step through the gates, Edward paused for a moment and looked at her with his searching brown eyes.

'The road is clear,' he said, 'So unless there's any further reasons you can't possibly leave shall we be on our way?'

For a second she almost blurted it all out. It would be a relief to share what had happened with someone, to tell the whole sordid tale. She wondered how Edward would react, if he would respond kindly and calmly, or push her away. Maybe he would let her stay, take pity on her and agree to shelter her from the world. Or maybe he would turn her over to whoever was hunting her down.

Unconsciously she raised a hand to her throat, rubbing the skin of her neck at the thought of a noose tightening around her throat.

'Nothing,' she replied eventually. She would be safer if no one else knew what she had done.

'The coach runs to London in one direction and

Brighton the other,' Edward said, disturbing Amelia from her thoughts.

She nodded absentmindedly.

'Would you prefer to go to Brighton or London?'

Dear Lord, not Brighton, Amelia thought.

'London. Definitely London.'

'Do you have any family there?'

Amelia shook her head. It was a lie, but a necessary one. It wasn't as though she could turn up on her aunt's doorstep, it would be the first place a magistrate would look for her.

'How about friends?'

Again Amelia shook her head.

'Where are your family?'

She sensed Edward was starting to feel a modicum of responsibility for her. He might not want to let her stay in his strange house, but he wanted to make sure she was safe all the same.

'India.'

'Ah. I see.' He paused for a few seconds. 'Surely you didn't come over here on your own?'

Amelia stopped walking and waited for Edward to turn.

'I'm out of your house and soon I'll be out of your life,' she said coolly. 'After today you will never have to think of me again. I have no friends or family in this country, but as you have made clear, that is not your concern.'

She saw the flicker of hurt in Edward's eyes and for a moment she felt remorse. Her cousin Lizzie always said she had a sharp tongue and Amelia knew she often spoke before she'd had chance to think through what impact her words might have. Edward was kind, for all his brusque manner, and he had taken her in for the night when others might have thrown her out. It wasn't his fault she was in such a mess, but she was just wishing for a reprieve, a few days to decide what to do with her life, and Edward couldn't give that to her.

'Come on,' he said stiffly and began walking again.

Amelia watched his back for a few seconds before hurrying to catch up. He was a tall man, with broad shoulders, a strong man. He emanated power and Amelia found herself wishing to be enveloped in his arms, pressed up against his chest and kept safe.

Trying to suppress the thought as she drew level with him, Amelia risked a sidelong glance. In his own way he was handsome, she supposed, although not in the same way McNair had been handsome. Edward had strong features and kind eyes, but he had a slightly wild look about him with his tousled hair and creased shirts. McNair had always been beautifully presented, but thinking back there was a coldness about him, a calculating, detached look on his perfectly symmetrical face.

After ten minutes they reached the outskirts of the village, with a few simple cottages appearing on either side of the lane. Amelia felt herself instinctively hunch her shoulders, trying to appear less conspicuous. Although there wasn't anyone around at the moment, she felt nervous and frightened all at the same time.

The small cottages gave way to bigger dwellings once they reached the village proper and as they turned on to the high street Amelia froze. People were milling about, women walking arm in arm and talking, men going about their business with purpose. Beside her Amelia felt Edward go still at the same moment she did and she wondered fleetingly how long it had been since he'd visited the village.

All thoughts about Edward's lifestyle were swept away as he took her arm and guided her down the high street.

People were looking at them strangely, a couple of women actually pointed and stared, and Amelia knew it would only be a matter of seconds until some officer of the law clamped his hand on her shoulder and hauled her off to face the consequences of her crime.

As they reached the clock tower that stood proudly in the middle of the village square Amelia caught a glimpse of a smartly dressed man coming out of a small shop. He looked out of place in this small village, his clothes were too well tailored, his hair too well groomed. It was obvious from a single glance he was an outsider.

With a pounding heart Amelia grasped Edward's arm and pulled him behind the clock tower, squeezing her eyes shut as she did so, wishing she could just will the well-groomed man away.

'Amelia?' Edward asked, his voice a mixture of concern and irritation. He probably thought she was just trying to waste more time.

'Shh,' she hissed.

'What's wrong?'

'Everyone's looking at us.'

Edward chuckled, the first real laugh Amelia had heard him utter.

'Do you think it might be because you're acting so strangely?'

Amelia opened her eyes and looked up into Edward's face, frowning.

'They're looking at me,' she insisted.

He shook his head, a self-deprecating little smile playing on his lips.

'I think they're probably looking at me. I am rather notorious. The recluse of Beechwood Manor.'

Amelia paused and glanced out from behind the clock tower. No one was coming for her—in fact, everyone had just returned their attention to whatever it was they'd been doing. Maybe Edward was right, maybe it was him they had all been staring at.

'What are you afraid of, Amelia?' Edward asked.

He reached out and touched her gently on the arm and Amelia found herself looking up into his concerned face. Edward had been generous to her, she couldn't deny it. He'd allowed her to stay and ensured she was warm and dry for the night, but until now she hadn't really caught more than the occasional glimpse of his kind side. His outward demeanour had always been stern and distant, but right now there was warmth in his eyes, genuine concern and compassion. She sensed this was the man he really was, his true nature, and the gruffness was a wall he erected to keep everyone at bay.

For a moment the rest of the world disappeared, the noise of the villagers going about their daily lives faded into the background and it was just the two of them, hidden in their own little world behind the clock tower. Amelia wondered what it would be like to raise herself up on her toes and kiss Edward, to allow him to fold her in his strong arms and protect her from the world. She felt her body sway slightly, her lips part with anticipation, but just as she began to lean in McNair's face flashed before her eyes.

The last time she'd kissed a man it had ended in tragedy. She wouldn't allow it to happen again. She couldn't be trusted, her instincts had been proven to be wrong before and just the fact that she felt attracted to Edward should be enough to tell her to stay well away.

Edward saw the moment Amelia's eyes glazed over and her lips parted. He had been without female company for a long time, but in his youth he'd experienced enough to know when a woman wanted to kiss him. She'd even began to lean in, swaying towards him, but then something had happened. Amelia had stiffened, a look of horror had passed over her face and now she'd backed away to a more respectable distance.

He found himself a little disappointed. He shouldn't want to kiss this enigmatic little minx, but the idea of tasting her lips, just once, was rather enticing. Before he could stop the thought it had taken hold and all the guilt and feelings of betrayal it conjured up were right there with it. Quickly he balled both his hands into fists, digging his nails into his palms to try to distract himself. He knew his wife was dead and gone, nothing would ever bring her back, but he owed it to her to honour her memory.

'Shall we find the stagecoach?' Amelia said formally once she'd recovered some of her composure.

Edward stepped out from behind the clock tower and waited for Amelia to follow. Before she ventured out into the open square, she checked each direction, her head swivelling this way and that like a skittish horse.

'There's no one poised and waiting to attack you,' Edward said impatiently as she eventually stepped out into the square.

She gave him a withering look, still checking each direction every few seconds. He wondered what she was afraid of. There was an air of innocence about Amelia, the demeanour of someone who hadn't experienced much of the world on their own, so he couldn't imagine she'd got mixed up in anything too heinous, although maybe the bloodstains on her clothes were evidence against that opinion.

Edward gently took her hand and placed it in the crook of his arm and guided her further along the high street to the point where the stagecoach stopped to pick up passengers. Now they were nearing the point of farewell Edward felt a great weight being lifted from his shoulders. He had found it difficult sharing his home even just for one short night and was quite looking forward to getting back to the peace and quiet of an empty house. For a second he felt a pang of sadness. Once, long ago, he had enjoyed noise and company and laughter. With a sideways glance at Amelia he rallied. Now was not the time to waver in his resolution to put this troubled young woman on a stagecoach and wave her on her way.

If Jane were here, standing beside him and giving advice in that calm and sensible way of hers, she'd tell him to start living, to stop stagnating. She'd probably convince him to take pity on Amelia, shelter her from whatever trouble she was running from and learn once again to tolerate the company of others. Edward knew one day he would have to pick up the reins of his life again, to do more than spend his time sketching and reading, but with living came memories and he wasn't sure he was ready to confront those yet.

'You're looking rather serious,' Amelia said as they slowed to a stop at the side of the road.

'Do you need any money?' Edward asked, knowing he was avoiding Amelia's comment.

She bit her bottom lip and fidgeted a little. It was the curse of the human race not to be able to ask for monetary help when they needed it.

'Maybe just a little something to help you on your way,' he said, placing a hand into his coat pocket.

One second he was standing at the side of the road, reaching for his coin purse, the next he was lying in some rather prickly bushes with Amelia on top of him.

'What...?' he began, but Amelia pressed a finger against his lips.

He tried to speak again, but was silenced by the look

of pure terror in Amelia's eyes. For almost a minute they lay there, Amelia frozen by fear and he trapped under her body. They were half-hidden from the road, but if anyone walked passed they would have a lot of explaining to do.

When another minute had passed without Amelia explaining or letting him up Edward began to feel the damp from the ground soaking into his trousers.

'Will you tell me what's going on, woman?' he asked, quietly but firmly.

Amelia's eyes widened with shock and fear and immediately Edward regretted his tone of voice.

'Come, let's stand up,' he said more softly.

Amelia allowed him to help her to her feet, although he noticed she did not step back out on to the road, and her restraining hand on his arm stopped him from doing so too. For an instant Edward missed the warmth of her body as it had been pressed against his, but soon the feeling was replaced by irritation. The woman was crazy. First darting behind the clock tower and now wrestling him to the ground whilst they waited for the stagecoach.

'Is he still there?' Amelia hissed.

'Who?'

She didn't answer so Edward stepped forward and looked up and down the lane. It was completely empty. Maybe there was something not quite right in Amelia's head. She seemed normal, if not conventional, most of the time, but then she went and did things like this. Then he remembered the blood-soaked clothes and the state Amelia had been in the night before and softened slightly. Something bad had occurred in Amelia's life recently. That must be what was driving this fear.

'There's no one there.' Edward wondered if this was another of Amelia's time-wasting ploys, but the terror in her eyes convinced him otherwise.

Warily Amelia edged forward, peering out from the bushes until she was satisfied they were alone.

'I think you should tell me what's going on,' Edward said, in a voice that brooked no argument.

Amelia shook her head, tears forming in her eyes and spilling out to roll down her cheeks. Edward almost reached out to brush them away, but he stopped himself. It was an intimate gesture, too intimate. He couldn't believe he'd even contemplated it.

'Who did you think you saw?'

Again Amelia shook her head, still glancing furtively up and down the road.

Edward ran his hands through his hair and studied the young woman who stood before him. She was petrified, that much was clear. He didn't know if her demons were real or imaginary, but he did have experience with living with events he'd rather forget.

His brain screamed to let her go, to get back to his reclusive existence, but his heart recognised another wounded soul. He wanted to leave, to walk off down the road without as much as a backwards glance, but something was holding him back. Edward even tried placing one foot in front of another, but his body just wouldn't obey his commands. Something sparked inside him, something that he thought was long dead and buried. He wasn't sure if it was compassion or pity, but he realised he didn't have it in him to abandon Amelia here in such a state of dread. For years he might have suppressed his humanity through lack of interaction, but he'd been brought up to be kind and chivalrous and there were a few strands of those characteristics that refused to leave him despite years of disuse.

'Amelia, look at me.' He grasped her by the arms and turned her to face him. She looked distractedly around her. 'I will make you a bargain,' he said.

This caught her attention.

'You tell me exactly what is going on, what trouble you're in, and I promise to help you as much as I can.'

She shook her head, 'I can't.'

'Then you're on your own.'

Edward had only taken two steps before he felt her clutching at his sleeve.

'Please don't leave me here.'

It would be so easy to give in to her beseeching eyes, but Edward knew he had to stand strong.

'Then tell me what has you so scared.'

'I've done something terrible,' Amelia said quietly.

He looked at her youthful, innocent face, and wondered what it was she could have done that was making her quite so worried.

'What?'

He watched as her whole body began to tremble. With difficulty she rallied, squeezing her eyes tight for a few seconds before looking up at him with an expression full of pain and regret.

'I've killed a man.'

Chapter Four

Amelia sank back into the comfortable, worn armchair and closed her eyes for a few seconds. She felt exhausted, even though it wasn't yet midday. For the duration of the trip out to the village she had been petrified, in a state of high alert, seeing danger where there was none and ready to flee at the slightest provocation.

When she'd leaped into the bushes at the side of the road, taking Edward with her, she really had thought someone was looking for her. A tall, serious man with an official-looking uniform had started walking down the lane towards them and Amelia had been convinced this man had tracked her across the South Downs and was here to take her away to face justice. When she'd pointed him out to Edward on their return dash through the village he'd actually laughed before telling her he was the local postman.

After her confession Edward had gone quiet, studied her for some time, then started to lead her back through the village.

'We'll talk back at the house,' he'd said and hardly uttered a word after that.

Amelia wondered if she should be scared. He might be summoning the local magistrate right now, eager to hand

over the murderer sitting in his cosy armchair and be done
with the drama she had brought into his life. Although she
hardly knew the man, Amelia couldn't find it in herself to
be overly worried. He seemed fair and honourable, and she
thought he would at least give her the chance to explain
the circumstances before deciding what to do with her.

'Whisky,' Edward said as he entered the room, 'and
biscuits, it's been quite a morning.'

Amelia watched as he poured out two glasses of whisky
and handed her one. Cautiously she sniffed the rich, caramel-coloured liquid before taking a gulp.

'Careful,' he cautioned.

She felt the wonderful burn in her throat followed by a
warm sensation in her stomach and felt herself relax a little.

'Not the first time you've had whisky?'

She shook her head. 'Back home in India the soldiers
were always happy to share.'

'So you actually did grow up in India?'

'I've lived there my whole life. Until I disembarked the
ship a week ago I'd never been to England before.'

'I think you should start at the beginning,' Edward said
quietly. 'Tell me everything and then we will decide what
is to be done.'

Amelia felt herself complying with his order and bristled. She didn't like being told what to do and especially
not by a man who she barely knew, but there was something authoritative about his tone, something that promised to sort things out, that made her relax back into the
chair and do as he suggested.

She wasn't quite sure where the beginning was. In all
honesty she probably would have to start far back in her
childhood to make complete sense, but she felt Edward
might lose patience if she began recalling the details of

her mother's death and the emptiness that followed. He wasn't a man to hide his irritation.

'Two years ago I met a man out in India. My father is a retired colonel and he still has much to do with the army and the officers stationed in India. He hosted a ball and it was there I met Captain McNair.'

Amelia didn't confess how she'd been swept off her feet immediately by his easygoing manner and charming façade. She had been bored, tired of the same routine day in and day out, and she'd been ripe for a seduction.

'We met in secret, in the months following the ball, and after a few meetings McNair professed his love for me.'

'Why the secrecy?' Edward asked, getting to the point in that calm, shrewd, way of his.

Amelia felt her cheeks start to colour with the shame of her naivety. At the time she'd believed McNair's wishy-washy excuses to keep their relationship a secret; his desire to gain a promotion before approaching her father, not wanting to conduct their courtship under his commanding officer's watchful eye. Amelia had believed him because she'd wanted to believe him. At first she'd even kept the relationship secret from her cousin Lizzie, her closest confidant.

'I was young and naive and I thought he wanted to marry me,' Amelia said simply.

He had *wanted* to marry her, of course—most men in India did when they discovered she was the wealthiest heiress in the subcontinent.

'We courted in secret for almost eight months, snatching precious moments whenever we could, and then suddenly he disappeared. I waited for him, searched for him and eventually found out he had been sent back to England. I even wrote to his commanding officer for information, but his reply was a curt note telling me to forget about Captain McNair.'

Amelia glanced at Edward sitting across from her. It felt strange to be admitting all this to a virtual stranger, especially when she hadn't even told her nearest and dearest the truth.

'Can I surmise you didn't take the commanding officer's advice?'

Amelia shook her head. 'I couldn't forget about him. I thought we were meant to be together.'

It was galling, really, when she thought of how much time and energy she had wasted trying to track McNair down.

'My behaviour became a little…erratic, and after some time my father decided to send me to England to stay with my aunt and have a London Season.'

And find a respectable husband. The words had never been explicitly said by her father, but he'd made it quite clear he wanted her happy and settled, and that he expected a good match from her. Edward leaned back in his chair and watched her intently as she told her story. There was something searching and assessing in his gaze, and she had the impression he was committing her to memory, maybe for one of his sketches he seemed so fond of.

'When I got to England I persuaded my cousin Lizzie to assume my identity for a few weeks whilst I slipped away. I'd found McNair's address and was determined for us to be reunited.'

Amelia didn't recount the dizzy anticipation she'd felt on her journey to Brighton. Her thoughts had been full of breathless reunions, impassioned kisses and romantic vows never to be apart. The reality had been so much different.

'When I got to his address McNair was more than a little shocked to see me, but he recovered quickly.'

She closed her eyes as she remembered the honeyed words he'd used to placate her after his first expression had not been of complete pleasure. He'd led her into his rooms, entwining his fingers with hers and had whispered all manner of scandalous endearments in her ear. Amelia had fallen for him all over again, her infatuation deepening every minute she was in his company.

Amelia glanced at Edward, unsure how much to say. He seemed to pick up on her hesitation and wordlessly stood, crossed the short distance between them and re-filled her glass with whisky. Amelia took a fortifying sip as she remembered McNair's kiss, the way his lips had trailed over her skin, the light dance of his fingertips over her back and the warmth of his body pressed close to hers.

She would have given herself to him, completely and utterly. It was only pure luck that she had not fallen into bed with the man she'd thought she loved.

'We were disturbed and McNair left the room for some moments. Whilst he was gone I wandered around, looking at this and that. Then I saw the will on his desk.'

She'd stared at it for a whole minute, uncomprehending. Reading the letters, but their meaning not fully sinking in.

'It was his wife's will. It transpires that she had become unwell just over a year ago, coinciding with McNair's return to England. She had passed away at the end of last month.'

'You didn't know he was married?'

Amelia shook her head. She'd stared at the piece of paper detailing McNair's wife's bequests to certain charitable organisations and she'd felt as though her heart was actually ripping in two. Years of flirtation and infatuation had immediately soured and as McNair had walked back into the room she'd finally seen him for what he was: a trickster, an adulterer. She'd hated him in an instant, but more than that, she had felt all of her self-confidence and trust in her own judgement destroyed in one fell swoop. She'd allowed herself to be taken in by this villain and that hurt almost as much as the scoundrel's betrayal.

'I confronted him when he returned and at first he tried to deny it. I became a little hysterical and suddenly he turned nasty.'

He'd shown his true colours then. Gone was the man who had whispered his desire to spend eternity in her arms and the real McNair replaced him. This McNair snapped and snarled like a wounded animal and let her know it was just her father's substantial fortune he was interested in.

'He admitted his plan had been to seduce me, entice me to run away with him, then extort money from my father for my safe and scandal-free return.'

It had been the ultimate humiliation. Just one more man who wanted her for her money.

'What a bastard,' Edward said, not apologising for his language. Amelia felt her spirits buoy a little as she continued. It was the most animated she'd seen him.

'I threatened to expose him as a scoundrel and a liar, empty words, but I think he had a new scheme afoot, some new girl he was trying to con, for he became enraged.'

Amelia raised a hand to her cheek where McNair had left his mark.

'He hit you?'

She nodded. 'He punched me, right on the cheek. He was livid, like a wild beast.'

It was no excuse, not for what she'd done, but Amelia truly had been afraid for her life.

'There was a fancy letter opener on his desk and I grabbed it, thinking to brandish it and warn him away, but he just laughed at my efforts and came at me again.'

She closed her eyes as she relived the moment the blade

had sunk into McNair's flesh, the soft resistance, the warm trickle of blood that had flowed over her hand, McNair's surprised exhalation before he collapsed on to the ground.

'I stabbed him,' she said so quietly she wasn't sure Edward would hear her words.

She couldn't open her eyes, couldn't bear to see what another person thought of her taking a man's life and all because of a seduction gone wrong.

'I stabbed him and I killed him.'

Some men would come and take her hand, try to comfort her despite there being nothing that could change the fact she was a killer. Some men would chastise and condemn her, even restrain her until they could summon a magistrate. Edward did neither. He sat in the chair across from her in silence, giving her time to collect herself, to steady her nerves and to continue.

'I fled, I ran as far as I could as fast as I could, then when I couldn't run any more I kept walking.'

'And that's how you came to be here, on the night of the storm.'

Amelia looked up at him, trying to read his expression, to garner exactly what he thought of her.

'How long was this letter opener?' he asked, taking her by surprise.

She measured out a few inches with her fingers, trying to recall the look of the blade before it had been covered in blood.

'And where did you stab him?'

'What does it matter?' she asked, feeling sick.

'The blade was small. Unless you hit a vital organ I think it unlikely you killed the man.'

She shook her head. She'd killed him. No one could bleed that much and not be dead.

'He collapsed to the floor...there was blood every-where.'

'Did you check to see if he was breathing? If he had a pulse?'

She hadn't. In fact, she hadn't been able to look at his body at all once the blood had started seeping from the wound around her fingers.

'There was too much blood,' she repeated.

Edward fell silent, seeming to realise if he pushed her much further Amelia wouldn't be able to keep her tenuous grip on her composure.

'What do you want to happen now, Amelia?' Edward asked.

'I don't want to hang.'

A smile tugged at the corner of his lips. Amelia watched as Edward fought it and returned his expression to the more familiar frown.

'An admirable ambition. I don't think any judge would hang you.'

Amelia wasn't sure. And even if she wasn't sentenced to death, a long spell in one of the country's notorious prisons was just about as bad as the noose.

'It was self-defence. You're a young woman of a good family and by all accounts McNair seems to be a known scoundrel.'

It sounded as though Edward was justifying handing her over to the magistrate to face the penalty for what she'd done.

'It's up to you, of course, but if you run then you will spend your entire life looking over your shoulder, wondering whether this crime will catch up with you.'

Amelia hadn't thought of that. She'd been so preoccupied with the here and now, avoiding being apprehended for murder and getting as far away from the scene as possible, she hadn't thought what her life would be like with this always hanging over her. She would always be a murderer. Even if she returned to India, to her father's protection, she would never be able to undo what she had done.

'I want to go home,' Amelia said in a small voice.

She wanted her father, with his gruff voice and stiff embraces. She wanted the rolling hills of Bombay with the humid heat and monsoon rains.

'To India?'

She nodded. He looked thoughtful.

'You can stay a couple of days,' he said eventually. 'I will summon my steward and instruct him to make discreet enquiries, see what the state of affairs is with this McNair. We will make a further decision when we have all the facts.'

She didn't know how he could reduce her momentous revelation to such a cool, calculating plan, but as his words sunk in Amelia felt a surge of hope blossom inside her. He was going to help her and, more importantly, he was going to let her stay.

With a yelp of relief Amelia sprang from her chair and launched herself across the room at Edward. He was stiff under her embrace and momentarily Amelia remembered how his body had moulded to hers the night before as she lay in bed shivering from the cold. He was capable of warmth and closeness, but he wasn't comfortable with it.

'There are conditions,' Edward said quickly. 'I don't like to be disturbed. We shall take dinner together and nothing more. The rest of the time you may do as you please, but you will not venture into the East Wing. Is that clear?'

Amelia nodded, willing to agree to anything if it meant she could stay. For a while at least she was safe. She would remain hidden in this strange, half-empty house until they could be sure exactly what the situation was with McNair's death. It was a reprieve, the sanctuary she had hoped for during her mad dash over the Downs. Of course it wouldn't bring McNair back to life, wouldn't change the fact that she was a murderer, but for now she would have to be content with safety over absolution for her crime.

Amelia pulled away, pausing as she got to arm's length. Something made her stop, to hesitate. Her eyes met Edward's and for a second there was a spark, a flare, between them. Amelia felt skin begin to tingle and her blood rushing around her body. She was aware of every tiny movement, every breath, every muscle. There was something captivating about this gruff, generous man, something not obvious at first glance, but hidden beneath his cool exterior.

Then Edward shifted and the moment was lost. Amelia stood, turning away to cover her confusion. She wasn't sure what had just passed between them, but she did know she had no right to experience whatever it was. Taking a deep breath, she forced a smile to her lips before turning back to face Edward.

Chapter Five

As Edward's pencil danced over the paper he felt all the tension and worry from the last couple of days flow from his shoulders. Drawing preserved his sanity, it was a hobby that had become much more. In the last few years he had lost himself in his sketches, picking up his pencils whenever his grief or solitude threatened to overwhelm him. Sometimes he drew from memory, a person from his childhood or scene from the village. Often he would sketch faces, allowing his pencils to flow over the familiar lines of the faces of the people he had lost over the years.

Today he was sitting by the window, drawing the view he could see. He'd needed this time alone, some space to regroup and sort through the events of the last couple of days. So he had retreated to his rooms soon after Amelia had finished telling him her story.

It was strange having another person in the house. Ever since he had dismissed the servants a few weeks after the fire he had lived alone. Edward knew he'd turned the house into a sort of mausoleum, a place of memorial for all that had he had lost. Maybe it wasn't the healthiest way of dealing with his grief, but he'd never felt he deserved anything more than the loneliness he had imposed on himself.

Now, with Amelia's presence, he felt uncomfortable and guilty. It should be Jane here with him, not some pretty young woman.

He didn't believe for a second Amelia had actually killed this Captain of hers. A petite little thing like her wouldn't be able to best a seasoned soldier with just a letter opener. Far more likely the scoundrel was still alive and hell-bent on vengeance. That was the real reason he'd allowed her to stay, to ensure she was kept hidden from McNair and whatever plans he had for the woman who'd injured him. Part of him had wanted to hold back and send her on her way, but he knew his conscience couldn't bear the burden of another death.

So he had promised to look into Amelia's claims and before he had retired to his rooms he'd walked to the edge of the estate and found a willing boy to deliver a message to his steward for a couple of shiny coins. Hopefully the man would visit later and they could get the business sorted as soon as possible.

Then life can return to normal. Edward grimaced. As if anything in his life could be termed normal.

Mulling his future over in his mind, Edward glanced out the window again, his hand with the pencil in falling to his lap as he saw Amelia pacing about the garden. As he watched he saw her heft a spade from the ground and start to dig.

For years the lawn had been overgrown, but covered in lush, green grass. Now it was beginning to be peppered with several muddy holes of varying depths all scattered about in front of the flower bed. It looked a complete mess.

It wasn't the mess, however, that made Edward spring up from his chair, it was the realisation of exactly where she was digging. Now there was only a thorny tangle of overgrown bushes and Edward couldn't remember the last time he'd seen a flower, but he knew for certain the area she was attacking had once been the rose garden. The rose garden Jane had once loved so much. With a growl of displeasure Edward stood, pushing his sketches to one side, and quickly made his way downstairs. Out in the garden the full extent of the damage became apparent.

'What are you doing?' he asked, not bothering to hide his exasperation.

'Digging,' came Amelia's cheery reply.

She carried on plunging the spade into the ground, a look of steely determination on her face.

'Why are you digging?'

'To rescue the roses.'

She didn't look up at him as she spoke, too intent on her task.

'Stop,' he said, adding a quiet 'please' as an afterthought.

'Won't be long now.'

She carried on wielding the spade.

'Stop now.'

The hole in front of them got a little larger and Edward's shoes were sprinkled with mud.

'Stop,' he bellowed.

Amelia halted, the spade frozen in mid-air, and looked at him with puzzlement.

'What's wrong?' she asked.

'What's wrong? What's wrong?' Edward tried to keep his temper in check, but as he looked around at the devastation in front of him he lost the battle. 'You've destroyed my garden.'

Amelia took a step back, but Edward couldn't regret the volume of his outburst. She had desecrated the rose garden, the patch of ground he and Jane had spent hours planting and tending together.

'It was a mess to begin with.'

Edward felt guilty. He knew he had neglected a lot in the past three years, allowing the house and gardens to fall into disrepair. He regretted allowing the garden he and Jane had planted so lovingly become this overgrown mess of tangled brambles, but that did not give Amelia the right to swoop in and attack it with a spade.

'If I had wanted it any different, I would have done it myself.'

'Like the rest of the house?' Amelia challenged him.

He could see she regretted her comment as soon as she'd said it, even going so far as clamping her hands over her mouth as if trying to pull the words back in.

'Do not touch anything else,' Edward said, his voice low and dangerous. 'Now leave.'

She hesitated for just a second and then dropped the spade and hurried back to the house.

'I'm sorry,' Edward whispered, closing his eyes. 'I'm sorry for letting things get like this.'

He knew the house and gardens were in a terrible state. No one could live there and be unaware of the dust and the weeds and the crumbling stone, but over time he had become used to it. Each time he'd noticed another cobweb or another fault he'd closed his eyes to it and tried to forget. He knew this was partly due to his need to punish himself. The problems arose when he realised he'd let the things Jane had loved fall into disrepair. He should have been a better custodian.

Carefully he began replacing the clumps of earth Amelia had dug up, patting the turf on top and trying to return the grass to how it had looked before. Once he had finished he sat back and regarded the overgrown rose bushes thoughtfully. After a few minutes he got up, walked to one of the outbuildings and began his search for the gardening equipment.

* * *

Half an hour later his fingers were scratched and bleeding, but the tangle of rose bushes had been trimmed back to a more respectable size. Each individual plant was distinguishable from its neighbour now, and although there were no buds on the bushes it looked more like the garden it had once been.

As he sat back on his knees he sensed Amelia's presence behind him.

'They must look beautiful when the flowers are in bloom,' she said quietly.

They had been beautiful. The whole garden had been beautiful. He and Jane had often taken evening strolls through the grounds in the summer months, stopping to admire the roses or sniff the fragrant flowers.

He turned to face her, trying to work out what to say. Amelia was already walking back towards the house, her head held high, but the slight hunching of her shoulders belying the burden she was carrying.

Amelia didn't want to return inside just yet. She had been shocked by Edward's reaction to her trying to do a spot of gardening and was still smarting from his harsh words. She couldn't quite understand why he had reacted in such a fashion; it was only a rose garden. Part of her had wanted to be helpful, to repay Edward's kindness with an act to show she was grateful for him letting her stay. Her other motivation for wanting to attack the flowerbeds was much more selfish.

Amelia couldn't bear to be idle, not at the moment. Every second she wasn't occupied with some task or other her mind wandered back to the encounter with McNair in his study. Over and over she would relive the moment he had lunged at her and she'd plunged the letter opener into his abdomen. It made her feel sick and light headed, but no amount of willpower could stop her from dwelling on her crime.

Only when she was occupied, preferably doing something physically demanding, did her mind take a break from brooding over the events of earlier in the week. So she'd decided to attack the flowerbeds, thinking Edward would be pleased to see some part of the estate tidy and thriving.

Amelia kicked at a pebble on the path, taking her frustration out on the small stone. She wanted to be angry with Edward for speaking to her in such a tone, but part of her wondered what had fuelled the outburst. There was something deeper going on at Beechwood Manor, something she didn't quite understand yet. Edward was a damaged soul—no one shut themselves away from the world like he did without a good reason. She rather suspected he had lost someone close to him and that loss had prevented him from moving on with his life.

Ever since she had first arrived Amelia had felt the grief and heartache emanating from Edward, but she had felt something else as well. There was a power there, a sense of authority that made Amelia wish he would just fold her in his arms and keep her safe from the world.

Pausing, Amelia flopped down on a bench and closed her eyes. Here she went again, jumping to conclusions about people before she really knew them. With McNair she had been taken in by his good looks and easy charm. She'd fallen for him within ten minutes of meeting him and declared her undying love less than a week later. Her judgement when it came to men couldn't be trusted. She didn't know Edward, not really, and she wouldn't allow herself to ever fall victim to a man ever again. From now on she wouldn't pin her hopes on anyone but herself.

'Good afternoon, miss.'

A voice startled Amelia from her reverie. She sprang to her feet, ready to flee if the need arose, and was confronted by a stout, portly man in his sixties. Slowly Amelia relaxed. If he did pose a threat she rather thought she would outpace him with nothing more than a brisk walk.

Forcing her racing pulse to slow, Amelia smiled warily at the newcomer.

'Tobias Guthry at your service, miss, and what a pleasure it is to meet you.'

Amelia took his proffered hand, allowing his podgy fingers to enclose hers briefly.

'I am Sir Edward's steward, been summoned by the master himself. Sorry if I startled you at all.'

Mr Guthry was looking increasingly anxious and Amelia decided he was most likely harmless.

'You must forgive me, Mr Guthry, I was miles away and I wasn't expecting anyone.'

'You gave me quite a surprise yourself, miss. In the past three years I've been working for the master I've not seen a single other person about the grounds.'

'Yes, I understand Sir Edward is a very private person,' Amelia said, wondering if this amiable little man might be willing to tell her any more about her host.

'Oh, very private, miss, the most private a man could be.'

'Tell me, has he always been this way?'

Mr Guthry gave her a sidelong look and his already pink complexion turned beetroot.

'I wouldn't like to speculate, miss, I've only known him since after the...er...the incident.'

He glanced at the fire-damaged portion of the building as he spoke.

So the fire had been the turning point in Edward's life.

She wondered if he'd been injured in it, or whether he'd lost someone he loved as she had first suspected. A slither of guilt slid into Amelia's consciousness. After all he was doing for her she ought to know more about him and the reasons behind his peculiar choice of lifestyle. The worst thing was he'd probably dropped hints, even alluded to whatever terrible event had affected him so badly, but she had been too caught up in her own world to notice.

'Do you come to see Sir Edward often?' Amelia asked, changing tack.

'Only every couple of months.'

She was surprised at this. Edward seemed the sort of man who liked to be in charge of things, completely in control. True, to manage an estate such as this, which must encompass land outside the boundaries of Beechwood Manor with tenants and farmers and livestock, you would have to not live in such reclusive circumstances, but all the same she couldn't picture him giving up complete control.

'Sir Edward must trust you very much, Mr Guthry.'

The portly man visibly swelled with pride at Amelia's words.

'Come inside and please make yourself comfortable, I will let Sir Edward know you are here.'

Amelia ushered him into the sitting room she'd entered the night before. It was the only room in the main part of the house vaguely suitable for guests. At least the chairs were no longer covered in dust sheets, but still there was rather a ghostly feel to the room.

She left Mr Guthry wiggling his ample backside into one of the armchairs and set off in search of Edward.

Cautiously she knocked on the door to his set of rooms in the West Wing, and when there was no answer after a few seconds she took a few steps inside. Edward's sketches were scattered across the desk, with an open pad of paper resting on the windowsill, but there was no sign of Edward. Amelia knew he wasn't outside or in the main portion of the house, which only left the fire-damaged East Wing.

Quickly Amelia padded along the landing, feeling like a rebellious child for even thinking about venturing into the East Wing. His warning never to enter that part of the house was ringing in her ears, but she couldn't exactly leave Mr Guthry waiting indefinitely.

At the end of the landing another long corridor swept off at an angle to the main house, identical upstairs and down. Amelia paused before stepping over the threshold, a shiver travelling down her spine and making her glance back over her shoulder to check she was alone.

She took a step and then another. Already the fire damage was evident: blackened walls, the faint smell of smoke, damaged paintings hanging over the peeling wallpaper.

'I told you not to enter the East Wing.' Edward's voice made Amelia jump with fright.

He emerged from the shadows like a phantom, taking Amelia firmly by the arm and guiding her quickly back to the main section of the house.

'You are never to enter the East Wing.'

Amelia was about to protest, about to question why, but she saw the haunted look in Edward's eyes and decided for once to keep her mouth securely shut. She waited for him to reprimand her further but he just continued to lead her away from the fire damaged corridor.

'There's a Mr Guthry waiting to see you,' she said, once her heart had stopped pounding and she'd caught her breath.

The normality of her response, or the familiarity of Mr Guthry's name, seemed to pull Edward back from whatever precipice he was teetering over. Slowly he regained his focus and Amelia was relieved to see the haunted look fade from his eyes.

'Good,' he grunted as they descended the main staircase, 'He can find the proof all this murder business is nonsense and then you can be on your way.'

Normally Amelia would have bristled at his tone and his dismissive attitude towards her plight, but even she could recognise a man who had just confronted some past demon and deserved a little forgiveness for his sharp manner, so instead of making a withering retort she led Edward calmly to Mr Guthry, all the time wondering what it was in the East Wing that Edward didn't want her to see.

With Edward and Mr Guthry ensconced in the sitting room Amelia wandered the house for a few minutes before finding herself back in the homely West Wing. Safe in the knowledge that Edward would be busy for at least the next half an hour Amelia ventured into his bedroom, the room they had both shared the night before, and made her way to the desk. Trying her hardest not to pry any further through his personal documents, she sat and rummaged through the drawers until she found a blank sheet of paper and a pen.

Amelia was not a keen writer of letters. Sitting and constructing beautifully worded, descriptive prose was not in her character, she much preferred to be outside doing something. Nevertheless today she would grit her teeth and get on with her task.

Dearest Lizzie,
How long it seems since I left you in London and how much has happened during that time. I hope you are faring better than I, and that my aunt has not discovered our deception and is treating you well.

Amelia paused, sucking on the end of the pen as she wondered how best to word the description of what had happened over the past few weeks. She did not want to trouble her cousin more than was necessary, but Lizzie was currently masquerading as Amelia Eastway and, if Edward was right and there was a chance McNair had survived, her cousin could become a target.

A hundred times I have wished for you to be by my side these past few days. I have been sorely in need of your calm words and sensible cautions. As you had suspected, McNair was not the man I had hoped and ever since I tracked him down in Brighton a series of unspeakable events have occurred.

I cannot go into detail on paper, but I hope we will be reunited soon and I will tell you everything then.

The most important thing, dearest Lizzie, is for you to be vigilant. I fear I am being hunted, most likely by a magistrate or one of his officers, but also possibly by McNair. As you are currently going by the name Amelia Eastway I urge you to be careful. I could never forgive myself if something happened to you because of my foolishness.

I will write again soon, hopefully with a solution to this predicament rather than all these concerns, but until then know that I am safe. A gentleman has given me shelter in his old dilapidated house for a few days until things have settled down. I feel peculiarly safe here.

All my love,

Amelia

Chapter Six

Edward wanted some privacy, but with Amelia hovering outside the door he knew he wasn't going to get much time to himself.

'Come in, Amelia,' he bellowed after she'd strolled past the open door for the twelfth time.

'Am I disturbing you?' she asked innocently.

'Yes.'

'Oh.' She looked taken aback. 'I can leave.'

She turned back towards the door and Edward sighed, knowing she would just pace up and down until he agreed to listen to whatever it was she had to say.

'Stay,' he said more softly.

Hesitantly Amelia perched on the edge of one of the sofas, sitting primly as no doubt her governess taught her all society ladies sat.

Edward waited, knowing she would come out and tell him what she wanted eventually.

'How did it go with Mr Guthry?' she asked.

Under her poised veneer Edward could detect a hint of nervousness. She nibbled on her lower lip in that distracted manner of hers and one of her legs was fidgeting up and down under her skirts.

'He's a very sensible man, Amelia, you have nothing to worry about.'

She nodded. 'But he could be linked back to you and then the magistrate would know exactly where to find me.'

'Mr Guthry will be discreet in his enquiries.'

Again Amelia nodded, but Edward could tell she wasn't convinced. He wanted to reach out and place a hand on her knee to stop the constant jittering, but instead leaned back in his chair.

'Someone might wonder why he is asking questions.'

'We need to know what the situation is,' Edward said a tad impatiently.

Amelia fell silent and Edward wondered if it would be unforgivably rude to usher her out so he could get the privacy he was so in need of. His head was in a spin, memories of the night of the fire sparring with regrets of letting the estate fall into such disrepair.

'It's getting late,' Amelia said after a few minutes, 'I was just wondering where I would sleep tonight.'

The memory of her soft body pressed up against his sprang uninvited to Edward's mind. He felt the hot flash of desire, a primal urge encouraging him to sweep Amelia up and hold her close to him again. It lasted only a moment, but it was enough to trigger a cascade of guilt and self-loathing.

'Of course, there are plenty of bedrooms. You may take your pick.' He paused, but chivalry made him continue, 'Unless of course you would prefer my bedroom and I will find another.'

'No, I'm sure I will find a suitable room.'

He expected her to stand and go off in search of a room to call her own for the next few days, but she remained perched on the edge of the sofa.

'Was there something else?' he asked.

Most people would understand the comment to mean he wanted to be left in peace, but Amelia cocked her head and smiled.

'Come and help me choose a room,' she said.

Edward looked down at the papers scattered across his desk and wondered how offended she would be if he just said no.

'Ten minutes,' Amelia pressed. 'And then you can go back to ignoring me for the rest of the day.'

Years ago Edward had known how to play the generous host. He had entertained and amused his guests and ensured they were never left feeling uncomfortable in his home. He supposed that was why he felt a little uneasy at leaving Amelia to amuse herself whilst he continued with his life as if nothing had changed, but it wasn't as though she were an invited guest.

'You can spare me ten minutes,' Amelia said. 'Just grit your teeth and show me the bedrooms.'

Edward felt the beginnings of a smile start to form on his lips and quickly suppressed it. In a world where people tiptoed around others it was refreshing to have someone speak quite so bluntly.

He stood, stretched, and then offered her his arm, feeling the unfamiliar wave of contentment as she slipped her delicate fingers into the crook of his elbow. He'd forgotten what it felt like to have a woman's hand rest trustingly on his forearm.

'The house has sixteen bedrooms,' Edward said, 'but four are in the East Wing. There's two in the West Wing, one of which is mine, and ten in the main part of the house.'

As they walked up the stairs he tried to remember the last time any of the rooms were occupied. There had been a garden party a couple of months before the fire, family and friends had gathered to celebrate some occasion or other and as they'd stayed long into the balmy evening his wife had offered most of their guests a room for the night. Edward doubted anyone had set foot in many of the bedrooms since then. He certainly hadn't.

Amelia poked her head into each of the bedrooms Edward indicated, glancing around for a few moments before returning to him in the corridor. In one room she hesitated for a little longer and Edward found himself stepping in after her.

He had to reach out and hold on to the door frame for support as he crossed the threshold.

'Edward?' Amelia's voice seemed to come from a long way away even though she was standing right in front of him.

As if in a trance he moved further into the room, trailing his fingers across the faded wallpaper and feeling his feet sink into the plush carpet. He hadn't stepped into this room since the fire, hadn't been able to face the memories of the chamber he'd shared with his wife for their four years of marriage. Unlike many couples they hadn't kept separate rooms, preferring instead to come together at the end of the day, and this had been their meeting place. A place where they had shared their hopes and fears and their love for each other.

With a heavy heart Edward sat down on the bed, placing a hand on the embroidered covers and remembering the last night they had spent together.

'Please, leave me,' Edward said, his voice coming out as a hoarse croak.

Instead of following his orders, Amelia sat down beside him, her petite form perched on the edge of the mattress. Gently she took his hand and without a word folded it in her own.

His memories were private and still raw, his grief was

overwhelming at times, and he knew that over the past three years he had coped by hiding from the pain rather than confronting it.

They sat side by side, hand in hand for a good long time and slowly Edward felt the grief begin to subside and the pull of reality build. Standing, he began to look around the room, allowing different objects and pictures to spark fond memories and even pausing before the small portrait of his late wife he used to keep on his bedside table. Gently he ran his fingers over her face, tracing the lines that had once been so familiar.

'I would rather you didn't choose this room to make your own,' he said.

'Of course.'

With one final glance behind him Edward led Amelia from the bedroom, closing the door firmly after her.

'We could—' Amelia began to say, but Edward cut her off with a shake of his head.

He didn't want to talk, didn't want to share his memories.

'Let's find you a bedroom,' Edward said resolutely.

He led Amelia through the house to the West Wing. His current bedroom and sitting room were in this part of the house and he had a feeling Amelia subconsciously wanted the security of being close to him at night. Although maybe not as close as they had been the previous night.

'This room is quite small,' he said, opening the door to the only other bedroom in the West Wing.

It was small but beautiful. Two large windows let in bright streams of sunlight and a four-poster bed dominated the room. Dainty furniture was squeezed into the rest of the space and the whole room had a definite feminine feel to it.

'I love it,' Amelia declared, walking over to the bed and

perching on the edge. Carefully she inspected the bedcovers and when all was to her satisfaction she smiled with pleasure. 'It's just perfect.'

And only a door away from his room. Probably too close for comfort, but at least there were two heavy wooden door separating them.

With the sunlight reflecting off the golden highlights in her hair and the smile lighting up her face Amelia looked like some goddess from mythology.

'I will leave you to get settled in,' he said. 'I have a few things I need to do.'

Quickly Edward left and made his way into his own rooms. There was a sense of urgency building inside him, the need to capture something special, almost magical. For years his sketching had been about losing himself in something that occupied his mind and allowed him to escape from his memories, or a way to relieve stress and tension, but before that, long ago, he'd drawn because he'd *had* to draw. Something or someone had inspired him and he couldn't help but put pencil to paper.

Just now, looking at Amelia, for the first time in years he had that feeling again. It was a primal need, something Edward had to satisfy, and as he picked up his pencils and a fresh sheet of paper he allowed himself to enjoy the warm buzz that was building inside him.

Chapter Seven

Amelia wandered downstairs, feeling a little lost. She was pleased that she had a room of her own now and a very comfortable room at that, despite a small part of her craving the warmth and protection she'd felt the previous night in Edward's arms. As a well brought-up young lady Amelia knew her even just being in this house alone with Edward would destroy her reputation and, if anyone ever found out they'd actually shared a bed, there would be moral outrage. Even so, Amelia had felt particularly safe with Edward's strong arms wrapped around her and it wasn't as though anything inappropriate *had* happened.

With a sigh Amelia admitted to herself her reputation would already be in tatters because of her crime. She would never be able to go out in society again, never take tea with respectable ladies, never whirl around ballrooms or flirt with eligible bachelors. Her life as it had been before was over. The best she could hope for was to escape back to India where no doubt she would have to live a life of quiet repentance. It was against her character and against her spirit, but Amelia had to acknowledge if it kept her from doing something awful again maybe it would be worth it.

Even now as Amelia wandered through the house her

mind kept returning to Edward. Strong, safe Edward. A man she had known for only a day and already she found herself trusting him as though he were her guardian angel. She was too quick to trust, she too easily judged a man honourable based on very little information. Edward had a powerful physical presence and when she caught him in a moment when the frown dropped from his face he was a very attractive man, but that shouldn't be enough to make her trust him. Amelia knew her attraction to McNair had been primarily due to his good looks and easy charm— surely she should have learnt from that experience.

As she reached the hallway Amelia froze. Someone was pushing the door open and with Edward retired to his rooms it couldn't be anyone good.

'Golly gosh, what a fright you gave me,' a plump woman in her late fifties said as she bustled through the door.

Amelia felt herself relaxing a little. The older woman looked no more of a threat than a fluffy pussycat.

'Not in all my years have I ever felt my heart beat so fast.'

'I'm sorry for startling you,' Amelia said, recovering enough herself to move forward and greet the woman properly.

'No harm done, my little ducky, I'll live to see another day. I'm Mrs Henshaw, but why don't you just call me Goody? Everyone else does, except the master, of course, but rules are different for some folk.'

Goody bustled through the hallway, took Amelia by the arm and began to lead her through the house. Already the half-derelict mansion felt more alive, even warmer somehow, with the older woman's presence.

'Now you must tell me who you are and what on earth you are doing here.'

Amelia thought about lying, she knew she shouldn't let

another person in on her secret, but Goody's kindly face
made her want to spill every secret she had.

'I'm Amelia,' she said as she was directed to sit on one
of the wooden stools in the kitchen. Next to her Goody
began unpacking a small sack, placing a loaf of bread and
various other foodstuffs on the table. 'I'm in a bit of trouble
and Edward, Sir Edward, is letting me stay for a few days.'

That made Goody stop what she was doing and stare at
Amelia for a few seconds.

'Well, I never,' Goody said eventually. 'I never thought
the day would come.'

Tears began to fill the older woman's eyes and immediately Amelia wondered just what was going on.

'What day? What do you mean?'

Goody shook her head and patted Amelia kindly on
the hand.

'I'm just glad to see the master being roused by something. By someone. Now why don't I fetch us some biscuits and make a nice cup of tea and you can tell me all
about yourself.'

Goody busied herself lighting the stove and boiling the
kettle and after a few minutes she set a steaming cup of
tea in front of Amelia, accompanied by a large plate of
biscuits.

'I baked them fresh this morning.'

'Goody, have you known Sir Edward for long?' Amelia asked as she took a bite of one of the buttery biscuits.

'Oh, Lordy, yes. I can remember when he was no more
than a lad, must have been about seven or eight. That was
when I joined the family.'

Amelia knew she shouldn't pry, but Edward intrigued
her and with his often monosyllabic conversation she
wouldn't get much information from him.

'You worked for his parents?'

'Indeed I did, worked for the late Sir Edward and Lady Gray for twelve years. And then when they passed away I carried on as housekeeper for young Master Edward.'

'Edward must have been young when his parents passed away.'

Goody nodded sadly, the tears springing to her eyes again. Amelia wondered what this family had done to earn such love and loyalty from a former servant.

'He was only twenty when his father died, still at university studying, of course. And then poor Lady Gray died not two months later. It was all very sudden, a great loss.'

So at one point in his life Edward had been out enjoying the world, studying and gaining an education. Something had changed him, pushed him into this reclusive state. She assumed it was the fire that had ravaged the East Wing, but it was interesting to hear how he had been when he was a younger man.

'That's when Edward inherited the house and the estate?'

Goody beamed proudly as if she had brought Edward up herself. 'He was such a good master and landlord, despite his young age. All of his tenants agreed he was just and fair, and you can't ask for more than that, ducky.'

Amelia reached out and took another biscuit from the plate, crumbling it before popping a small piece into her mouth.

'Was it the fire? Was that what changed everything?' Amelia had never been good at being subtle in her approach and she decided now just to come out and ask the question she wanted to know the answer to.

'Mrs Henshaw, I didn't realise you had arrived.' Edward's deep voice made Amelia jump guiltily up from her seat. 'I see you have met my guest.'

Amelia swallowed nervously and wondered how long he had been standing there.

'What a lovely young lady she is, sir.' Goody paused, and then pressed on. 'I don't wish to speak out of turn, master, but have you spared a thought for her reputation? A young lady staying with just a man for company...I wouldn't want there to be gossip.'

Edward waved a dismissive hand, but smiled indulgently at his old housekeeper.

'Always looking out for me, Mrs Henshaw. I don't deserve you. However, I think it would be fair to say Amelia has bigger problems to worry about than her reputation.'

Amelia marvelled at the change the older woman brought about in Sir Edward. There was a fondness there, an easy companionship that came of knowing someone for a very long time. Amelia wondered if it was the first time she'd seen Edward smile properly and glanced at the old housekeeper again. She must be a special woman to have this effect on her guarded host.

'Ah, that's easy for you to say, sir, but a young woman always has to think about her reputation. Miss Amelia is young and no doubt one day she will want to marry. A woman can find even a small stain on her reputation a significant impediment.'

Edward looked at Amelia and raised an eyebrow.

'I honestly don't mind,' Amelia said, 'It is very kind of Sir Edward to let me stay here. He shouldn't have to disrupt his life in any other way.'

'I could come to stay for a little while, sir,' Goody pushed on. 'No one could say anything improper was going on with me in the house. And it would give me a chance to tidy up a little at the same time.'

Amelia saw the determined glint in the older woman's eyes and wondered if she was just the excuse Mrs Hen-

shaw had been looking for to ensure her old master was
properly looked after.

'I wouldn't like to inconvenience you,' Edward said.

'Nonsense. I'll pack my bags this evening and return
tomorrow.'

Edward gave a curt nod and then turned his attention
back to Amelia.

'Would you grant me a moment of your time, Amelia?'

It was an order rather than a request and immediately
Amelia felt her heart begin to pound in her chest. Slipping
from her perch on the kitchen stool, she followed Edward
from the room and into the sitting room she'd first met
him in the night before.

'Is there something you want to ask me, Amelia?' Edward asked, turning to face her.

He was standing close to her, so close it emphasised
their difference in stature and build. Amelia felt small
compared to Edward, but despite his powerful build
and obvious physical advantages over her she didn't
feel threatened at all. There was an underlying gentle-
ness about Edward, obvious even through his gruff exterior. However angry he might become, however much
she might irk him, Amelia knew he would never raise a
hand to her.

She shook her head.

'Are you sure? I would rather you ask anything of me
directly than gossip with anyone else.'

Amelia felt the heat begin to rise in her cheeks as the
shame and embarrassment washed over her. She was selfish and sometimes she didn't think how her actions affected other people. Amelia knew her flaws well, but it
didn't seem to stop her from acting or speaking before she
had considered the impact on other people.

'I was wondering why you keep yourself shut up here, away from the world,' Amelia said eventually.

Edward turned away from her and stared out the window for a long couple of minutes. Amelia was convinced he wasn't going to answer her, but finally he exhaled and cleared his throat.

'Sometimes something happens in life that even the strongest person finds it difficult to deal with,' he said slowly, 'My solution was to shut myself off from the world, to deal with my pain in my own time without anyone making it worse by inadvertently reminding me of things I didn't want to remember.'

Amelia wanted to push him, wanted to ask him just what pain he was recovering from, but something made her hold back. Edward would tell her when he was ready, pressing him now would only make him close up completely. This was the most frank conversation they had shared since her arrival.

'Has it worked?' Amelia asked instead.

Edward turned back to face her, a small smile tugging at his lips.

'Do you know, I've no idea? Who is to say what I would be feeling if I'd done things differently?'

Amelia felt an urge to reach out and take his hand, to reassure him everything would get better, but she knew she was not in a position to give that reassurance. He seemed lost and empty, as if he had strayed from his path in life and was now struggling to find his way back. Amelia wanted to help. Despite her preoccupation with her own problems, she wanted to guide him to a place where he could be happy.

Quietly she snorted. All her life she had been pampered and protected. Everyone had done her bidding and she could count on one hand the times she had not got her own way How could she, a now disgraced socialite, hope to comfort a man who had obviously suffered greatly?

Edward leaned back from his desk and admired the drawing in front of him. Whatever disruption Amelia might have brought into his life he could not deny she was doing wonders for his creativity. The sketch sitting on his desk was one of the best pieces he had ever done. It was a portrait of Amelia and he had managed to capture some of her essence, some of her vitality on the page. In the drawing she was captured in motion and he'd even managed to reproduce the little frown that furrowed her brow when things weren't quite going her way.

Carefully he set the drawing down, reluctantly acknowledging he could do no more by candlelight and the finer details would have to wait until morning.

He was tired now, but he doubted he would sleep. So much had changed in the course of a couple of days, his entire life had been turned upside down. From tomorrow he would have two people living in his house alongside him, but despite his grumblings Edward had welcomed Mrs Henshaw's suggestion she come to stay. Amelia would have someone else to talk to and he would be doing his bit to protect her reputation. Although he would have to get used to the idea of even more social interaction.

Edward sighed. He knew his manners sometimes left something to be desired. He could be abrupt and blunt and believed in using the fewest words possible to get his point across. More than once he had seen the shock in Amelia's eyes as he didn't soften his words for her ears. He supposed if she would be staying for a few days he would get used to socialising again, maybe even used to considering someone else's needs.

Slipping into bed, Edward allowed himself to consider

the future for the first time in three years. Ever since the fire he had lived day by day, focusing on surviving rather than enjoying his life. Looking back, he could see it had been necessary for him, the best way for him to grieve and process all of the emotions that had threatened to suffocate him in the months after his bereavement, but today Amelia had made him question how he coped with things and what came next.

Edward sat, moulded his pillow into a more comfortable shape and then laid down again. Maybe his coping strategies weren't the healthiest or the most robust, but they had kept him from falling into the deepest pit of despair over the past few years. For now that would have to be enough.

Edward awoke with a start. There was a scream, followed closely by another one. Quickly he jumped out of bed, his reflexes sharp despite years of living on his own. He'd reached the door before he realised he was naked and, cursing for the delay it caused him, he quickly pulled on his dressing gown.

Amelia's room was next to his, the only other bedroom in this part of the house. His heart was pounding as he threw open her door, wondering what he was going to find. Thoughts of an intruder attacking Amelia crowded his mind and as he dashed into the room he was ready to fight whoever was there.

The room was empty apart from Amelia's small form under the bedcovers. She was still lying down, curled up like a small child in bed, screaming in her sleep.

For a moment Edward didn't know what to do, but then his instincts took over and he was by her side immediately.

Gently he scooped Amelia into his arms and held her firmly, but not tightly. He murmured soothing sounds and stroked her hair, all the time making sure she could feel the strength and safety of his body.

As soon as he'd gathered her to him the screams had stopped to be replaced by sobs that racked her whole body. Edward held Amelia whilst she whimpered and nuzzled into him, wondering what memory or event had caused such terror.

'I'm sorry,' Amelia whispered after a few minutes. She'd woken up at some point during the ordeal, but Edward just continued to soothe her.

'Hush,' he said gently. 'Nothing to be sorry about.'

It felt oddly right to be sitting with Amelia in his arms in the middle of the night. Edward felt useful again, as if he had made a difference to someone's life, and that feeling was beyond compare.

'Do you want to tell me about it?' he asked.

For a long time Amelia just sat with her head resting against his chest, but Edward didn't push the matter. He knew all about nightmares, all about the very real terror they could inspire in you. For well over a year after the fire he had woken up certain his bedsheets were burning. He would hear screams in his sleep and be convinced the fire was raging all over again. Dreams and nightmares were not something to be easily dismissed, they could have a big impact on your mental state and ability to cope with events.

'I can hear your heart beat,' Amelia said, tilting her head slightly to look up at him.

Edward held her a little tighter and wondered whether he would have coped better with his bereavement if he'd had someone to hold him and help him through.

As Amelia stared up into his eyes Edward had the urge to bend down and kiss her. It wasn't lust, just an urge to touch his lips to hers, to connect with her.

'It was McNair,' Amelia said eventually.

'You dreamed about him?'

Hesitantly she nodded.

'It felt so real, as if I were back there in the room with him.'

Edward was well acquainted with the pounding heart and sweaty palms that accompanied these sorts of dreams, the features that made you question what was real and what was imagined.

'It's over now,' he said soothingly.

'Every time I close my eyes I can see my hand holding the letter opener.' Amelia gave a little sob. 'And I can see the blood oozing out of his body.'

As she nuzzled in closer to him Edward felt his body begin to respond. Trying to distract himself, he ran a hand up and down her back, but found the warmth of her body having the opposite effect.

'It's normal to have nightmares and flashbacks after such a traumatic event,' Edward said, trying to keep his voice neutral. 'It will get better with time.'

Amelia looked up at him with such trust and hope in her eyes that Edward felt the weight of responsibility he had for her.

'You promise?'

'I promise.'

She didn't push him as to how he knew, didn't ask for his personal experience even though Edward suspected she knew more about his circumstances than he'd told her.

Sighing, Amelia rested her head back on his chest and Edward found himself dropping a quick kiss on her tousled hair. It was intimate and immediately he regretted it, but Amelia didn't seem to notice.

As she relaxed into him, her body growing heavy as she slipped back into sleep, Edward continued to hold her.

She wouldn't sleep unless she felt safe and after the terror of her nightmares she needed to rest.

After a few minutes of Amelia's steady breathing Edward closed his eyes. He knew he would not sleep, but he tried to force himself to relax. His mind was a hive of activity, thoughts and doubts and self-recriminations.

Amelia shifted in his arms, making a little mewl of contentment as she slept. It felt good to be the one who had made such a difference to her, the one that could make her feel safe. He knew he had become a little self-absorbed during his years of solitude—with only his grief for company it was difficult not to. As much as he grumbled about having Amelia invade his privacy he wondered whether maybe it was a good thing to challenge himself, just for a couple of days.

With these thoughts circling his head Edward settled himself back against the headboard, trying to ignore the warm glow he felt inside from holding Amelia in his arms.

Chapter Eight

Amelia brushed the dust from her hands and stood back to admire her handiwork. Slowly she looked around the room and frowned. Things weren't going quite how she'd envisioned them.

That morning she'd woken once again in Edward's arms. Memories of her nightmares the night before had flooded back and she'd felt a supreme sense of gratitude towards Edward for comforting her. When she was a child Amelia had experienced night terrors, awful dreams about the monsters coming to hurt her and her family, and every night her cousin Lizzie had climbed into bed with her and held her until Amelia had banished the bad dreams. The night before had been the worst nightmare she'd ever had, so vivid and detailed it had been as though she were back in McNair's lodgings, plunging the small blade into his flesh once again.

At the memory Amelia shook herself. Edward had gathered her up and held her close and soon the nightmare had been weakened to a faint echo. She felt inexplicably safe with him and when he'd released her from his grip that morning she'd heard herself suppressing a murmur of protest.

As Edward had slipped away and Amelia had woken fully she had felt a crashing sense of unease. She had wanted Edward to remain holding her all morning, wrapping her in his arms and never letting go. Her body had stirred as he'd moved against her and Amelia felt that familiar heat rising all the way up from her toes.

The last time she'd reacted like that was when she'd fallen for McNair.

Not wanting to examine her feelings too deeply, Amelia had thrown herself into a flurry of physical tasks. Today she was tackling the sitting room. If she was going to stay with Edward whilst Mr Guthry made enquiries about McNair and the authorities then she had decided she would help brighten the place up a little. After the initial disaster in the rose beds yesterday Amelia was not going to be deterred. She had seen Edward's wistful look as he took in the dust and grime as they'd searched through the bedrooms the day before. He might not know he wanted the house to be spruced up, but Amelia was sure deep down it was the truth.

Not having any budget to work with, or any means of obtaining new furnishings, Amelia had decided to first strip back the room to the bare essentials and then forage around the house for items to brighten the place up and replace what she had removed. In her mind she had pictured a wondrous transformation. The reality was a little disappointing.

Grimacing, Amelia wiped her dusty hand on her dress and swept her hair from her face. She knew she must look a state, but that was one advantage of living such a life of solitude, she did not have to care too much about her appearance. Apart from for Edward, of course.

There it was again, that rebellious thought about her host. There were many emotions when Amelia thought of Edward, gratitude and relief being in the top five, but there was something else, something deeper, too. Considering she had only met the man a few days ago, she felt a connection with him, despite the myriad of obvious differences between them. When she caught him looking at her a warmth swept through her body and he made her feel safe and secure even in these most difficult times. Then there were her reactions to him holding her close, the subtle quickening of her pulse, the warming of her skin. She knew he had only held her to comfort her from her dreams, but it had been so lovely to feel another person's arms wrapped round her, especially as that person was Edward. It was almost devastating to think none of these feelings could be trusted.

'Dear Lord, what on earth has happened here?' Goody gasped as she bustled into the room.

Amelia looked around sheepishly.

'I wanted to brighten the place up a little, to do something for Edward, Sir Edward.'

Goody patted her kindly on the hand whilst still looking around in horror.

'Well, I'm sure he will see you have the best of intentions, my dear. That's what counts.'

'I want him to know I really appreciate him taking me in.'

'You should just tell him, ducky. And never forget he is getting something out of this arrangement, too.'

Amelia looked at her, puzzled. As far as she could tell Edward was taking all the risk sheltering her for no real benefit. It wasn't as though she had any money to pay him for her lodgings, or any contacts in this country to see him justly rewarded for his kindness.

'He gets your company,' Goody said. 'Something he sorely needed,' she added half under her breath.

Amelia had to smile. Although Goody was very polite to Edward and acted in many ways the good family servant, she did have quite strong opinions about her former master with regard to his well-being.

'Why don't we get these dust sheets cleared out of here and you can help me give the room a good airing?' Goody suggested. 'After that we can worry about putting things back together.'

Amelia relished the physical work of folding the dust sheets into neat squares which they stacked in one corner and then cleaning and polishing the furniture that had dulled with disuse. As they worked Goody chatted away, talking about life in the village and giving Amelia the gossip on the locals. It made Amelia feel normal for a while and part of her craved this sort of life. A life where she belonged somewhere, where people knew her. In India she had felt at home for many years, she had a loving if distant father and her cousin Lizzie was her closest friend and confidant in the world. True, she missed her mother who had died when Amelia had been just seven, but she hadn't been unhappy, not until McNair had come along and seduced her with his honeyed words. Then she couldn't wait to get away, to chase after the man she'd thought she'd been in love with. The rolling green hills and dusty tracks that surrounded her home had lost their charm and Amelia had lost interest in the people who surrounded her. Now, looking back, she could see how self-absorbed she'd been. No wonder her father had despaired and sent her to England for a Season in London.

As she worked she wondered what she wanted from her future. The things that had once seemed so important to her, excitement and adventure, now felt soured and naive. If she could have anything it would be to turn back time, to have never met McNair, never fallen under his spell and never followed him back to England. She would give anything not to have his death on her conscience. No matter what Edward said, she still believed she must surely have killed him.

'I think that's enough for today,' Goody said when they had wiped down all the surfaces and rid the room of dust. 'Tomorrow we can work on the carpet and curtains. I've got dinner to prepare now and you look as though you could do with a bath.'

At the suggestion Amelia almost squealed with delight. A bath would be glorious. She had managed to scrub most of the grime from her body with cold water, but it had not been a pleasant or relaxing experience. Now she was covered in dust and certainly not looking or feeling her best.

'Would it be possible?'

Goody laughed at her hopeful expression and took her by the arm.

'It won't be the most glamorous bath ever, but it's possible.'

Edward regarded the house with a critical eye. When he had woken this morning, stiff from holding Amelia in a sitting position all night, he'd felt the need to clear the cobwebs from his head. Donning his heavy boots and a coat to barricade him from the cold, he'd set out to take a walk about the estate. It had been an eye-opening experience.

Although he had left the house in the past three years he had never really done so with an appraising eye. Today he'd forced himself to look at the overgrown garden, the tumbledown portions of the house and the neglected estate, despite the feelings of regret they inspired inside him. Edward knew he'd let things go, stopped caring about what had once been so important to him. For a long while he hadn't seen the point of worrying about the state of his birthright, his estate, as he had lost his family, the people he had worked so hard to give a good lifestyle. His family would no longer grow up in Beechwood Manor and to Edward that had been a good enough reason to let it fall into disrepair.

Sighing, he acknowledged all the work that needed to be done to get the estate back to its former glory. It seemed almost insurmountable and, if he had been faced with such a challenge even a couple of weeks ago, then he would have retreated back to his rooms and tried to forget about it. But he wondered whether he needed a project to focus on, something that he could be proud of. For too long he had allowed himself to languish and now he could see just how his estate had suffered.

Knowing he didn't need to make a final decision on what to start with straight away, Edward re-entered the house. Maybe it was enough that he was acknowledging the disrepair and the damage, one day he would decide what he needed to do. The idea of employing a gardener or an architect to fix the structural damage filled him with dread, but part of him wondered if he needed to take the first step to restoring the house he had once been so happy in.

Hearing a soft, sweet melody coming from the direction of the kitchen, Edward stopped where he was and listened for just a second. In all the years Mrs Henshaw had been his housekeeper he had never heard her sing. The dulcet tones must be coming from Amelia.

Suddenly he wanted to talk to her, share some of his plans for the estate. He hesitated, nearly heading for the solitude of his rooms anyway, but decisively he changed direction and made his way towards the kitchen. There was no harm in talking to her about the house and gardens.

Maybe Mrs Henshaw would have a plate of warm, buttery biscuits he always remembered so fondly from his youth.

As he pushed open the door to the kitchen the humidity hit him and made him pause. It was a warm, damp heat, not usual for this part of the house. Inside there was a big screen pulled across one half of the kitchen and the sound of soft splashing and Amelia singing coming from behind it.

Edward swallowed, looking around for Mrs Henshaw. She was nowhere to be seen.

The scene was so domestic, so routine, but Edward felt his senses heighten and his blood begin to rush around his body. It was natural for Amelia to be taking a bath. In fact, if he was any kind of host he would have provided her with the means to bathe earlier after her dash over the stormy Sussex Downs. What was not natural was his presence in this room with her. He should leave, slip out before Amelia or Mrs Henshaw found him here.

With once last glance at the screen Edward left the room, stopping to rest his forehead on the cool plaster of the wall outside. He could still hear Amelia's singing, the sweet soft tones drifting from the kitchen and trying to entice him back in like a siren's call.

Part of him wanted to deny the physical reaction he was experiencing at this very moment, but it was not the first time he had responded in this way to Amelia. That very first time he'd laid eyes on her as her wet dress slipped from her shoulders he'd felt the same. And again each time he'd held her body close to him at night. This was not a one-off.

The cool wall against his forehead was helping to disperse the vivid images racing through his imagination and the pictures of Amelia drizzling water over her naked body in the bath started to fade. Edward stood up straighter, turned and almost collided with Mrs Henshaw.

'Are you well, Sir Edward?' the kindly older woman asked with real concern in her voice.

Edward managed an unconvincing nod.

'You look like you've seen a ghost.'

Not seen, Edward thought, just aware of. Everything he did, every decision he made, his late wife's presence was there with him. He had loved Jane and he had lost her, and now he was defiling her memory by feeling desire for a woman he barely knew.

'What have you got there?' Edward asked, trying to distract himself.

'Three dresses for Amelia. I took the liberty of purchasing them from the dressmaker's in the village. They'll be far too big, of course, but I can adjust them.' She paused for a second. 'Amelia doesn't want to be walking around in Jane's clothes.'

Edward nodded. He supposed he should have thought of it himself.

'They're a present from you,' Mrs Henshaw said with a smile, patting him on the arm in a motherly fashion.

'How generous of me.'

'I'll be serving dinner in the dining room at eight,' Mrs Henshaw said, opening the door to the kitchen. Edward managed to restrain himself from peering over her shoulder, balling his hand into a fist and digging his nails into his palm.

'The dining room?'

'Second door on the left in the main hallway.'

He remembered where it was, he'd eaten in there enough throughout his life.

'It's shut up.'

'Not any more. I cleaned it earlier today. You can't expect Miss Amelia to take all her meals down here in the kitchen with me.'

Edward thought Mrs Henshaw would likely be better company than him.

'Anyway, it'll do you good to dress for dinner. How long has it been since you put on your full dress suit?'

Years. In fact, it had probably been eaten by moths many moons ago.

'It will be too much trouble for you to make dinner and serve it, after you seem to have spent the day cleaning as well,' Edward said.

'Don't worry, Sir Edward, I'm hardy,' Mrs Henshaw said cheerfully. 'Although I wouldn't say no to an extra pair of hands to help around the place. Maybe a maid or an odd-jobs boy, just someone to do the fetching and carrying my old arms are too tired for.'

There was a mischievous glint in his old housekeeper's eyes and Edward began to wonder how long she had been planning her assault on his life. Mrs Henshaw had been with his family for more years than he could remember. She cared about him, that he knew, and throughout the years of his seclusion she had insisted in keeping the house ticking over even if he hadn't kept on any other staff.

'You wouldn't want to see me suffer in my old age, would you, sir?'

Was it his imagination or had she become more stooped in the last thirty seconds? He watched as she grimaced and steadied her back with one hand.

'You are hardly old, Mrs Henshaw, I have a feeling you will outlive us all.'

This made the older woman smile.

'But about that maid?'

Edward had a soft spot for Mrs Henshaw and her overt

meddling didn't annoy him as it would if it came from anyone else.

'Fine. One maid. But she'd better keep out of my way and not touch my sketches. And make it clear it is only a short-term post, just whilst Amelia remains here.'

Mrs Henshaw immediately straightened and almost skipped with glee into the kitchen. As much as he'd never admit it, it felt warming to have someone worrying about his well-being.

Chapter Nine

Edward struggled with the fabric of his neckcloth and growled softly. He couldn't remember getting dressed for dinner to be such a complicated and arduous task, but he supposed in the days they'd hosted house parties and had friends over he'd had a valet to ensure he was properly presented.

With a grimace he glanced in the small mirror on his wall, pushing his hair back from his forehead as it flopped into his eyes. He was far from the debonair figure he was sure was popular in today's society, but he had to admit he did look smart even if his waistcoat was a little crumpled and his neckcloth not completely straight.

As he walked from his room towards the main part of the house he felt a moment of nerves and had to chastise himself softly. This was purely a dinner with the young woman he was assisting in her plight, nothing more. There was no need to worry his polite conversation might be too rusty or his manners too abrupt. Amelia was not some woman he was trying to impress. If he said or did the wrong thing it would not matter.

All thoughts of his lack of social graces fled his mind as he reached the bottom of the stairs and turned to find

Amelia beginning to descend behind him. She was dressed in a gown of deep red and, although it was once again too big for her petite frame, tonight someone had expertly pinned it to pull tight against her curves and sit well on her body. Her skin was pink and fresh and her hair still a little damp, with a few stray curls bobbing as she walked.

Amelia's eyes met his and immediately she smiled, an unfettered, instinctive smile of warmth and pleasure. Edward felt something snap inside him and found himself smiling back.

'Thank you for inviting me to dine with you,' Amelia said.

He hadn't, but of course he didn't say anything. Mrs Henshaw would be mortified if he ruined her cunning plan at the first hurdle.

'Thank you for the dresses. Mrs Henshaw has just pinned this one to fit for now, but she said she would adjust them for me,' she said, pulling at the material of the dress. She was obviously a little uncomfortable wearing a garment that didn't quite fit, but Edward thought she looked exquisite all the same.

'You look fine,' he said.

'Oh, good.'

He cursed himself for his lack of ability to compliment her, but Amelia recovered quickly.

'Mrs Henshaw filled me a bath this afternoon,' she said, placing her hand into the crook of Edward's elbow, 'It felt divine to finally wash all the mud and grime off properly.'

Edward grunted, trying not to blurt out that he'd walked in on her having the bath and nearly been ungentlemanly enough to venture round the screen.

'And whilst I was in the kitchen I took a peek at what Mrs Henshaw was cooking up for dinner. It looked incredible and smelled absolutely delicious.'

'Good. I'm hungry.'

Amelia fell silent and Edward wondered if he'd always been so clumsy in making polite conversation. He didn't think he'd struggled at university and of course with Jane things had been different. He'd known her since they were both young children, barely any effort had been needed.

Silently Edward escorted Amelia to her seat and pulled the chair out for her, ensuring she was comfortable before he sat down himself. Reaching across the table, he poured out two glasses of red wine, pushing Amelia's towards her before taking a large gulp.

'I saw you outside today,' Amelia said as she toyed with the stem of her wine glass. She was always moving, always fidgeting, and sometimes Edward just wanted to reach out and place his hand over hers to show her how to keep still.

Edward nodded.

'What were you doing?'

'Just looking. At the house.' And thinking. All the plans he'd once had for the estate, all the work he'd undertaken to improve the house and gardens.

'Did you like what you saw?'

He looked at Amelia sharply, wondering if she was trying to provoke him. She was a little minx sometimes and he wouldn't be surprised if she was goading him into blurting something out just to get him to talk to her. He hadn't exactly been stellar company so far.

'Your home in India—have you always lived there?' Edward asked.

Amelia frowned as she tried to follow his trail of thought. 'Yes, my father built it before I was born.'

'Then you will understand how one's memories can be tied to a building, a place. A lifetime of good times and bad times, all contained within one house.'

'Is it the good times or the bad times you think of when you look at Beechwood Manor?'

'Both.' Edward paused and considered his answer further. 'I suppose all the good memories are tainted with the bad, though.'

Amelia reached across the table and took Edward's hand, her soft, warm skin connecting with the sensitive pads of his fingertips.

Guiltily they sprung apart as Mrs Henshaw entered the room with two steaming bowls of soup, setting them down in front of Edward and Amelia before bustling back out. Edward waited for Amelia to start, but although she picked up her spoon she did not dip it into her bowl.

'What happened here, Edward?' she asked.

He could have pretended to misunderstand her question, or just refused to answer, but Amelia was not the sort of person to let something go.

'There was a fire.' *A terrible fire.*

'In the East Wing?' she prompted.

'Yes.' He nodded curtly, to try and signal that the conversation was over.

'You were here when it happened?'

Edward gripped the edge of the table, the memories of the heat and the flames taking over his mind.

'You lost someone, didn't you?' Amelia asked gently.

Edward stared down into his bowl of soup before closing his eyes. Then abruptly he stood and strode from the room.

Amelia finished her dinner alone, shrugging as Mrs Henshaw brought the main course and enquired where Edward had gone. She'd upset him and that hurt her. She hadn't meant to be so insensitive, but she knew herself how cathartic it was to talk about these things. Edward bottled everything up, if he would just rant and rave about what had gone wrong in his life, let it all out, then maybe he might be able to start healing.

After dinner she roamed around the house, too restless to go to bed and too preoccupied to settle to any particular task. Once or twice she picked up a book, but put it down again almost immediately. Still there was no sign of Edward. With resolute steps she turned her attention to the West Wing. If he wouldn't come to her she would go to him. It wasn't as though she was going to sleep until she had seen he was at least partially recovered.

She knocked on his door, softly at first and then a little louder. When there was no reply she gently pushed it open. His bedroom and the small sitting room off it were empty. It didn't look as though Edward had returned since dinner. Amelia hesitated, knowing she should not trespass in his private rooms, but the temptation of the desk, and the piles of papers on top of it, was too much.

Carefully she leafed through Edward's sketches, feeling the warmth spread through her body as she realised all of the recent ones were of her. He had sketched her digging in the garden, strolling through the rosebushes and even just lounging on one of the chairs in the sitting room. His drawings were good, even Amelia's amateur eye could see that, and he had caught something deeper than just her physical likeness on the paper.

As she reached the bottom of the pile she placed the drawings back on the desk and made her way out of the room. If Edward wasn't in the main part of the house or the West Wing then he must be in the East Wing. Despite him warning her to stay out of the fire-damaged Wing, Amelia barely hesitated before stepping into the corridor.

The light of her candle flickered and cast long shadows in the darkness of the East Wing and Amelia found herself creeping silently down the long corridor. There were doors off to either side, bedrooms most likely, but something drew Amelia further down the corridor to where the fire damage was at its worst.

Here an entire portion of the house had been ravaged by the fire, the walls still blackened with soot and even the faint aroma of smoke remained. As the floorboards creaked underneath her feet Amelia had visions of plummeting through the damaged floor to the hard flagstones of the ground below.

Amelia paused beside an open door, every fibre in her body telling her this was where she would find answers and maybe Edward, too.

As she stepped inside the room it took her a moment to work out exactly what it had been before the fire, and then as her eyes rested on a half-burned rocking horse she heard herself gasp softly.

It was a nursery. A beautiful, fire-ravaged nursery. Amelia bit her lip as suddenly she understood the depth of Edward's pain and suffering. No one should have to lose a child, not like this.

Her eyes began to adjust to the gloom and she could make out other features, familiar shapes morphed and warped by the fire. There was a small bed, the remains of a rocking chair and a pile of what Amelia could only assume had once been toys. A sooty teddy bear sat on the bedsheets as if sadly waiting for an owner who would never return.

Amelia spun around as a noise from by the window startled her. Edward's silhouette was outlined against the glass, his shoulders hunched as if he was physically trying to block out the pain. She hesitated, wondering if he would explode in anger at her for venturing into the forbidden East Wing, for trespassing on his grief and memories, but when he remained silent Amelia crossed the room and wrapped her arms around him.

'What was his name?' she asked quietly.

'Thomas.'

She felt him drop his head and rest his chin on top of her hair, allowing her to hold him tight. Amelia couldn't even begin to imagine his suffering and knew whatever she said would never be enough. No wonder he had locked himself away.

'Come,' Edward said after a few minutes, leading her out of the room and back to the main part of the house. He held her hand, his large fist enveloping her small one, but the pressure of his fingers were light on hers.

'You don't need to tell me anything,' she said as they reached the West Wing and their bedrooms. Edward hesitated a moment, and then pulled her gently into his rooms.

'Sit,' he instructed, motioning to the armchair by the fire she had sat on a few nights previously.

Amelia obeyed. She knew it was entirely inappropriate to be in Edward's bedroom, especially at this time of night, but in truth they had overstepped the line between appropriate and scandalous days ago. This little indiscretion was just another in a long list.

Edward pulled his desk chair over beside her and sat looking at the embers glowing in the grate for a few minutes.

'I shouldn't have pried,' Amelia said eventually. She wanted to know what had happened, wanted to know every detail of how Edward had lost everything dear to him so she could better understand him, but not if retelling it was going to cause him pain.

'Thomas would be six now,' Edward said softly.

'Thomas was your son?'

He nodded and Amelia saw the flash of pride and love cross his face.

'He was the sweetest little boy, mischievous and playful, but ever so loving.'

Amelia remembered the drawings of the young boy she'd seen on her first morning at Beechwood Manor.

'I was so happy. We were so happy. Our lives were complete, we had each other and we had Thomas, I never wanted anything more than that.'

And it had all been ripped away from him. Amelia felt a wistful longing. She doubted she would ever feel love and satisfaction like that, not now her life would be spent always in the shadow of her crime. One day she might marry, but it would be to a second-rate suitor, someone who had flaws of his own so would overlook her past.

'The fire...' Edward trailed off, running a hand over his brow.

Amelia slipped from her chair and knelt on the floor in front of him, her hand resting gently on his arm. She wanted him to know he didn't need to tell her anything, but she sensed now they were here, now Amelia had seen the scorched nursery, he wanted to share his pain with someone.

'Thomas had been ill. We were taking it in turns to sleep in his nursery at night whilst he recovered.'

Of course Edward would be a wonderful and caring parent. Amelia thought back to all the ways he had looked after her during their short acquaintance. He was a kind and giving person underneath the sometimes gruff demeanour.

'It was your wife's turn?' Amelia prompted.

He nodded. 'I still remember kissing them both goodnight. I never thought...'

Amelia couldn't even begin to imagine what it would

feel like to wake up every day knowing those you loved were no longer in the world. No wonder Edward had shut himself away for these three years.

'No one could tell how the fire started, but it was in the nursery. By the time the alarm was raised a good portion of the East Wing was on fire.'

She could see the panic in his eyes as he relived the memory in his mind.

'I went in through the flames and they were just lying there on the bed, side by side.'

Amelia could imagine him charging to the rescue, battling the fire and the smoke to save the people he loved the most.

'I carried them out, but it was too late. The doctor said the smoke killed them while they slept, that they wouldn't have suffered...'

Edward fell silent, his head dipped and his eyes closed. Amelia wished she could reach up and smooth the pain away, but she knew nothing she said or did would make much of a difference. Every day Edward would have to mourn his wife and his son and every day the pain would rip him apart.

Suddenly Amelia felt helpless. She wanted to do something, say something. When she had confessed her crime to Edward he had listened carefully and then made a sensible and reassuring plan. He was the reason she wasn't mentally falling apart, or worse, festering, rotting in a cell somewhere. Now he needed her, he'd trusted her with this emotional wound and she didn't know what to say to him.

'A day lasts until it's chased away but love lasts until the grave,' she said eventually. Edward opened his eyes and looked down at her. 'It's an old Indian proverb, my nanny used to say when I was a child. It means no matter what you never stop loving those close to you until the day you die.' Amelia felt the colour rising to her cheeks and wondered if she had spoken out of turn.

'A day lasts until it's chased away but love lasts until the grave,' Edward repeated, nodding slowly. 'Very apt.'

'Do you have any other family, anyone to help you mourn?' Amelia asked softly.

Edward shook his head, 'I pushed everyone away. I couldn't bear the looks of pity in their eyes.'

They fell silent, both lost in their own thoughts. Amelia wondered whether anyone could ever recover from a loss like this. Edward was a good man, a kind man, and if anyone deserved a second chance at life it was he. He'd taken her in and protected her when she was a complete stranger. She just wished there was something she could do to help him, but part of her wondered if he would ever be able to enjoy himself without feeling guilty because his wife and son weren't there beside him.

'I can see why you shut yourself away,' Amelia said eventually.

'I doubt it was the right thing to do.'

'Maybe at the time it was the only way for you to cope.'

Edward seemed to think about this for a while. 'It just seemed impossible to carry on life as normal when I'd lost...' He trailed off and Amelia squeezed his arm.

Amelia couldn't tell how long they sat like that, with her curled by Edward's feet, her head resting on the arm of the chair, but eventually she must have nodded off for the next thing she remembered was Edward's arms lifting her up gently and carrying her to her own bed. She was still half-asleep as he lay her down carefully on top of the sheets, paused and then kissed her softly on the cheek. As the door closed behind him Amelia lifted her fingers to where he had kissed her. Her skin was tingling and she had the urge to preserve the moment, but slowly her body relaxed and she slipped into a dreamless sleep.

Chapter Ten

Edward prowled through the house, a frown on his face. He'd agreed to one maid, one harmless young woman to help dust and tidy around the place. He should have known things would spiral from there. In the past week Mrs Henshaw had taken full advantage of her return to the house and now the place was practically crawling with people.

He sighed. He wasn't angry with Mrs Henshaw, he couldn't be when he knew she had his best interests at heart, but he just wanted a little privacy.

'Good morning, sir.' A maid curtsied as he walked past.

Edward grunted and then regretted his surliness. 'Good morning, Betty.'

All in all there were now five members of staff at Beechwood Manor, including Mrs Henshaw. Two maids, one upstairs and one in the kitchen, a footman and a gardener. Edward had argued against the need for each one, but as the house began to regain some of its old sparkle and lustre he had to admit they were doing a good job. Mrs Henshaw always had run a tight household.

As Edward stepped outside he saw Smith, the gardener, hurrying towards him.

'Good morning, sir. Might I just have a quick word?' Smith said, pulling his flat cap from his head as he spoke.

'What can I do for you, Smith?'

'It's a delicate matter, my lord…don't want to offend.'

'Go ahead,' Edward prompted, with a sinking feeling in his stomach. He knew what this was going to be about and there wasn't an easy solution.

'Well, I don't wish to cause offence, but it's the young lady, sir, your guest.'

They had agreed to keep Amelia's identity a secret from the staff for now, after taking Mrs Henshaw into their confidences. Amelia had been introduced to the staff as a friend and guest, staying with him for a few weeks to take in the country air.

'I keep finding her digging up my flowerbeds, sir.'

Edward had noticed. Each afternoon Amelia would return to the house covered in mud, looking rather dirty and dishevelled. He often sat by the window in his bedroom, just watching her as she worked. There was something so energetic about Amelia, so alive. Often he would draw her whilst he observed, but sometimes he just found himself watching. Sometimes an hour would pass without him quite knowing how.

'I wouldn't mind at all, sir. Soil always needs a good turning over and who am I to say what a guest of the master can do? But…' The gardener trailed off, his cheeks flushing.

'But she's disturbing the plants?'

'Exactly, sir.' Mr Smith sounded relieved.

Edward looked around the garden with a critical eye. He couldn't deny Mr Smith had worked miracles in a matter of days. The middle-aged man had only been in Edward's employ for less than a week and already the garden was transformed. Overgrown bushes had been trimmed, weeds pulled and he had just made a start on planting a few new flowers.

'Miss Amelia likes to keep busy,' Edward said. 'I wonder whether there might be an area of the garden where you would be happy for her attention to be directed. Somewhere she can focus on without getting in your way.'

The gardener's face broke into a wide grin, 'What an excellent idea, sir. I knew you'd have the solution.' He slowly perused the garden, his lips moving as if weighing up where would be best to redirect Amelia's efforts. 'How about near the old gazebo, sir? There's a patch of flower-beds there where she could dig as much as she wanted.'

'Wonderful. I'll let Miss Amelia know when I next see her.'

Just as the gardener turned away Edward saw a flurry of colour heading towards him and found for the first time in a long time he didn't have the urge to avoid any further human interaction. Amelia was a frenzy of pent-up energy, always on the move, always eager to do something to occupy herself. He knew much of it came from her feelings of guilt over what had happened in Brighton. She still thought she had killed a man and Edward could see that was eating away at her. By exhausting herself during the day she didn't leave much time to dwell on her feelings and was so tired by the time she got to bed she managed to sleep at least a little.

On four separate occasions this week Edward had needed to go into her room at night and soothe her screams and tears. She seemed to be reliving the events leading up to her crime and each night it was distressing her even more. Sometimes she would wake up as he held her, but most nights she just burrowed into his chest and calmed as he wrapped his arms tightly around her.

Edward hoped Mr Guthry returned soon with good

news concerning the young Captain Amelia thought she had killed. If she could hear the scoundrel was still alive, still going about his daily life, then no doubt her guilt would ease.

'Edward,' Amelia said, coming to a stop a few feet away. 'I've got something to show you.'

She grasped his hand and began pulling him back towards the house.

'What is it?'

'A surprise. Now come on.'

Edward began to grumble something, but Amelia flashed him a withering look and he promptly fell quiet.

'Close your eyes,' Amelia instructed.

'Why?'

'Stop being so difficult and close your eyes.'

He didn't doubt Amelia had ever had a problem with getting her own way. She had a confidence in her voice that suggested she hadn't often been challenged.

Edward heard a door open and Amelia's hands on his back guiding him into a room.

'Open your eyes.'

Edward obeyed. They were in the sitting room, the one he had first found Amelia in, stripping off her sodden clothes. In front of him Amelia was smiling proudly and looking around, waiting for his reaction.

Edward felt his body freeze and time slow down. An uncontrollable urge to storm out almost overtook him, but he struggled and managed to remain still.

'You don't like it?' Amelia asked, her face dropping.

'You did this?'

She nodded, biting her lower lip.

'You changed the furniture and the curtains and even the damn rugs.'

Again Amelia nodded.

'What made you think you had the right to do that?'

A small part of him knew he was being churlish and unnecessarily harsh. True, she hadn't asked his permission to renovate the sitting room, but she didn't know what it meant to him.

'You didn't even stop and think, did you? You didn't even consider this room might be preserved in a certain way for a reason.'

'I…' Amelia tried to speak, but Edward held up his hand, silencing her.

'You're so self-centred, so absorbed in your own little world. You didn't even consider asking me if it would be a problem.'

'I can put it back,' Amelia stuttered.

Some part of her anguish must have penetrated through the red haze of Edward's anger because he felt himself deflating, the anger subsiding as if he had been popped with a pin.

'No,' he said, running a hand through his hair. 'Leave it. It doesn't matter.'

Edward knew many women would flee the room in tears after an incident such as this. He wouldn't have blamed her for doing so, he was acting so brutishly, but Amelia stood her ground. Slowly he saw some of her normal confidence return. Her shoulders squared, her chin raised up a notch and she looked as though she were about to do battle. Edward didn't know if he could bear having Amelia berate him for his behaviour, not now. He was just about to apologise and leave quickly when she lunged forward and grabbed his hand. Too late. He was trapped.

Amelia knew sometimes she was not the most aware of or sensitive to other people's feelings. She supposed it came from being a spoiled only child, always the one to get her way. She'd never really had to consider anyone else before, but right now she was having a moment of clarity.

'Come and sit with me, Edward,' she said softly.

She knew the look in his eye—he was weighing up whether he could get away with fleeing the room, locking himself away in his sanctuary and avoiding the confrontation that was to come. It wasn't a healthy way to deal with things and Amelia was determined to get to the bottom of Edward's outburst one way or another.

'I apologise,' Edward said.

Not good enough. She wanted to know more, only then could she actually make a difference to his life the same way he was to hers.

'Yes, yes,' Amelia said, pulling Edward towards the sofa, 'apology accepted. We all get a little ratty sometimes.'

'I need to go.'

'No. You need to stay and talk to me.'

At the suggestion a look of panic crossed Edward's face.

'I really don't think that's necessary.'

'You've just snapped at me for rearranging a few pieces of furniture,' Amelia reprimanded. 'I think it is necessary.'

'I said I was sorry.'

'It's your wife, isn't it?' Amelia plunged in with the question that had been on the tip of her tongue for the last few minutes.

Edward recoiled a little, but wouldn't meet her eye.

'Did she decorate this room?'

For a while Edward just sat silently, looking around at the changes Amelia had made. Slowly he nodded.

'And then I came along and charged in without even thinking.'

'It doesn't matter.'

'It does to you. And that means it matters to me.'

Amelia wanted to reach out and embrace him, to fold

him in her arms and show him he wasn't alone. The memories of his family and his solitary existence in this ghost of a house for the past few years would be enough to drive anyone a little mad. She had to remember she'd exploded into his life, changed so much in a short space of time. He had been remarkably patient with her; Amelia knew she was difficult to live with sometimes, but Edward had barely complained.

'Tell me about her.'

For a moment Amelia wondered if he would refuse. She knew she was pushing him, forcing him to face up to some of the grief he had been hoarding inside for years, but Amelia couldn't help it. Edward needed something to change in his life or he would spend his days in a never-ending cycle of guilt and regret. Maybe, just maybe, she could help him start living in the present. It was no less than what he'd done for her.

'She was kind,' Edward said eventually. 'Probably the kindest person I've ever met.'

'How did you meet?'

Edward smiled softly as if remembering. 'We were just children. Jane's family moved into the area and soon after our parents introduced us.' He shrugged. 'There was always the plan we would marry when we were an appropriate age.'

Amelia resisted the temptation to screw her face up in response. Her father had threatened her with an arranged marriage on a couple of occasions when she had particularly vexed him, but she'd known he would never go through with it. To her not having at least some say in who she spent the rest of her life with was the worst possible scenario. Although she had to concede her judgement when it came to matters of the heart was maybe not as reliable as she had once thought. McNair's face flashed before her eyes and for a moment Amelia felt the light-headed panicky sensation she always did when she thought of him. Focusing on Edward, she tried to push the building anxiety away.

'So that's what you did?' Amelia asked.

'When I came back from university we married as had always been planned.'

It wasn't the most romantic of stories, but Amelia could sense there was more to come.

'When did you fall in love?'

Edward looked at her strangely, then gave a low chuckle. 'You know, no one has ever asked me that before.' He paused as if thinking. 'We weren't in love when we married. I liked Jane, was very fond of her, but then I didn't love her. I suppose it crept up on me slowly. I just remember when Thomas was born looking down at him in my arms and realising how much I loved the woman who shared him with me.'

Amelia felt the tears spring to her eyes. She wasn't normally emotional. Sometimes her cousin Lizzie even said she was the least sentimental person in India, but she knew she could never hope for a love like Edward's.

'You must have been very happy.'

'We were. I spent my days running the estate. Jane looked after Thomas and in the afternoons we would all come together.'

It sounded like the perfect little family. No wonder losing his wife and son had hit Edward so hard. It wasn't as though he were an absentee husband or father, living it up in the city whilst his family festered on the country estate. They had been a proper family.

Edward closed his eyes as if remembering the good times and Amelia wondered if she had pushed him too far.

'I'm sorry for rearranging the room without asking you first,' she said softly.

Edward opened his eyes and looked at her for a long minute before nodding as if accepting her apology.

There was a rawness about his expression, something pained and resigned at the same time, and Amelia just wanted to smooth away the pain. Slowly she reached up and placed a hand on his cheek, running her fingers over the light stubble that was already growing after his morning shave. Their eyes met and for a long while they just sat, their bodies close together, Amelia's hand on his face.

Amelia knew she should get up and walk away. Nothing good could come out of gazing into Edward's eyes and wishing for something that he could never give her. He was a good man, probably the kindest man she had ever met. Part of her knew that she was still rebounding from her experience with McNair, looking for someone who was the polar opposite of that brutal, lying scoundrel, but deep down Amelia could acknowledge that wasn't all that was going on here. Edward had rescued her, swept her away from danger and cocooned her in the safety of his protection. There was something rather intoxicating about that.

Against her better judgement Amelia felt her body sway forward. Her eyes were still locked on his and she thought she saw a mutual spark of desire and affection burning there. Maybe he wouldn't reject her.

For a moment she thought there was a softness to Edward's face and then his expression hardened into something more akin to disgust. He pushed himself back, away from her, and shot to his feet.

'Edward?' she said, hating the pleading tone in her voice.

'Good day Amelia,' he said stiffly, all the intimacy and closeness of just a few minutes ago gone from his voice.

As she watched him give a curt bow and leave the room she felt embarrassment and anger and shame. Her anger wasn't directed towards Edward, he'd never given her a reason to think he wanted anything more than to do his civic duty and give her a safe place to stay. No, she was furious with herself.

Chapter Eleven

As she tossed and turned in bed Amelia realised she was full of regrets. Regret that she had ever trusted or cared for McNair, regret that she had so foolhardily followed his trail to Brighton, regret that she had confronted him over his lies and, of course, the climax of those events: picking up that letter opener to defend herself with.

However, her biggest regret of all didn't centre around McNair, or the myriad of mistakes she'd made with him, it was about the events of yesterday morning with Edward.

She'd finally felt as though she were getting through to him; he'd opened up a little about his wife, showing her snippets of the life he had once lived. Slowly and surely Amelia had thought he was softening towards her. She'd learnt to ignore his gruff moments and his requests to be left alone and had thought she detected a blossoming of affection.

Well, that would be all gone now. Amelia closed her eyes and once again saw the look of disgust on his face as she'd swayed towards him. Yet again she had thrown herself at a man she barely knew and hadn't considered the consequences.

She felt disappointed in herself. Ever since the moment

in McNair's study she had vowed to be more careful and considered. She couldn't take back how she had acted with McNair, but she could learn from it. For a long time she had allowed her attraction to the Captain to cloud her judgement, refusing to see him for what he really was. It was only when she was presented with indisputable proof McNair was a scoundrel that she had believed it.

Amelia sighed, not that she thought Edward was a scoundrel, far from it. His behaviour over the past week had been beyond reproach. He'd allowed her, a complete stranger, to stay in his house at her moment of need and had acted like a gentleman, albeit an aloof one, for the entire time.

With a dramatic groan Amelia sat up and threw off the sheets. She'd never been very good at lying and mulling over her problems. She was an impulsive person, someone more likely to cause a scene than to quietly think through a solution, but tonight something was holding her back.

It was Edward, Amelia realised, kind, gruff Edward. The man of few words who had opened up to her about his wife and son. She didn't want to hurt him, didn't want to add to his already substantial pain. He had suffered the ultimate loss, the loss of a beloved wife and child. It didn't matter it had been three years, Amelia rather suspected it could be thirty years and the pain would still be acute. She felt the blood rush to her cheeks as she relived the moment of embarrassment she'd felt before Edward had left the sitting room yesterday morning. How could she even begin to think she would be good enough to occupy a place in his heart alongside his treasured late wife and son?

She was a murderess, a wanted woman. He was the type of man to mourn his family for three years and to take in a desperate stranger; a good man, a kind man. In reality there was no comparison between them and Amelia found a bubble of hysterical laughter fighting to escape as she realised how ridiculous it had been to think Edward would ever want her.

The funny thing was Amelia had found herself imagining all kinds of domestic situations, situations she had no right to want. It had surprised her as she had never really thought about settling down. With McNair she had been dazzled by the promise of adventure and glamour, but yesterday morning as she'd sat in the sitting room with Edward she'd found herself wondering what a life of quiet domesticity would be if Edward was by her side.

Amelia snorted. That was something she certainly had no right dreaming about. Her circumstances meant she had no right to even fantasise about a life like that—besides, Edward would never love her. He'd not once given her any indication that he might be interested in her romantically, but still Amelia had found herself wishing for something that could never be.

He still loved his wife and probably thought one love in a lifetime was more than many people got to experience, he wouldn't be looking for a second. And if he was it certainly wouldn't be with a foolish murderess as his mate.

Amelia pulled a shawl around her shoulders and paced gloomily to the window and then back to the bed. She felt the tears begin to prick at her eyes and knew she would struggle to face Edward again. He was a gentleman and wouldn't bring up the moment they had shared in the sitting room, but it would always be hanging quietly there between them.

Maybe she should just leave. It would pre-empt any awkwardness and she would no longer be a burden to the man who has treated her so well. The idea of fending for herself again in a strange country made her stomach flip over with nerves and for a moment she almost threw herself back under the bedsheets. She knew Edward would struggle to look at her in the same way again, he'd probably wonder when she would next throw herself at him. His love for his late wife was all-encompassing, but even so Amelia knew he would never blame her, he was too good, too self-condemning. Edward would probably find a way to punish himself for her moment of weakness.

Amelia wandered back over to the window and leant on the sill, looking out at the garden she had tried to desecrate, and suddenly she realised what she must do. For once in her life she had to put someone else first.

Edward would not ever want her, he wasn't gaining anything from this arrangement. Amelia might want to stay, to hide in the sanctuary of Beechwood Manor and enjoy Edward's company, but for once she would not put herself first. It would be a hard step to take, but after all he had done for her Edward deserved it. Besides, she knew if she stayed her feeling for Edward might develop into something more and Amelia didn't know if she could bear to experience any more heartache. Finding out what sort of man McNair really was had almost broken her. Her heart wasn't strong enough to be rejected again.

Her decision made, Amelia gathered up her paltry belongings and swept out of the room before she could change her mind.

'You're up early, ducky, are the bad dreams troubling you again?' Goody bustled along the hallway as Amelia crept downstairs.

'I thought I'd get some air,' Amelia said, the words catching in her throat.

'At this time in the morning? You'll catch a deadly chill. Come and sit in the kitchen and I'll make you a nice warm glass of milk.'

'No,' Amelia said, more forcefully than she meant to. 'I really need to go outside.'

Goody looked at her appraisingly and then led her firmly towards the kitchen.

'There isn't a problem in the world that can't be sorted by a bellyful of warm milk and a seat by a newly lit fire.'

Amelia allowed herself to be led into the kitchen, all the time wondering if she should just break away and run. If Goody said one more kind thing to her, she might just break down and cry and then her resolve would waver.

'You sit there, ducky, and I'll be right back.'

Amelia watched as Goody bustled around the kitchen and before long a cup of warm milk and a plate of biscuits had been set down in front of her. Not knowing when her next meal might be, Amelia tucked in.

'You're thinking of leaving,' Goody said as she pulled out a stool and sat down opposite Amelia.

Amelia froze, mid-bite of a biscuit. The woman was a mind-reader.

'I...'

'Don't worry, my dear, it's not my place to talk you out of going.'

Amelia found herself a little disappointed. Maybe she did want someone to talk her out of fleeing the only place she had felt safe in the last few weeks.

'Now, I don't know what's happened to prompt this change and I'm sure you've already thought through all the consequences, but I couldn't have you leaving on an empty stomach.'

Amelia looked down into the frothy cup of milk and wondered if she had considered all the consequences. She had still killed a man, there would still be people out there looking for her, that hadn't changed just because she had foolishly developed feelings for Edward that could never be reciprocated.

'*Have* you thought through all the consequences?' Goody prompted softly.

'All my life I've put myself first,' Amelia said softly. 'Do you know I begged my cousin to swap identities with me so I could chase after Captain McNair? I didn't even consider the difficulties she would face, the lies she would have to tell, all for me.'

'She agreed?' Goody asked.

Amelia smiled. 'Lizzie is the kindest, most generous person I know. She'd do anything for me.' She paused, feeling a lump building in her throat. She wished Lizzie was here now, her cousin would know what to do, what to say, how to make everything right again. 'I guess I want to be more like her.'

'We are who we are,' Goody said quietly. 'It's no use wishing to change.'

'But I can be kinder, more thoughtful. I can put others' needs before my own.'

Goody looked at her thoughtfully. 'You're worried about the master.'

Amelia couldn't meet the older woman's eye. Goody had known Edward when his wife was alive, she'd run his household when it had been inhabited by a happy, living family. She wouldn't approve of Amelia pining after Edward, of her sullying the memory of his marriage.

'I don't know what has passed between you and it's not my place to know, but I do want to say this: Master Edward has been barely surviving these past three years. He has shut himself away from the world, retreated into his rooms and refused to move on. Now I understand grief, truly I do, but what he was doing was not healthy.' Goody leaned forward and took Amelia's hand. 'It has been good for him to have someone else to think about, to worry about. It's reminded him what it is to be human, to be alive. You've done more for him in a week than anyone has been able to do in three years.'

'But I haven't *done* anything.'

'Maybe nothing out of the ordinary. But you've showed him how to care again, how to break free from the constant cycle of grief and guilt and think of something else for a while. Don't underestimate the value of that. So whatever it is you think you've done wrong, just remember the good you've achieved by being in his life.'

Goody gave her one last pat on the hand, then got up and bustled out of the room, leaving Amelia to her thoughts. She wanted to believe Goody's words, wanted to think maybe she could make a difference to Edward's life. Even if she could bring him just a moment of happiness that would be worth a lot of sacrifice, but then she thought of the look on his face as she'd swayed towards him and she knew she couldn't stay. Far from easing his grief she had only made it more acute, reminded him how much he missed his family. She couldn't have his pain on her conscience along with everything else.

Nevertheless deep down she wanted to stay—in fact, she couldn't think of anywhere she would rather be. Even the rolling hills of Bombay didn't hold the same appeal as staying here with Edward where she felt safe.

Amelia almost surrendered to her desires, but something held her back. She thought of Lizzie, her kind and selfless cousin, and wondered what she would do. Lizzie always put others first, considered their needs long before her own. And if Amelia was honest with herself she knew Lizzie would leave. She would unobtrusively walk away and let Edward carry on with his new lease of life unhindered by her own emotional baggage.

Slipping out of the kitchen, Amelia felt the tears start to run down her face. Although she'd only been here just over a week it felt like home and she would be sad to leave Beechwood Manor and the people in it. Before she could change her mind Amelia pushed open the heavy wooden door and left the house, wondering what the next stage of her life would hold.

Chapter Twelve

Edward prowled round the house like a wounded bear, growling at any staff that crossed his path. He had barely slept and now something didn't feel right. The house felt empty, deserted, despite there being the maids and other servants present that Mrs Henshaw had hired. He had spent the time since he'd woken up alternating between wanting to seek Amelia out and wanting to avoid her at all costs.

He didn't blame her for the moment they shared the morning before. He had told her things he'd never told anyone else and a closeness, an intimacy, had followed. That in itself wasn't a problem, it was his reaction to her that had caused him to toss and turn all night.

Edward pictured her eyes fluttering closed, the delicate eyelashes resting on her cheeks, and her swaying towards him. His body reacted instantly to the memory, a coil tightening inside him and a surge of desire flowing all the way to his very core.

This was what disgusted him. He was still mourning the deaths of his wife and son. They would never laugh or cry or shout with joy again and here he was sullying their memory with a fantasy about the first pretty young woman who came along. Every day since the fire Edward had wished it had been him who had been taken and not them. He knew his retreat from the world had partially been from grief, but also stemmed from a need to punish himself. Then Amelia had crashed into his life and everything had changed. Yesterday wasn't the first time he'd felt the hot burn of desire for his houseguest and he didn't know how to cope with it.

Most of him wanted to retreat further, to punish himself for the betrayal of his wife and son's memories, but a small rebellious part kept asking what he was so disgusted with himself about. Jane wouldn't want him to live like this, she'd much rather he enjoyed the company of others, but that didn't mean he had permission to lust after Amelia.

'Good morning, sir,' Mrs Henshaw said as she bustled out of the kitchen.

'Good morning.'

'Would it be too bold to venture that you're looking for Miss Amelia, sir?'

Edward tried not to let the surprise show on his face as his housekeeper asked the question.

'Has she said something?' he asked abruptly.

'Nothing at all, sir, and it's not my place to pry.'

Edward saw the knowing glint in Mrs Henshaw's eyes and wondered if there were any goings on in his household she wasn't aware of.

'It's just Miss Amelia left early this morning. I thought you might like to know.'

Edward froze, every muscle in his body seizing up at once.

'She left?'

'Yes, sir. At about half past seven. She wasn't to be swayed from her decision to leave.'

Edward let out a growl of frustration. He'd driven her away.

'Maybe it's for the best,' Edward said quietly. He

couldn't quite bring himself to believe his own words, though. Amelia was out there on her own, scared and vulnerable, at the mercy of strangers. All because of him. He'd seen the expression in her eyes as he'd backed away from her, the hurt and confusion. He should have uttered a few words of comfort.

'Maybe it is, sir. As long as that scoundrel doesn't find her, of course. Or the law doesn't catch up with her. Or she doesn't starve or freeze to death.'

Edward was too caught up in his own thoughts to reply immediately. McNair, the villainous cad who had seduced Amelia, struck her and provoked her into self-defence, was most likely somewhere out there. Either that or someone would be looking for Amelia for his murder. Whichever scenario was true, things were grim for Amelia and he'd just pushed her away from the one place she'd felt safe.

'Of course you could go and get her back,' Mrs Henshaw said nonchalantly. 'The first coach doesn't leave until noon and, unless she plans on walking to London, I doubt she's got further than the village.'

Part of Edward wondered if it would be easier just to let her go. Then he wouldn't have to deal with the maelstrom of feelings building inside him. If Amelia was out of his life he could go back to just feeling guilty about the fire and his lack of ability to protect those he cared most about. Edward snorted. He knew this was no way to live, but the guilt had been part of his life for so long he didn't know how to live without it.

He loved his late wife, he missed her every day, but now he had agreed to help Amelia he felt a modicum of responsibility for her. If she was put in danger because of him, he wouldn't be able to forgive himself.

'I'll just check she's not wanting for anything,' Edward

said, half to himself, as he pulled on his overcoat and strode towards the door.

'I'll make lunch for two, then, shall I?' he heard Mrs Henshaw shout cheerily after him before the heavy wooden door closed behind him.

As he hurried through the estate towards the village Edward felt a knot of tension building in his stomach. He was worried about her safety, but that wasn't all that was troubling him. After all, how much trouble could one young woman get into in a couple of hours? No, he realised he was also worrying that she might refuse to return to Beechwood Manor with him.

He didn't want to admit it but he had got used to having Amelia around the house. Where a week ago he was irritated by her soft voice humming as he tried to focus on his accounts or her incessant chatter over dinner, now he quite looked forward to meeting her in the hallway or watching her as she strolled through the gardens.

Within fifteen minutes he was on the outskirts of the village and he slowed his pace a little so as not to attract any undue attention. Already he knew the whole village was gossiping about how he'd finally been seen out and about and how he'd opened the house up once again, employing staff and allowing the gardens to be tended. He didn't need any additional gossip about him dashing through the narrow streets like a madman.

Keeping vigilant for anyone who looked out of place, Edward made his way to the village square, wondering if Amelia would be waiting for the coach or if she had resumed her journey across the Downs by foot. A momentary wave of panic engulfed him as he pictured her caught in another storm, drenched to the bone and shivering in a ditch somewhere, and he decided not to examine the depth of his concern in too much detail.

As he caught sight of the clock tower Edward saw a familiar flash of light blue fabric rounding a corner at the end of the street. Amelia came into view and Edward found himself suffused with relief. He'd found her. She wasn't injured in a ditch or halfway to London or in the hands of the evil scoundrel who had seduced her. Within a few minutes they would be on their way back home and he could ensure she was safe once again.

Just as he was about to raise his hand to catch her attention a man in a bright blue jacket and crisp white shirt caught his eye. The man was young, handsome and very well presented. As he walked through the village Edward could see some of the young women surreptitiously following his movements and glancing in his direction.

Suddenly Edward knew this man was McNair. He knew it as surely as if they'd been introduced. There was an arrogant air about him, an irritating swagger, and Edward could see innocent young women would be taken in by his easy charm and good looks. Simmering underneath all of that was a restrained anger and a sense of purpose and Edward knew this was a man he had to protect Amelia from at all costs.

With a spurt of speed Edward strode past the man he thought to be McNair and hurried towards Amelia. She was unaware of either man approaching yet, distracted by something in a shop window, and Edward just hoped he could get to her before she spotted the man she thought she'd murdered. Knowing Amelia, she would make a scene.

He reached her just as she turned away from the shop window, threw an arm around her waist and barrelled her into a small alleyway.

'Edward,' Amelia exclaimed, with a loud exhalation, her body shaking with the shock of being manhandled and taken by surprise.

His body had pressed up against hers in an entirely inappropriate way and for a few seconds Edward lost the ability to speak. She was soft and warm and every curve of her body seemed to fit his perfectly. Rousing himself, he pulled away a little, but only as far as to maintain an appropriate distance between their bodies whilst still being able to talk quietly to her.

'He's here,' he said quietly, hearing the strain in his own voice.

Amelia understood immediately and the colour drained from her face.

'He can't be. He's dead. I killed him.' There was a slight note of hysteria in her voice and Edward saw her begin to panic. 'You must be mistaken, you don't know what he looks like.'

'Amelia, he's here. I need you to keep calm.'

She writhed, pressing herself away from the wall and against him, seemingly unaware of the contact between their bodies. Edward forced himself to focus, waiting until she collapsed back against the bricks, her body going limp. Edward knew he had a limited amount of time before she either dashed out into the street or made such a fuss other people would come to investigate.

'Amelia, you need to take a look and tell me if it's him or not,' Edward said. 'But you need to do it carefully.'

'He's dead.'

'Well, let's reassess that after you've looked at this man.'

'He's dead.'

Edward leaned forward and gently cupped her chin with his hand, his large fingers feeling oversized and clumsy against her delicate features. He waited until her eyes met his and until the panic had subsided.

'Whoever this man is, I won't let him hurt you. I just need you to have a look.'

He watched as she regained control of herself, noting her squared shoulder, straightened back and raised chin. She was ready.

'When I last saw him he was heading towards the clock tower on this side of the street,' Edward said.

Amelia edged towards the end of the alleyway and cautiously peered out. She looked left and right, her entire body tense as if ready to flee at the slightest hint of danger. Slowly Edward could see her relax as she studied the people in the village square and along the shopfronts without seeing anyone she recognised. Then she stiffened. Edward heard a sharp intake of breath and quickly pulled her back towards him. She allowed him to scoop her in to his chest and as he held her body against his Edward could feel her shuddering.

'He was dead,' she whispered.

Although Amelia was in shock now, Edward knew seeing McNair would be a good thing in the long run. Here was the proof she needed to know she hadn't killed a man. For days Edward had watched her as she suffered, not knowing how to ease the guilt and regret she was living with. Now, although they had to worry about McNair seeking revenge, Amelia would at least be able to move on with her life.

And move on from you, a rebellious little voice said inside Edward's head. He squashed it down, but the seed had been planted. She could move on from Beechwood Manor now. He would get what he'd wished for on numerous occasions in the past week: his house back to himself and a life of solitude again.

'What do we do?' Amelia asked, turning her beseeching blue eyes up towards him.

'Let's get you home,' Edward said, taking charge of the situation. 'He hasn't seen you and no one knows you're here. There should be no reason for him to tarry in the village for more than a day. We'll keep you hidden until he's passed through.'

He could see his words were having a soothing effect on Amelia and was relieved when she nodded in agreement.

'Come with me.' Edward took her hand and led her further down the alleyway between the shops and round the corner at the back. They had to scramble over some old crates, but after a few minutes they were out of the village and on the path back to Beechwood Manor.

'Why is he here?' Amelia asked as they walked. Every few seconds she would turn and glance over her shoulder as if checking if they were being followed.

Edward shrugged. 'It's the logical place to start looking for you, a village on the route to London. You'd have to pass through if you took the stagecoach. He's probably trying to trace your movements.'

Amelia fell silent. As she moved closer in towards Edward, taking his arm as she stepped across a puddle, Edward felt inordinately pleased at the implied trust in her gesture. She wanted him close, she wanted him to be the one to protect her. He'd forgotten quite how intoxicating being needed could feel.

Chapter Thirteen

Amelia was a mess. She'd been a bundle of nerves for the last few days and it didn't seem to be getting any better. She knew she should be pleased—after seeing McNair in the village it was quite clear she hadn't killed the man, but that fact did leave him alive and most likely looking for revenge.

'Amelia,' Edward called as she roamed through the house aimlessly. 'Come here. I have a surprise for you.'

Relieved she wouldn't have to be alone with her thoughts any longer Amelia hurried to the hallway where Edward was waiting for her.

He grabbed her hand, obviously excited by whatever it was he wanted to show her, and pulled her outside. Amelia was aware of the tingle in her fingers as his skin met hers and wondered if any woman would be strong enough *not* to fall for him in these circumstances. He was her knight, her hero, and it was so typically unfair that she could never have him.

'Where are we going, Edward?' Amelia laughed as he pulled her along. She hadn't seen him this excited before, there was something boyish and carefree about his demeanour. It suited him.

'You'll see.'

They dodged the gardener, who stared after them with a raise of his eyebrows and a knowing expression, and continued on to the outbuildings.

'Here we are,' Edward said, as he pushed open the door to one of the huge barns.

'A barn?' Amelia asked. 'This is my surprise.'

Ever since Edward had tracked her to the village and escorted her back to the house Amelia had sensed a change in him. It wasn't huge or obvious, but she noticed he was allowing himself to smile a little more, to spend a few more minutes conversing with her rather than hurrying off to his private rooms. It was as though he'd realised he was allowed to enjoy her company, that the threat of her leaving had been enough to prompt him to appreciate how human contact could enhance his life.

'It's what's inside the barn.' He pulled her inside and whilst her eyes adjusted to the darkness Amelia let her imagination run wild, hoping Edward might take advantage of the low light and kiss her just as she wanted him to. Of course it didn't happen, Edward clearly didn't see her as a romantic prospect, but since he'd brought her back from the village there was a greater sense of companionship, maybe even friendship between them.

In the gloom she heard a rustling noise and then a louder tapping, as if a hoof was hitting the floor.

Edward pulled her forward again and directed her to a stall. Amelia peered in and let out a squeal of delight. Inside was a beautiful light bay horse with a glossy coat and silky black mane.

More stomping and a quiet whinny was enough to tear Amelia away from the first stall and to look into the second. Inside was a massive black stallion, standing proud and tall and just a little bit haughty. All in all the perfect horse for Edward.

'You bought two horses.' Amelia turned to Edward with a smile. He glanced guiltily at the stall on the end.

'Well...' Edward said with a sheepish smile. 'I actually bought three.'

Amelia was over there immediately and couldn't help but smile. Inside the third stall was a heavily pregnant mare, barely able to stand but munching away happily on some fresh hay.

'Who buys a pregnant horse?' Amelia asked with a laugh.

'I didn't want to separate them,' Edward said a little uncomfortably.

Amelia glanced back in at the black stallion and realised the depth of love the man standing before her was capable of. He'd even bought a pregnant mare just so his new stallion wouldn't be separated from the foal. Edward might appear stern and sombre, but over the past week Amelia had caught glimpses of the man underneath, the man who sheltered damsels in distress, inspired loyalty in his servants and bought a pregnant mare for sentimental reasons.

'And they threw her in for free with the other two.'

Amelia knew Edward would have bought her even if she had been at a premium.

'Afternoon, sir,' a young man said as he pushed open the door to the stable.

'Amelia, this is Tom, our new groom. Tom, this is Miss Amelia.'

He doffed his cap and gave a little bow, before going straight in to see the pregnant mare.

'Would you like to take the horses out, sir?' he called from the stall, all the while petting and soothing the heavy horse.

Edward looked at Amelia with a raised eyebrow and allowed himself a low chuckle at her enthusiastic response.

'I think the lady would.'

Amelia watched as the groom fitted the saddle on to the bay mare and Edward did the same with the stallion. He talked softly to the huge horse throughout, running his large hands over its back and calming the great beast. Amelia took one last look at the heavily pregnant mare still lying in her stall and sent a quick prayer that the foal would be delivered safely, then she helped to lead the two horses out into the yard.

Edward handed the reins of the stallion over to the groom and came up behind her.

'Can you ride?' he asked.

Amelia loved riding. There was an unrivalled freedom on horseback. In India she would often saddle up her horse, persuade someone to join her and roam the countryside for hours at a time.

'I can ride,' Amelia said. 'The real question is can you keep up?'

As Edward helped her mount her horse Amelia felt some of the tension from the day slipping from her shoulders. Soon it would just be her and Edward and the open countryside. She wouldn't have to worry about McNair or the future or even her burgeoning feelings for Edward.

'Let's ride,' Edward said as he swung himself up on to his horse.

Amelia soon found her confidence in the saddle, despite not being correctly attired for riding and it being her first ride out for a few months. They rode in silence for a while, both enjoying the crisp, fresh country air and the sun on their faces.

'We'll stick to the estate,' Edward informed her, 'so

there's no need to worry about bumping into anyone we don't wish to.'

'Thank you,' Amelia said quietly.

For now she just wanted to ride. She wanted to forget the feeling of dread that had planted itself deep inside her when she'd caught sight of McNair, she wanted to forget the sadness that had led to her leaving Beechwood Manor, sadness that she could never mean as much to Edward as his late wife. No, later she could dwell on all of that, but for now she was going to enjoy the fresh air and freedom being on horseback allowed.

Edward was a surprisingly good host, pointing out all the features of the estate, grimacing as he saw how some parts were overgrown or walls had fallen into disrepair, but generally cheerful. Amelia knew he was doing this all for her, trying to instil some normality into her life after the supremely stressful episode a few days ago. He didn't bring up their encounter in the village whilst they rode, or the reason why she had left, but instead stuck to more mundane subjects.

'This wall marks the edge of the estate,' Edward explained as they reached the top of a small hill. 'Those cottages over there are tenant cottages and the farm you can see in the distance belongs to the estate, too.'

Amelia noticed the long silence that followed as Edward surveyed his domain. She wondered if this was the first time he'd been out this far since the fire and whether he regretted his decision to ride up here.

'I haven't been to see my tenants for three years,' he said after a few minutes.

'I'm sure they understand.'

'Mr Guthry ensures the cottages are well looked after and collects the rent, but I always imagined myself a hands-on landlord.'

'You've had a lot to deal with.'

Edward fell silent and then turned his horse away so he was facing back towards his estate and the house. From up here there was a good view of the rolling countryside and Beechwood Manor in the middle. Amelia grimaced as she, too, turned around and saw they were looking at the East Wing of the house.

'I need to get that repaired,' Edward said quietly. 'One day.'

Amelia leaned over and placed a hand on his arm. Edward stiffened for a second, but did not shake her off.

'Why did you leave?' Edward asked eventually.

Amelia had known this question would come and Edward deserved an answer, but she wasn't sure if she could tell him the truth.

'I didn't think you'd want me around,' she said.

'I don't want you to ever put yourself at risk like that again.'

Amelia sensed he wanted to say more, but something was holding him back. She willed him to open up, to tell her he felt *something* for her, but he remained quiet. Allowing herself a moment of sadness, Amelia knew it was too much to expect. She should be content that Edward had realised he was allowed to enjoy her company, that they could live side by side in easy companionship—anything else was just pure fantasy on her part.

'What do we do about McNair?' Amelia asked.

'Nothing. At least nothing for now. No one knows you're here, apart from Mrs Henshaw and she's the most loyal person I know.'

'One of the servants might talk.'

Edward shook his head. 'They don't know who you are and they would have no cause to talk to McNair anyway.'

'I thought I'd killed him.'

Edward must have heard the tremor in her voice because immediately he dismounted, took her horse's reins in his hand and lifted her out of the saddle. His strong hands encircled her waist and once again Amelia felt safe and secure.

'You didn't kill him,' Edward said softly. 'And even if you had it was self-defence. He struck you, he hurt you. A man like that doesn't deserve your pity or your regrets.'

Once again Amelia could picture the letter opener slipping into McNair's flesh, the warm trickle of blood over her hand.

'Stop it,' Edward said sharply. 'Whatever you're thinking, stop it.'

'Why is he here? Why is he looking for me?'

'I don't know the man, but I've encountered enough of his type in my life. To him a physical wound won't be anywhere near as bad as a wound to his pride. You got the better of him and I'm sure he wants revenge for that.'

Amelia felt herself shiver. The murderous look that had flashed in McNair's eyes just before he'd struck her was enough to scare someone much braver than her.

'But he won't get anywhere near you. I promise I will not let him hurt you.'

As Amelia gazed up into Edward's eyes she believed him and some of the fear and the worry began to ebb away.

'But—' Amelia began, but Edward cut her off, tilting her chin up with a gentle finger so she had to meet his eye again.

'I promise I will protect you.'

Amelia had been about to ask when she had to leave Beechwood Manor, but all thoughts were dashed from her head as Edward's fingers touched the skin of her chin. For a moment she thought he might kiss her and her entire body willed him to dip his head and claim her as his, but it was not to be so.

Slowly Edward stepped away and Amelia fought to hide her disappointment. It was for the best. At least that was what she had to keep telling herself. Not that she truly believed that in her heart. If Edward leaned forward and kissed her she would be smiling for the rest of her days. Amelia knew she had doubted her burgeoning feelings for Edward these past couple of weeks, telling herself that her judgement couldn't be trusted, that she'd fallen for a scoundrel before, but ever since Edward had promised not to let McNair hurt her Amelia had known the truth. He was a good man, a man no one would ever regret loving, if he loved you back, of course.

As Edward helped her back into the saddle he smiled up at her softly and a little sadly and Amelia wondered if he were thinking about his wife and son. Maybe wishing it was them he was out riding with instead of her.

'I was thinking about your cousin,' Edward said as they began the ride home.

Amelia frowned, wondering why on earth he would be thinking about Lizzie.

'You said you had swapped identities to allow you to travel to Brighton.'

'Yes, I hadn't seen my aunt since I was very young so Lizzie was going to pretend to be me until I returned to London.'

'Would you like me to ask Mr Guthry to send someone to check on her well-being? I doubt McNair would harm her, but if he pays someone else to look into the matter for him they might fall for your ruse and think your cousin is you.'

Suddenly all the blood drained from Amelia's face and

she felt a little light headed. Had she underestimated the danger Lizzie was in? She loved her cousin more than anyone in the entire world and she wanted to protect her from this mess above anything else. The letter she had penned a week ago would hopefully be well on its way to Lizzie by now, but maybe that wasn't enough.

'I'll write again when we get back to the house. Perhaps Mr Guthry could pass on my letter so I know Lizzie receives it.'

'I received a note from Mr Guthry yesterday. He is still following McNair's trail, but promises to come and update us in the next couple of days. We shall ask him to organise someone to check on Lizzie's safety then,' Edward said decisively.

Amelia felt the tears welling in her eyes and tried to suppress them. Edward was thoughtful and considerate, he was even thinking of the safety of a woman he'd never met, and from what she had heard about his late wife she had been the same. Amelia would never be able to live up to her character, it was ridiculous to even dream she might.

As soon as they returned to Beechwood Manor, Amelia excused herself, went to her room and hurriedly began writing to Lizzie, hoping that nothing befell her cousin before the warning reached her.

Dearest Lizzie,
I do not know if you received my last letter, but I am in a perilous position and am worried for your safety, too. Captain McNair turned out to be exactly the scoundrel you suspected and as always I wish I had listened to you at the time. Then this entire mess could have been avoided.

Lizzie, I did something terrible, something I cannot bear to write down, and now McNair is out for revenge. I worry for you, for your safety as you pretend to be me. Please be careful.

Do not expend too much energy worrying for me. For now, at least, I am safe and cared for. When I was fleeing from Brighton I stumbled upon an old house inhabited by a gentleman. Edward has sheltered me and cared for me over the past two weeks and I could not ask for a better host.

Oh, he grumbles and sometimes is a little crabby. In fact he reminds me of that bear we saw once in the marketplace in Aska. Of course he's completely harmless...in fact, underneath it all he's one of the kindest people I've ever met.

Not that I mind his bearish demeanour. He's been beset by tragedy. Three years ago he lost his wife and young son in a fire. Until I came into his life I think he'd barely spoken to another person for years. It's terrible how such a kind and generous person can be struck by such sad circumstances.

Oh, Lizzie, I wish you were here with me. I need your sensible counsel, your words of wisdom. I think I might be falling for Edward.

I know, I know... I hardly know the man. But if you only could see him, Lizzie, and understand what he's done for me already I truly think this time you would approve.

Of course none of that matters. Edward still mourns his wife and his son. His late wife sounds so lovely, so kind. I know I could never live up to her. And Edward does not deserve second-best. I am aware of all of this, but still my heart sings every time I see him.

What should I do?

Please keep yourself safe and I hope we will be reunited soon.

All my love,

Amelia

Chapter Fourteen

Three days later Mr Guthry made an appearance. Edward had been sitting at his old desk in the study, a room he hadn't entered for at least two years. The furniture was recently polished and the room aired, but there was still a slight musty, disused feel about it.

He had spread out a number of documents pertaining to the estate and was going over his accounts for the past twelve months. Although he had kept abreast of what was happening to his birthright, Edward knew he had been a neglectful owner these past few years. It was the small things, like the Richardsons, who were one of his tenant-farmer families. They'd had to source someone to repair their roof when it had collapsed the previous year. In the past Edward would have never let one of his properties fall into such a state that a roof might even threaten to fall in. Someone could have been hurt.

A tap at the door made him look up from his papers.

'Mr Guthry here to see you, sir,' one of the new maids said with a deferential curtsy.

'Show him in. And have you seen Miss Amelia?'

'I think she's out with the horses, sir.'

He hadn't been sure of himself when he'd bought the

horses, it had been an impulsive action, one that he hadn't quite thought through. After chasing Amelia into the village of Denton he had allowed himself to acknowledge he actually enjoyed her company. When he had noticed the advertisement for the sale of the horses from a neighbouring estate he had felt an urge to do something to take her mind off McNair and what the rogue wanted with her. It had worked. Amelia had fallen in love with the three beasts and spent a lot of time out there rubbing them down or riding.

Mr Guthry entered and shook Edward's hand, his face grim.

'Miss Amelia should hear what I have to say,' he said with a grimace as Edward indicated the man should sit.

Edward thought about screening the information his steward was bringing first, but decided it was Amelia's future at stake, so instead strode outside to find her.

She was hurrying back towards the house from the stables, her hair windswept and her cheeks rosy from the fresh air. She looked happy, the fear that had been stalking her for the past few days was finally lifting, and Edward was loathe to shatter that happiness.

'Mr Guthry's here,' Edward said as they met.

Immediately the worry was back. He could see it in the small frown lines between her eyebrows and the way she sucked in her lower lip.

'What did he say?'

'He hasn't told me anything yet. I thought we should hear whatever he has to say together.'

Edward wondered if he'd made the right decision. When Jane was alive he had always dealt with any unsavoury business without involving her. He'd protected her from the worst in the world, but Amelia was stronger than Jane had been. She'd been through so much in the last few weeks and was still fighting. It only seemed right to let her hear what Guthry had to say first hand. It was her life after all.

Mr Guthry was waiting for them and looked anxious to begin.

'Well, firstly, McNair is alive. I thought you'd like to know straight off. But I have some worrying news, miss… worrying news indeed. I don't wish to alarm you, but I need to warn you. I'd never forgive myself if something happened and I hadn't warned you.'

'Start at the beginning, Mr Guthry,' Edward said sooth-ingly. He glanced at Amelia and saw she had initially blanched at Guthry's warning, but had managed to re-gain her composure.

'Well, I travelled to Brighton to track down this fellow of yours, Captain McNair. It wasn't all that difficult to find where he resided, but the man himself was long gone.'

Edward supposed McNair had set off after Amelia soon after he had recovered from the wound she had inflicted upon him.

'I started to ask around, try to build up a picture of the man, and I can tell you it wasn't good.' Guthry shook his head vehemently and clasped his hands together.

'He's in debt with everyone, a gambler and a drinker, and no one would come out and say it, but I gathered he's seduced one or two women he shouldn't have.' Guthry's ears turned pink as he glanced at Amelia. 'Begging your pardon, miss, but that's what I was told.'

Amelia gestured for him to continue, her face impas-sive and only her stiff posture betraying the tension she must be feeling.

'It took me a while to pick up his trail, but after a few days I caught up with him in the village of Southease. He was asking everyone if they had seen a young woman fit-ting your description.'

Edward knew the village well. It was only a few miles away and he supposed McNair must have followed Amelia's trail from there to here.

'I bought some of the locals drinks to find out what he'd been asking them and it turns out McNair was rather vocal when under the influence of a few too many cups of ale. He said he was tracking his wife, who had attacked him and then fled, and that when he caught up with her then her life wouldn't be worth living.' Guthry flicked an apologetic glance in Amelia's direction. 'I'm sorry, miss, I wish I had better news.'

Amelia shook her head. 'You've been very diligent, Mr Guthry. Thank you for everything you have done.'

'There's one more thing, miss. One of the locals told him they'd seen a young woman covered in blood about a week previously. Pointed him in this direction.'

Which explained why McNair had been in the village a few days ago.

'I've spent the last few days travelling backwards and forward between the local villages, trying to pick up his trail again, but he's disappeared.'

'Thank you, Mr Guthry, you've been very thorough,' Edward said.

'My pleasure, Sir Edward. I only wish I had better news.'

'I have another request, Mr Guthry, if you don't mind.'

The portly man nodded, his face serious and his demeanour showing he was ready to do whatever was asked of him.

'Miss Amelia's cousin is currently residing in London. I won't go into details, but she has assumed Miss Amelia's identity for a few weeks. We are concerned that there is a small chance she may be in danger from McNair due to her relationship with Miss Amelia.'

'I'll travel to London straight away,' Mr Guthry said.

'It would be enough to send a trusted associate,' Edward said. 'We may well need you here in the next couple of weeks.'

'I have a young assistant who is much faster on a horse and would be honoured to assist us in this matter,' Mr Guthry said, 'I will ensure he sets out as soon as I return.'

'Thank you,' Amelia said, taking Mr Guthry's hand and squeezing it warmly. 'Here are the details he will need to find Lizzie and this is a letter outlining the circumstances for her.' She handed over the envelope and the name and address of her aunt in London.

Edward showed Mr Guthry out, asking his steward to return in a day or two to discuss estate business, but for now he knew he needed to check Amelia was not too shaken by Guthry's account.

Amelia was slumped in one of the comfortable armchairs he had moved himself from his rooms in the West Wing to his newly re-opened study.

'Amelia…' he began, not sure where to start.

'I'm a terrible person,' she wailed, taking Edward by surprise. He had expected fear, uncertainty, maybe even gratitude for the confirmation she wasn't a murderess, but not this.

'You're not a terrible person.'

She levelled him with a black look and Edward had to contain a sigh. He had thought Amelia's dramatic outbursts were a thing of the past. He glanced a little wistfully at the pile of simple, undramatic papers on his desk before turning his attention back to Amelia.

'I am a terrible person. I wished him dead,' she whispered this last part. 'I wished that I had killed him. Even when I saw him with my own eyes I wished McNair dead.'

Edward collapsed in the armchair opposite her and regarded the woman in front of him for a minute. His instinct was to flee, to leave her to work through this dilemma on her own, but something kept him in the chair. He knew all about guilt, about punishing oneself for things that were not your fault. He knew how it could eat away at a person, strip them of hope of happiness and make them question their reasons for living.

'The man tricked you, stole away your innocence, struck you and threatened your life. Show me a hundred people McNair has injured like you and I'll show you a hundred people who wished him dead.'

'But for weeks I've hated myself for killing him...' Amelia paused and then corrected herself. 'Well, thinking that I'd killed him.'

'And if you didn't show remorse for your actions I would be much more concerned I was sheltering a monster,' Edward said, trying to inject some joviality into the room.

'Do you think I'm a monster?' Amelia asked quietly, her face pale and her lips trembling.

Edward silently cursed his choice of words and resisted the temptation to lever himself out of his chair and take her hand. Amelia was the sort of woman who stirred a man's protective side, but it wasn't his place to comfort her. He had promised to shelter her, to provide her somewhere safe to stay whilst she worked out what to do, and he would even go so far as to protect her from the cad that had seduced and betrayed her, but he could not allow himself to go any further than that. If he took her hand, well, Edward didn't want to think of how his body might react and that would lead to the now familiar feelings of grief and self-reproach. So instead he remained where he was, but spoke softly and kindly.

'You're not a monster, Amelia. You're a wonderful, fun, kind person who was treated very badly by that scoundrel.

It is human nature to want him punished, just as it is human nature to regret actions taken on the spur of the moment.'

'I'm scared, Edward. What does he want from me?'

Edward was all too aware of what McNair wanted from Amelia. In all likelihood he wanted to hurt her as she had hurt him, wound her pride just as his had been wounded.

'It doesn't matter what he wants, he's not going to find you.'

Amelia bit her lip and nodded unconvincingly.

'He's not going to find you, Amelia. You have to believe that.'

'But he was right here, in the village.'

'That was three days ago. If he'd picked up your trail, if he knew you were here with me, then he would have made his move by now.'

She looked as though she were digesting that piece of information, weighing it up and looking for flaws.

'He's not going to give up.'

Edward had to agree with her there. He didn't know the man, but he'd come across plenty like him in his time. McNair wouldn't rest until Amelia had paid for her attack on him.

'It doesn't matter. He has no idea where you are and by now he would have moved on, somewhere further away.'

'I'll always have to be looking over my shoulder.'

Edward grimaced. She was right, her life would be spent waiting for McNair to catch up with her.

'I don't know what to do, Edward.'

'Stay here with me, at least for a while longer,' he said with authority. 'Write to your father, explain exactly what has happened and ask for his assistance.'

As soon as the words were out of his mouth Edward found himself gawping. He had never meant to ask her to stay a while longer.

'Run back to India?'

Something inside him wanted to withdraw the invitation for her to stay with him whilst she awaited her father's reply, it had been issued spontaneously without him fully thinking through the consequences, but he kept quiet. Amelia was alone and in danger, he couldn't be the man to turn her out into the world. And after all it was only a few weeks, maybe a couple of months, and then Beechwood Manor would become his private sanctuary again.

She looked down at him with those piercing blue eyes, an uncharacteristic uncertainty behind them.

'I can stay here, with you, until my father sends for me?'

'I suppose I have the space for you,' Edward said.

Amelia launched herself out of the chair and into his arms. After his initial shock Edward found himself instinctively embracing her, pulling her closer. She was warm and soft and inviting and as Edward held her in his arms he felt his heart begin to hammer faster in his chest.

'Thank you, thank you, thank you,' Amelia said, pulling away a little.

Their eyes met and Edward felt a spark fly between them, but then Amelia looked away, stiffening slightly. She stood, gave a hurried little curtsy, something she'd never done before in his presence, and fled the room.

Chapter Fifteen

Amelia read through the letter to her father one last time, grimaced and then signed her name. She was glad she wouldn't be there to see his reaction first hand. No doubt he would curse and shout when he read she wasn't in London finding herself a well-to-do husband.

Dearest Papa,

I hope you are keeping well. I miss you and find myself wishing I could be back in the hills of Bombay, awaiting the first of the monsoon rains with you. Do you remember when Mama was still alive and we would sit on the veranda watching the first heavy drops hit the dusty ground? I can still smell that earthy scent Mama used to love so much as if it were yesterday.

Papa, I'm so ashamed to have to write this, but I need your help. I'm in trouble and, although I know you will be angry and disappointed, you are the only person I can turn to. On arriving in London I did a silly thing: I asked Lizzie to assume my identity for a few days whilst I travelled on to Brighton alone.

I don't know if you remember Captain McNair

from the regiment in Bombay, but I am ashamed to admit I was a little infatuated with him. I thought ours would be a wonderful reunion after the time we spent together last year, but I judged him wrongly.

After travelling down to Brighton to find Captain McNair I discovered he had been married all the time I had known him in India. He was planning on seducing me, convincing me to run away with him and then extorting money from you for my scandal-free return. Only the intervention of his commanding officer saved me from my fate and McNair was sent home to his ailing wife.

When I found this out on arriving in Brighton I threatened to expose him as a scoundrel and things got a little heated. I did something awful, Papa. I stabbed him with a letter opener.

Now I do not know what to do. I am currently staying with a gentleman by the name of Sir Edward Gray. He is sheltering me from McNair, who I think will be seeking revenge. I regret my actions every minute of every day, but I am scared of what McNair will do to me.

Papa, I know I have been foolish and I know I have been selfish, but I truly need your help.

I was hoping you might be able to find a way to organise a passage back to India. If I could come home to you, I promise to try and be a more docile and obedient daughter.

Please help me, Papa.
I love you and miss you.
Amelia

Folding the letter, Amelia then slipped it into an envelope and wrote the address on the front before making her way to the kitchens to find how Goody was getting on with the favour she'd asked of her.

Amelia hovered around the kitchen whilst Goody bustled backwards and forward, chatting away at the same time. It was relaxing being in here with Goody. The woman was content to carry out a conversation with just the minimum of prompting, allowing Amelia's mind to wander but without her being able to focus too long on one thing.

'We've got jams, fresh bread, a fruit cake and some pickles. I think the tenants will be delighted with the hampers.'

Amelia peered inside, wondering if it was a good idea to spend the entire day out and about with Edward. She wanted to do something to say thank you, to show she appreciated him letting her stay whilst she awaited a reply from her father, but maybe an activity that threw them together all day was not the best idea. She hated to admit that she yearned for him, when he wasn't close by she missed him physically.

She wanted him to look at her the way he looked when he spoke of his late wife and son, that adoration, that eternal love, but it was clear that would never happen. Over the past week Edward had opened up a little, shown her more of his real self, and Amelia had just found herself wanting him even more, but today she would suppress all those feelings and focus on being a good guest and friend.

Once Goody indicated everything was ready Amelia gathered up the baskets and thanked the older woman for all her hard work. Whatever she felt for Edward she still wanted to say thank you to him for letting her stay. She'd seen the regret and wistfulness in his face a few days previously when he'd talked of how he had neglected his tenants and this was an area where Amelia could excel.

She loved entertaining and meeting new people. She

was naturally confident and outgoing, whereas Edward was more reserved. He might struggle to approach the tenants he'd neglected for so long on his own, but he would feel increasingly guilty the longer he left it. Amelia thought she could help smooth the way and take some of the awkwardness out of the situation.

'Knock-knock,' Mr Guthry said as he peered round the kitchen door and smiled sheepishly as he caught sight of the two women.

'Mr Guthry, what a pleasant surprise. I had no idea we were expecting you today.' Although Amelia greeted him warmly she felt a ball of dread settle in her stomach.

'I just popped by to discuss a few pieces of business with Sir Edward,' Mr Guthry said. 'He was eager to go through some new acquisitions.' He caught Amelia's worried expression and hastened to reassure her, 'I have no more news on that front, Miss Amelia, but you try not to fret. Sir Edward will look after you.'

'He will indeed.'

Goody patted Amelia on the arm and Amelia rallied. They were right, she couldn't go thinking the worst every time there was a visitor to the house.

'And my young associate is heading to London as we speak, ready to seek your cousin out and warn her of the potential danger she could be in.'

'Thank you, Mr Guthry.'

'My pleasure, Miss Amelia, I am truly delighted to be of service.'

'Would you like a drink, Mr Guthry?' Goody asked.

'Oh, that would be very kind, Mrs Henshaw, if it isn't too much trouble.' He paused and then pressed on. 'And maybe one of those delicious biscuits, if there are any left from the other day.'

'I'll see what I can do, Mr Guthry.'

Amelia watched as Goody fussed around the older man, pulling him out a stool and pouring him a cup of tea. Once a plate of biscuits was set on the table Goody took a seat opposite the land agent.

'I do declare these are the finest biscuits I've ever tasted,' Mr Guthry said as he devoured a buttery shortbread. 'And as you can probably tell I've tasted a fair few in my time.'

He patted his ample midsection and eyed up the plate.

'Go ahead and take another, Mr Guthry,' Goody said warmly. 'There's nothing wrong with a man with a healthy appetite.'

'I do believe you have a magical touch when it comes to baking, Mrs Henshaw. The fruitcake you sent me home with the other day was just divine. I have to confess I've polished it off already.'

Goody's cheeks shone at the compliment and Amelia wondered how many times Mr Guthry had come to visit the widowed housekeeper in the past few days. It was obvious he had a soft spot for her baking, but she had a feeling there might be something deeper pulling him back to the kitchen at Beechwood Manor.

'Well, I really had better get going,' Amelia said, deciding to let the housekeeper and the estate manager have a bit of privacy.

'Good luck, my dear,' Goody called after her.

Amelia knocked quietly on Edward's study door, wondering if he would agree to her plan. She felt surprisingly nervous and wondered if it was because she wanted today to be a success or if it was down to her remembering the urge she'd had to kiss Edward the last time they'd been in the study together.

'Come in.'

Pushing open the door, Amelia summoned up her courage and stepped inside.

'Are you busy?' she asked.

'Yes.' His answer was curt and he immediately returned his attention to the papers in front of him.

'I've got something planned for today. Will you join me?'

'I've got a lot to do.'

Amelia felt her heart sink, but rallied. Over the past few weeks she had become an expert in drawing Edward out. He was a reticent and solitary man, but Amelia had learnt that perseverance and a sunny smile often won over his initial reluctance to engage with her.

'I won't take no for an answer,' Amelia said, wondering whether he was regretting asking her to stay for the foreseeable future.

'What have you planned?' he asked eventually.

Amelia suddenly felt a little nervous, but bit her lower lip and ploughed on. 'I thought we would go and see your tenants. You were only saying the other day they were well overdue a visit.'

He regarded her in silence for almost a minute.

'What about keeping your presence here a secret?'

'You said yourself McNair will have moved on by now and we can be suitably vague when introducing me. Just give my name as Amelia and tell people I'm your guest.' Amelia didn't say it, but she rather thought the tenants would be more interested in their landlord and his emergence from Beechwood Manor after all these years.

Edward frowned and looked down at his papers for a minute and Amelia thought he might decline, then he gave a short, sharp nod of his head.

'Good idea.'

'Mrs Henshaw has made hampers for us to take.'

'Hampers?'

'With food. As a gift.'

Edward grunted, but she could see he appreciated the thought she had put into their outing.

Half an hour later Amelia was dressed in a riding habit that was a few sizes too large, but certainly much more comfortable to ride in than an ordinary dress. She was waiting for Edward in the courtyard by the barn that was currently stabling the horses.

'Are you ready?' Edward asked as he strode from the house and gave his horse a hearty pat on its flank.

Amelia was just about to answer when Tom, the new groom, came rushing from the barn, a look of panic on his face.

'Sorry to bother you, sir,' he said, his words tumbling out of his mouth as though they were being chased.

'What is it, Tom?'

'It's Milly, sir.' Tom blushed and quickly corrected himself. 'The pregnant mare.'

'What's wrong?'

'I think it's her time and I've only ever birthed one foal, sir.'

Amelia peered over his shoulder into the darkness of the barn, but could not see anything.

'Come on.' Edward grabbed her hand and pulled her forward, then he paused. 'You're not squeamish, are you?' he asked.

Amelia gave him a scornful look and brushed past him, following Tom back into the barn.

Milly, the heavily pregnant mare, was in her stall lying down. On the floor there was a copious amount of liquid soaking into the otherwise fresh hay. As they entered the horse let out a small whinny and stood clumsily, tossing her head and tottering a little.

'Her waters went about ten minutes ago,' Tom said quietly.

'What should we do?' Amelia asked. Although the barn was quiet and peaceful Amelia felt an awful sense of panic welling up inside her.

'Nothing. Mares have been birthing foals for hundreds of years without man's intervention. Just stay quiet and watch, and we'll be ready to step in if there are any problems.' Edward was calm and cool and Amelia wondered how many times he'd done this before.

They watched silently as the mare settled back down on the hay, breathing heavily.

Edward stood right next to her, leaning on the wooden gate and watching the horse in front of him. Amelia felt his shoulder brush against hers and cast a quick glance at his profile. She felt as though she were getting a glimpse of the man Edward had been before tragedy had struck his life. She'd seen this side to him before, usually when a situation needed a cool head and quick thinking. Then Edward would emerge from his protective shell and take control calmly and authoritatively. Now was no different. He had instantly soothed the panic-stricken groom and inserted himself into the barn unobtrusively in case anything went wrong.

'How long will it take?' Amelia asked as the mare gave a whinny of pain.

Edward shrugged, never taking his eyes off the horse. 'It varies.'

The mare was back on her feet now, snorting and stomping her front left hoof. Amelia found she was holding her breath as the horse seemed to become more and more agitated.

'What's wrong?' she whispered, biting her lip. She prayed nothing would go wrong for the mare and a foal would soon emerge alive and well.

'She's in pain and distressed,' Edward said, still focused on Milly.

He gripped hold of the gate and watched the horse whinny and snort for another thirty seconds before seeming to make up his mind. Quickly he vaulted over the wooden partition and into the stall, murmuring soothing words to Milly under his breath as he approached her. Amelia felt her heart begin to pound as he got within touching distance. One wrong move and he could be trampled by the distressed animal.

'Be careful,' she whispered quietly. 'Please don't get hurt.'

She might not ever be able to have Edward's heart or his love, but Amelia knew she would be completely devastated if anything happened to him.

Carefully Edward reached out and began to stroke Milly on the nose, all the time talking to her in his soft voice. Even just his presence by her side seemed to calm the mare and slowly she relaxed. After a couple of minutes Edward helped to guide her back into the hay. He sank down with the horse, stroking her flank and talking to her softly.

'Nearly there,' Amelia heard him say as the mare tensed and snorted. 'You can do it, girl.'

Amelia didn't know a single other landowner who would sit in the hay coaxing a labouring mare through giving birth. Every new thing she learnt about him made her care more, to want something that could never happen between them more.

'Look,' Amelia whispered suddenly. 'I can see a hoof.'

Sure enough one hoof and then another came into view, followed shortly by a nose. Amelia found she was holding her breath, waiting for a little more of the foal to appear with each contraction. For a moment she forgot her troubles and instead focused all her attention on the mare, willing the foal to be born safely and wishing there was something she could do to help.

Edward remained where he was, stroking and talking, but Amelia could see the excitement and anticipation in his eyes. He looked more alive than she'd ever seen him and she felt as though she wanted to capture this version of him and keep it with her for ever.

Suddenly, with a rush, the foal was born. Immediately he was moving, uncoordinated and unsteady, but moving. Milly looked back, exhausted, at her baby, and allowed it to nuzzle in to her.

'Foal should be up and about in half an hour or so,' Tom said, smiling now the danger had passed.

'That was miraculous,' Amelia said, unable to take her eyes off the mother and baby. They were curled together, both sticky and wet, but both two halves of a whole.

Edward stood up slowly, careful not to disturb the mare and her foal. With a backwards glance at the two animals he vaulted back over the fence and took Amelia by the arm.

'Come, let's leave them to bond,' Edward said quietly, leading Amelia away. 'We can return and see how they're doing later.'

Out in the courtyard Edward helped Amelia to mount her horse, boosting her up and holding her steady whilst she rearranged the heavy material of the riding habit.

'I've never seen anything so wonderful,' Amelia said, still unable to think of anything else but the new life inside the barn.

She'd never really considered children before, but seeing the foal cuddle up to its mother had sparked some hidden maternal part of her. When she had been infatuated with

McNair Amelia had never been overly keen on the idea of
a family of her own, it just hadn't really fit in to the idea
of soirées and parties that McNair had painted for her,
but maybe there was a part of her that would like to be a
mother. Only if she found the right man to be a father to
her children, of course.

Glancing quickly at Edward, Amelia tried to suppress
the image of him as a father. From how he had talked of
his son and the stories Goody had told her Amelia knew
Edward had been a wonderful father. He'd been loving and
involved, not distant like some. Just the sort of man she
would want to be father to her own children.

Pushing the fantasy away, Amelia smiled brightly and
urged her horse forward. Today was about Edward bonding
with his tenants. She wouldn't make it about her. Nothing
could distract her from her aim.

Edward was quiet as they rode over the green slopes and
Amelia left him to his thoughts for a while. As they approached the cottages she reined in her horse and slowed.

'Tell me about your tenants,' she said, wanting to know
just a little about the people they would be visiting.

'The estate owns twenty-four houses in total,' Edward
said, allowing himself a smile at the surprised look on
her face.

'I only brought three hampers.'

'Most of the houses are in the village itself. The cottages we saw the other day are rented out to the farmer
labourers and their families.'

'The ones that work on Beechwood Farm?'

It was the farm surrounding the quaint farmhouse Edward had pointed out the other day.

'Exactly.'

'So who lives in each?'

Edward thought for a minute, his fingers tapping the leather of the reins gently as he stared off into the distance.

'The first cottage is rented to the Wilsons. They are a young couple without any children, or at least they didn't have any when I last saw them. In the second cottage are the Turners, Mr Turner has worked for the family for many years. They have seven children in total, but I think the eldest three have left home.'

'There's six of them living in that tiny cottage?'

'You have led a sheltered life. That's considered spacious for some families.'

Amelia bristled slightly. She'd probably seen more poverty than Edward could imagine. In India whole families often lived in one room with no access to clean water or sanitary facilities. Disease spread quickly in the heat and it wasn't uncommon to have whole villages wiped out in the course of a week.

The difference of course was the weather. Although whole families might only have one room, most of the living was done outside. Cooking, washing, sometimes even sleeping when the nights were clear and balmy. What she couldn't imagine was being cooped up in a gloomy cottage with so many other people in the dark, cold days of an English winter.

'And the third cottage?'

Edward grimaced and looked a little bashful.

'Mrs Locke and her three daughters live there.'

'I thought you said the cottages were for farm labourers.'

'They are. Mrs Locke's husband worked at Beechwood Farm until he died five years ago.'

'How awful.'

'I've never had the heart to turf them out, even though

it means some of the other farm labourers living further away in the village.'

'How do they pay their rent?' Amelia asked a little suspiciously.

Edward coughed and urged his horse forward.

'Mrs Locke takes in sewing and I think the eldest daughter has just got a job as a maid.'

'You don't make them pay, do you?'

'No.'

Amelia suppressed a smile. He'd been brought up to be a fair landlord, she was sure, but also to ensure his properties were profitable. She didn't think many men would take pity on a widow and her daughters for so many years.

They stopped outside the first cottage and Edward dismounted before helping Amelia down. Expertly he secured both horses to a fence and led Amelia carefully up the neat little stone path.

A woman in her late twenties opened the door with a baby in her arms and a toddler clinging on to her skirts. As she realised who was visiting her eyes widened with shock and she dipped into a nervous curtsy.

'Sir... Sir Edward,' she managed to stutter.

'Good morning, Mrs Wilson. I hope we haven't come at an inconvenient time.'

'Oh, no, of course not, my lord, it is a pleasure to welcome you into our home at any time.'

She stood aside and ushered them into a small kitchen with a few solid pieces of wooden furniture.

'May I introduce Miss Amelia? A friend who is currently staying with me at Beechwood Manor.'

'It's lovely to meet you, miss.' Mrs Wilson paused, switched the baby to her other hip and then ploughed on nervously. 'And may I say it is wonderful to see you out and about, my lord. I pray every week for your family.'

She blushed, wrung her hands and looked at Amelia beseechingly as if worried she had said too much.

Edward remained silent and Amelia could feel Mrs Wilson's concern building.

'That's very kind of you, Mrs Wilson. I know Sir Edward is grateful to everyone who has prayed or sent good wishes in these difficult times.'

'Would you like a cup of tea?'

'That would be wonderful, but you must let me make it. You have your hands full with these little darlings.'

Amelia and Mrs Wilson talked for twenty minutes about the children and by the time they were ready to leave the older woman had relaxed considerably.

'Is there anything you need, Mrs Wilson?' Edward asked on their way out the door.

Mrs Wilson glanced at Amelia, who smiled encouragingly.

'Well, the roof over our bedroom does leak a little. We've managed to patch it up for a while, but after the last storm it's got much worse. We never wanted to bother you, but it would be nice not to have a bucket in the middle of the room to catch the water.'

'I will send someone to look at it later this week,' Edward promised. 'And you must tell me if anything else ever needs doing. That is what I am here for.'

The second visit was just as successful, with Edward even relaxing enough to scoop one of the younger of the Turner children on to his shoulders whilst they were having a tour of the small garden.

Amelia watched him as the young boy gripped his hair and Edward laughed. He had picked the boy up so effortlessly, as if it were second nature to him. She could imagine him as a father, playing and laughing and loving his son. It made her heart constrict to realise just what he had lost.

'Will you be my horsey?' the little boy asked.

'Hush, Timothy, don't bother Sir Edward,' Mrs Turner said with an apologetic smile.

Edward tilted his head back, gave Timothy a mischievous smile and then began to trot around the garden, making the young boy squeal with delight.

'Faster, faster!' Timothy yelled.

Edward obliged, picking up speed and jiggling Timothy up and down until both man and boy collapsed panting and laughing.

Amelia realised it was the first time she'd seen Edward properly laugh. There had been a few self-deprecating chuckles, the odd smile and one or two twinkles of amusement in his eyes, but she'd never actually seen him let go and laugh like this.

'Sir Edward is a good man,' Mrs Turner said as they watched Edward and Timothy sit up, only to collapse back again on to the grass. 'And he's suffered so much.'

Amelia nodded wordlessly. Even when he'd told her about the loss of his wife and son Amelia hadn't realised quite how it must have destroyed his entire soul. Seeing him with the children showed her how he must have lived for his son.

After Edward had been completely exhausted by the Turner children and Amelia had eaten far too much of Mrs Turner's fruitcake they bid their farewells and moved on to their final visit of the day.

As they approached the last cottage the door opened before Edward could raise his fist to knock.

'Sir Edward,' the middle-aged woman said, with worry apparent in her voice.

'Mrs Locke, I hope you are well. This is Miss Amelia. She's a friend staying with me at Beechwood Manor at the moment.'

'Please come in.'

No sooner had the door closed than Mrs Locke was ushering them into the small kitchen and nervously tidying up around them. Two young girls peeked round the doorframe, both as anxious as their mother.

'You have a lovely home, Mrs Locke,' Amelia said, trying to put the older woman at ease.

'We're very grateful for all your generosity over the years, Sir Edward, and of course I understand the time has come for you to move one of the farm labourers into the cottage, but I beg you please let me find somewhere else for my girls first. I don't want them to end up in the workhouse.'

As she spoke the tears began running down her cheeks and her two youngest daughters rushed into the room to cling on to her.

'Mrs Locke,' Edward said, quietly but firmly, 'please don't worry. That is not why I am here.'

A glimmer of hope appeared in her eyes.

'It's not?'

'Your husband was a good man, a good worker, and it was a tragedy he lost his life so young. Believe me, I understand the suffering involved in losing one's spouse, one's life partner, and I have never had to worry about how I would provide for my family, too. I think you are an extremely brave and resourceful woman and I don't want you ever have to worry about losing your home, not whilst I am your landlord.'

'You don't want us to move out?'

'I don't want you to move out.'

'But we don't pay any rent.'

'Mrs Locke, if we can't show a little kindness to others in this world then what is the point of living? I don't want your money. I don't want you to leave.'

Mrs Locke threw herself at Edward and hugged him, encircling him with her skinny arms and sobbing like a child on his shoulder.

Amelia motioned for him to reciprocate and awkwardly he patted her softly on the back.

'Is there anything we can do to help, Mrs Locke?' Amelia asked.

The older woman released Edward and sniffled. 'You've been so kind. When I saw you coming up the path I thought...' She trailed off. 'I thought we were for the workhouse.'

'How old are your daughters?' Amelia asked, looking at the two skinny girls standing by their mother.

'Emily is fourteen and Ginny is ten. My eldest, Rebecca, is out at work. She's a maid over at Twittle House.'

Amelia glanced at Edward and tried to convey her idea with a flash of her eyes. He frowned at her.

'It won't be long until Emily is going out to work, too,' Amelia prompted.

'Oh, no, miss. As soon as we can find her a position she will be going into service.'

'I'm sure it would be a comfort to you if she could find a position locally.'

Understanding finally dawned on Edward's face.

'Mrs Henshaw, my esteemed housekeeper, is always telling me we need more staff at Beechwood Manor. I will have to check, but I can ask to see if she has a position for Emily.'

'Truly, Sir Edward?'

Edward retreated a little, as if expecting another hug, but managed a reassuring smile.

'Truly. I will talk to her later today.'

As they left the Lockes's cottage Amelia took Edward's arm and leaned in closer to him.

'What you said back there, to Mrs Locke, I think that's one of the kindest things I've ever heard.' Amelia could see the hint of colour in Edward's cheeks. 'You're a good man, Edward Gray.'

He opened his mouth to reply, but Amelia pressed a finger to his lips. She knew what sort of man he was and no amount of protestation on his behalf would change her mind.

Chapter Sixteen

'Stay right there,' Edward instructed, frowning as Amelia started to sit up. 'Don't move.'

'What…?' The question trailed off as Edward dashed from the room and disappeared down the hallway. He was back within a few minutes, sketchbook and set of pencils in hand.

'I want to draw you.'

'Like this? I look a state.'

'You look fine. Natural. Sit still.'

She was reclining on a *chaise longue* she had found in some distant part of the house and moved to the sitting room. It was a rainy Sunday afternoon and they'd been stuck in the house all day. Edward could see Amelia was getting restless; she kept running her hands through her hair and fiddling with her dress, all which gave her a natural and dishevelled look. A look Edward just had to catch on paper.

'Where should I look?' she asked, fidgeting.

'Just carry on reading your book and try to forget I'm even here.'

She was so easy to draw and as Edward let his pencil glide over the paper he felt all his tension and worries melt away. In this moment all that mattered was capturing Amelia's vitality, her sparkle, her aura of energy.

'Have you finished yet?'

'Be patient.' Edward smiled to himself. Patience wasn't one of Amelia's virtues. He was counting the minutes until she sprung up off the chair and declared she couldn't sit still for a moment longer.

A curl of hair slipped from its pin on top of her head and cascaded down over her shoulder. Edward closed his eyes for a moment before forcing himself to focus. He had felt unbalanced and restless ever since their trip to visit his tenants, and he'd hoped drawing would have its usual soothing effect on him.

'You've stopped drawing,' Amelia said accusingly.

'Just considering my next angle.'

In truth it had felt good to do something normal, something he had done for years before his self-imposed seclusion. Visiting his tenants, taking an interest in their lives... that was something he had been brought up to do and he found that he had missed it. He missed running the estate and getting out to talk to people, and for that one afternoon he caught a glimpse of how life could be.

In the moment he had thoroughly enjoyed himself, but ever since he'd been plagued by a nagging guilt. Before the fire he would have asked his wife to accompany him on tenant visits, or he would have taken Thomas out to explore the estate. Now he was taking enjoyment in the things they had done together when they would never get to do them again. Edward knew his entire life couldn't be governed by his guilt at surviving when his family had not, at allowing himself to smile and laugh when they weren't by his side, but he seemed unable to push through his regrets completely and leave them behind.

'Can I see?' Amelia asked, straining to catch a glimpse of her impromptu portrait.

'It's not finished. Sit still.'

Amelia flopped back into position, the neckline of her dress slipping a little with the movement and revealing a triangle of velvety skin underneath. Edward found himself not able to look away as she leisurely rearranged her dress, a hot wave of desire flooding through his body.

Forcing himself to return his attention to his sketch, Edward repeated the mantra that had become part of his daily ritual these past few days. *I do not desire Amelia,* he told himself, not risking another glance in her direction in case she could read his pained expression. *I will not desire Amelia.*

Every bone in his body wanted to cross over to the *chaise longue* and grip the hem of her dress that was currently carefully arranged to cover her legs. He wanted to gently lift her hem until the tops of her stockings were revealed, resting on those slender thighs. Now that would make a wonderful work of art.

I do not desire Amelia. I will not desire Amelia.

'I can't sit still for a moment longer,' Amelia declared, jumping up from her seat and gliding over to where Edward was still sketching. He liked her like this, animated and in motion. He wished there was some way to capture the essence of her movements on paper, but he had to make do with still portraits, not very realistic when you considered how much of the time Amelia spent moving about. Clearing his throat, Edward quickly made an effort to banish his inappropriate thoughts from his mind before she came into his personal space.

She leaned over the back of the chair and angled his sketch pad up towards her. Edward found himself holding his breath. He wanted her to like it. He hadn't shared his drawings with many people in his life and suddenly he felt nervous.

'Is that how you see me?' Amelia asked, her voice a little strained.

Edward glanced at the drawing. He couldn't quite tell if Amelia was upset or not, but something wasn't quite right.

Cautiously he nodded.

'You've made me beautiful.'

He mumbled something incomprehensible.

'Will you teach me?'

Edward blinked in surprise. He'd never expected her to ask that of him. Amelia was a restless, active person. Drawing took patience and serenity.

'What would you like to draw?'

'You.'

'Maybe we can start with something a little easier. That vase of flowers?'

Amelia shook her head. 'I've got no interest in those flowers. I want to draw you.'

Edward shrugged, laid out a pencil and paper for her and resumed his seat.

'No, no, no,' Amelia said, tapping the pencil on her lip. 'Something's not right.'

Edward raised an eyebrow, but shifted slightly.

'Maybe if you stand.'

He stood.

'Look out into the distance. Like a conquering hero.'

Edward looked, but kept his expression of mild irritation.

Amelia sketched, every so often pausing to pop the end of the pencil into her mouth and regard him for some minutes.

'This isn't going well,' she admitted eventually.

'Come here,' Edward instructed, pulling her to the floor to sit beside him.

He grimaced as he looked at her rudimentary pencil strokes and harsh lines. The perspective was all wrong, his body was out of proportion to his head and there were scribbles and dark lines where Amelia had obviously got frustrated.

'Let's go back to basics,' he said, picking up a clean sheet of paper and handing Amelia a fresh pencil. 'First of all, relax your grip. The pencil is an extension of your hand, allow the drawing to flow from you.'

Amelia giggled as she flopped her hand around a little, brandishing the pencil more like a weapon than an artistic instrument.

'Here.' Edward took her hand in his and adjusted her grip, his skin feeling rough against her satiny-smooth fingers. 'Press gently, allow yourself to relax and try long, smooth strokes.'

Carefully he guided her hand across the paper, showing her the ideal amount of pressure and control. She was sitting close to him, her body almost tucked into his chest, and Edward was acutely aware of her proximity. As Amelia tilted her head he felt his pulse quicken. A curl of her hair fell backwards and tickled Edward's neck and they were so close he could hear the soft intake of breath as she concentrated on her drawing.

After a long few minutes of torture Edward couldn't bear the anticipation any longer and reached out to trail a finger down the soft skin of the nape of her neck. Only at the last minute did he catch himself and stop, finger poised in mid-air.

He couldn't do that to her, she didn't deserve to be toyed with, subjected to a tormented man's uncontrolled desires and moods. It wouldn't be fair on her and it would only cause him further heartache.

Amelia turned and caught the haunted expression on his face.

'Do you think...?' Amelia began, but let the question trail off.

'What?'

She shook her head.

'Ask it.'

'Do you think you will ever be free?'

'Free?'

'From the guilt and the regret? Free to start building a normal life again?'

Edward saw the pity in her eyes and felt the squeeze in his chest as his heart constricted. Three years he had been in mourning, three years of pain and punishment and self-inflicted exile from the world. It would never be enough to make up for the guilt he felt at surviving when those he loved, those he should have protected, had perished.

'You wouldn't understand,' he said harshly.

He couldn't stand the sympathy and compassion in her eyes and suddenly he had the urge to push her away, to strike out with his words and wound her. Anything would be better than continuing to receive her pity. He didn't deserve it.

'Help me understand.'

'You'll never understand. How could you?' He hated the harsh tone of his voice and the hurt expression on Amelia's face as though he'd physically slapped her, but somewhere deep down Edward knew that was all he deserved.

'Maybe I couldn't,' Amelia said softly.

Sadly she reached up and placed a hand on Edward's cheek, tears springing to her eyes. She looked at him long and hard, as if committing his face to her memory, and then stood and left the room, leaving Edward wondering if he had lost the one thing which could bring him back to life.

Chapter Seventeen

'I do not know what you said or what you did, but for the love of everything that you hold dear, please make amends,' Goody was saying.

Amelia paused outside the door, intrigued by what was going on in the room. She heard Edward grunt and through the crack between the door and frame saw Goody level him with a look of despair.

'What makes you think *I've* done something?' Edward asked eventually.

'Sir Edward, I've known you since you were trawling the ponds for tadpoles. I know when you've done something wrong.'

Amelia knew she should leave, or at the very least make her presence known, but something held her in place. In the two weeks since she had pressed Edward about moving on with his life as they sat in the sitting room with him teaching her to draw, Amelia had barely laid eyes on him. Oh, they still dined together and occasionally passed each other on the stairs, and Edward still rescued her from her nightmares almost every night, but she hadn't properly talked to him. Not since she'd asked that question and ruined everything.

It was her impulsive nature that was to blame, of course. Most women would have just kept quiet and enjoyed his company, especially as Amelia suspected she was falling rather deeply in love with Edward, but of course she had to spoil everything. She'd pushed too hard, asked too much of him. Who was she to say when he should stop mourning his family? When he should move on and resume a more normal life? If only she'd kept quiet.

'You should do something nice to make up for it,' Goody suggested.

'Like what?'

'You're a grown man. I'm sure you don't need me to tell you what a young lady might enjoy by way of a treat. Maybe a little excursion, or a shopping trip. Miss Amelia strikes me as a young woman who follows fashion.'

Edward didn't answer and Amelia could see he was tracing patterns in some spilt flour on the kitchen table.

'Or maybe take her somewhere on those horses you two love so much. It doesn't really matter what you do, as long as you do something. Let her know you're sorry. Let her see you enjoy spending time with her.'

Amelia found she was holding her breath whilst waiting for Edward's response. Would he deny he wanted to spend time with her?

Goody's tone changed and her voice became much softer. 'I know it's hard, Sir Edward. I know these past three years have been the hardest challenge any person has to endure, but you have survived. I'm so proud of you.'

Goody's voice cracked and Amelia saw the older woman brushing tears from her cheeks.

'You've survived. Now it's time to start living.'

Amelia felt a lump form in her throat and quietly she turned and walked away. She shouldn't intrude on their private moment and if she entered the kitchen now she was likely to cry as soon as she saw Edward.

Flopping down into a chair, Amelia stared out the window morosely. It had been raining for the past four days, but today was dry at least. Every so often Amelia could even see a patch of blue in the sky. As she looked up she realised Goody was right; she would like a trip out. It wouldn't have to be anywhere special, but just to get out of the house, to see a bit more of the world than Beechwood Estate, would be wonderful. It might also stop her from worrying about the lack of news from Mr Guthry's man in London about her cousin. Lizzie should have received her letters by now and sent a reply, but there had been no word. Every day Amelia felt her levels of concern growing.

'Amelia,' Edward said as he entered the room, 'I have something to ask you.'

Amelia sat up quickly, rearranging her skirts and correcting her posture. She looked hopefully up at Edward.

'Do you fancy a trip to the seaside?'

The question threw her so completely Amelia sat with her mouth opening and closing like a fish out of water.

'The seaside?'

'Well, not Brighton, of course, and probably not anywhere too populated. I was thinking a quiet little cove not too far away.'

He was nervous, Amelia realised. Normally so blunt and to the point, Edward was nervous about asking her to accompany him on a trip out.

She hesitated, thinking of all the reasons she should refuse, make up an excuse and let Edward go back to avoiding her.

'I'd love to,' she said after a few seconds' pause.

Edward smiled then, a genuine smile of happiness and

relief, and Amelia saw the man he had once been, the carefree young man before his life had been destroyed by the fire.

'Mrs Henshaw is packing us a picnic. Shall we meet in the barn in an hour's time?' Edward suggested.

Amelia nodded and watched as Edward strode out, no doubt to gather his pencils and paper. She doubted he would go for such an excursion without them.

Two hours later and they were riding across the Downs in a bracing but warm breeze.

'Race you to the top of the hill,' Amelia shouted as she spurred her horse forward into a gallop. Behind her she heard Edward laugh and take up her challenge, hot on her heels as they mounted the top of the hill. 'Look at that view.'

They slowed for a minutes, regarding the rolling green hills before them with the sparkle of the sea in the distance.

'I love this part of the country,' Edward said. 'I couldn't imagine living anywhere else.'

'There's something captivating about it, isn't there?'

For a while they let the horses set the pace, plodding along whilst they enjoyed the scenery. It felt to Amelia that the further they got from Beechwood Manor the more Edward seemed to relax. It was as though out here he could become his own man again, not tied down by the painful memories of his past.

'Tell me about India,' he said as they started a gentle descent towards the chalky cliffs.

Amelia briefly closed her eyes and summoned a picture of home. When she felt scared or alone often she would picture she was sitting on the veranda of their house just outside Bombay, drinking a cool drink and fanning herself in the heat. From the veranda you could see the rolling green hills, thick with foliage, and the wonderfully blue sky above.

'I didn't realise England would be so completely different to India,' Amelia said eventually. 'Out there everything is bright and warm. There's no wind like this and when the rains come there's something almost magical about them. It's as though you're waiting for something to burst, a release, and suddenly the monsoon is there.'

Edward listened quietly and Amelia smiled as she remembered.

'I was so shocked when we disembarked our ship in London, I'd never seen anything like it before. The noise and the dirt and the sheer number of people.'

'But there are cities in India.'

'Father wasn't keen on me visiting the cities, or even the larger towns. He thought it was dangerous, even though I've never once felt threatened by anyone in India the way I have here. My world was made up of the sleepy little villages close to our home, the army base down the road and the small British community that lived nearby.'

'It sounds rather idyllic.'

'I didn't think so at the time. In fact, I couldn't wait to leave.'

'And now? Do you regret coming to England?'

Amelia considered the question. There was so much to regret: foolishly chasing after Captain McNair, losing control in his house, her need to live in fear now.

'No.' Quite simply if she hadn't come to England she wouldn't have met Edward and she wouldn't be here right now. 'I needed this,' she said. 'In India I was spoiled and bored. I caused havoc and I fear I was on a path to self-destruction.'

Amelia could see the problems with her behaviour now and she knew something had needed to change.

'I miss my home, and I miss my father, but I do not regret coming here.'

She glanced over at Edward, saw the small smile on his face and realised how much her answer meant to him. He didn't want her to be unhappy, even if it wasn't in his power to do much about it.

They had reached the cliff edge and Amelia gazed out to sea. Far from the brilliant blue waters she had seen during her voyage to England the sea here was moody and dark, a reflection of the clouds gathering above, but it was just as beautiful, just as striking, as the clear, calm waters of the Indian Ocean.

'It's rather dramatic,' Amelia commented, taking in the climbing white cliffs backed by rolling green hills and the crashing sea down below.

'Shall we go down?' Edward asked.

He helped Amelia to dismount, tied up the horses and led her down a narrow rocky path.

'You've been here before.'

'As a boy this was where my father would always bring me when we spent the day together. I know these paths as well as I know the hallways in Beechwood Manor.'

Amelia stumbled suddenly and Edward was immediately at her side. He took her hand to steady her, checking she was unhurt before leading her further down the path.

They reached the beach, a deep cove cut into the chalky rock face covered in large grey-and-brown pebbles. In front of them, close to the sea, was a narrow strip of sand leading round the cliffs in both directions.

'Where's the rest of the sand?' Amelia asked, frowning.

Edward laughed. 'This is a pretty generous amount of sand for beaches around here. Most just have pebbles and shingle. I'm sure it isn't anything as beautiful as the beaches in India.'

Amelia shook her head, 'It's more atmospheric.'

And she meant it. As she looked out to sea she could feel the salt on her face and the spray in the air. Here the coast was dramatic and almost alive. The sea looked powerful and even a little menacing, and Amelia knew nothing could entice her in for a swim.

'Shall we bathe?' Edward asked.

She realised he was joking just before he grinned, took her by the arm and pulled her closer to where the water was crashing into the sand.

'Can we head around the cliffs?'

Edward paused as if calculating something. 'You have to be careful not to be caught by the tide, but it's still on its way out so we should have an hour or two before it starts coming back in.'

With her hand tucked into the crook of Edward's elbow Amelia allowed him to lead her down the beach and round the base of the cliff. Here the strip of sand stretched along ahead of them for half a mile before disappearing as the cliff jutted out.

They walked until they reached a small cove bathed in the sunlight that was peeking through the clouds. Edward laid out the blanket he'd brought with them and set the basket Goody had prepared for them down in the middle.

Amelia watched as he sat down, pulled off his boots and socks and then sank his toes into the grainy sand. She giggled.

'Try it,' Edward said. 'It feels like freedom.'

Obligingly Amelia sat beside him and kicked off her boots, then paused.

'I won't peek.'

She looked at him with his eyes closed, face turned up to the sun, and wished he would.

Slowly Amelia peeled off her stockings, wriggled her toes and pressed them into the sand. He was right, it did feel like freedom.

As Edward lay with the sun warming his face he realised he felt content. For once everything felt good in the world. Mrs Henshaw had, of course, been right, he had needed to put things right with Amelia. These past two weeks had been uncomfortable and lonely, and he'd hated seeing her hopeful face fall every time he barely acknowledged her as they passed each other. The only time he had felt at least a little useful during the past fortnight was when he'd dashed in every night to hold Amelia as she sobbed in her sleep. She was still experiencing the nightmares about McNair. Edward had been hopeful they might dissipate once she knew the scoundrel was alive, but every night she was terrified by reliving the events in the Captain's house. Edward found himself anticipating the moment he got to wrap his arms around her sleepy body and comfort her whilst she calmed into a deep slumber. He didn't want to examine exactly what this meant, but for now it was enough to know his presence calmed her.

'Can we paddle?' Amelia asked.

Edward opened his eyes and looked up at her from his position reclined on the rug. As usual she was restless, eager to be moving about.

'It'll be cold.'

'Are you too much of a coward?'

'You injure me, Amelia.' Edward said, with mock indignation. He stood, pulled Amelia to her feet and without relinquishing her hand pulled her towards the sea. 'Mind you don't get your skirts wet, otherwise I've no doubt you'll moan the entire way home.'

Quickly he dodged as Amelia swatted him. As they neared the sea Amelia slowed.

'Are you regretting your challenge?'

'Of course not. How cold can it be?'

He wondered if she were imagining the beautiful warm waters of the Indian Ocean back home.

'Promise not to scream.'

She looked at him with defiance in her eyes, hitched up her skirts to reveal slender honey-coloured calves and dashed at the sea.

Edward laughed out loud as she uttered a string of expletives no young lady should even be aware of. She was out of the water in seconds, looking at him reproachfully. It felt good to laugh again. Out here, away from the memories of Beechwood Manor, Edward felt some of his light-heartedness returning after years of being locked away. Maybe once in a while it wasn't so bad to enjoy himself, to smile or feel pleasure in someone's company.

'I did warn you.'

'Not nearly well enough. That was really cold. My toes still hurt.'

'So you don't fancy a swim?'

'I'm not crazy, so, no.'

'I used to swim here all the time with my father, whatever the weather,' Edward said.

'Please don't let me stop you,' Amelia said, smiling sweetly.

'I think I'll just dip my toes,' Edward said, walking into the shallow water.

It was cold, so cold he felt his toes begin to go numb after about thirty seconds, but it was bracing and refreshing at the same time. The coldness gave him an unusual clarity, and, as he stood looking out into the grey foaming sea, he found himself wondering whether he'd judged things wrong over the past few years.

Turning back towards the cliffs, Edward returned to where the water just lapped on the sand and placed Amelia's hand in the crook of his elbow. For a while they just walked along together side by side, Edward allowing the small waves to surge over his feet whilst ensuring Amelia was always out of their reach.

As they got to the end of the cove they continued along the sand at the base of one of the high chalky cliffs. Edward realised he was wishing they could just carry on walking arm in arm for eternity, that way he wouldn't have this uncertainty about his decisions to face up to.

'Do you think Mr Guthry's man will return soon?' Amelia asked.

As Edward turned to look at her he realised how preoccupied with worry she was. He'd been so absorbed in his own concerns he hadn't even realised Amelia was thinking about her cousin so much.

'I'm sure he will. I do not know what has delayed him or any message from your cousin, but if there was bad news we would surely have heard by now.'

Amelia nodded and looked at least a little reassured by his words.

'I sent the letter to my father last week,' Amelia said as they strolled along. 'But I think it will be a while until he receives it and replies.'

Edward was just about to answer, to assure her nothing had changed and that she was welcome at Beechwood Manor for as long as she needed when there was a rumble from up above them. He looked up, frowning, but there was nothing to be seen.

'We should move away from the cliff,' he said, keeping his eyes fixed on the heavy rock above them. Rock-falls were common on this part of the coastline and he didn't want either of them to have their skulls caved in by a chunk of falling chalk.

'If you've changed your mind, I can find somewhere else to stay whilst I await his reply,' Amelia said.

Edward heard the anguish and uncertainty in her voice and momentarily took his eyes off the cliff above them to study her face.

'There's...' he began, but paused as there was another loud bang from over their heads. Edward looked up and his eyes widened as he saw the chunk of chalky cliff plummeting down towards them. Instinctively he pushed Amelia back against the cliff face, knowing she was unlikely to get hit there, then pushed his body against hers meaning to protect her from the worst of the falling rock.

He heard Amelia scream and then a bolt of pain shot through his head before the darkness descended.

Chapter Eighteen

Amelia screamed. She couldn't help herself. Then the scream was cut off as she watched Edward totter and collapse to the ground. There was a nasty gash in his forehead, and a steady stream of blood oozed from the wound and stained the sand.

'Edward,' Amelia whispered as she crouched down beside him.

He was dead, she was sure of it. His face was deathly pale and he wasn't moving at all. Amelia felt the despair and sorrow begin to overwhelm her and the sobs started to rack her body. She buried her head in Edward's chest and tried to will him back to life.

She couldn't lose him, even if he wasn't really hers to lose. Suddenly Amelia realised quite what Edward had come to mean to her over the past few weeks and felt an overwhelming sickness at the thought of never hearing his voice or seeing his smile again.

Just as she was about to become hysterical something made her sit up and pause for a moment. She'd already had a similar experience, convinced a man was dead when he was just badly injured. With a silent plea Amelia placed her ear to Edward's chest and listened. She almost cried with relief when she heard the steady beating of his heart and felt his chest gently rising and falling with each breath.

Open your eyes and I promise never to annoy you again, Amelia pleaded silently. *Just open your eyes, Edward, please.*

For some time she just sat beside him, stroking his hair and willing him to open his eyes and wake up. She wasn't sure how long he might be unconscious for, but she thought she'd heard somewhere people could remain unresponsive for days.

After what must have been almost an hour Amelia shifted slightly, stretching her legs out, but not relinquishing Edward's hand. With a shout of surprise Amelia turned to see the sea lapping at her feet. The bottom of her dress was soaking up the seawater and the icy water covering her toes. For a moment the implications of this didn't sink in, but slowly Amelia realised the tide had turned. The sea was on its way in.

'Edward!' Amelia shouted, shaking him by the shoulders. 'Wake up.'

No response.

'Edward, please wake up. The sea's coming in.'

He lay peacefully on the sand, his unconscious body not bothered by the approaching water.

Amelia stood, grabbed him under his arms and started to drag him across the wet sand back towards where they had left the picnic things. As she inched along she felt the first drops of rain splatter her and murmured a few uncomplimentary phrases about the English weather.

By the time they'd moved three steps Amelia's muscles were already screaming and her breath coming in laboured gasps.

Wake up, Edward, she begged, glancing back over her

shoulder to see just how far she had to drag him. It seemed
an impossible distance and for a moment Amelia felt despair crashing down on her. If only she'd told him how she
felt when he was still alive and well.

Gritting her teeth, Amelia tightened her grip and continued along the beach. She would not give up, not whilst
there was still a chance of saving him.

After a further fifteen minutes Amelia had managed
to pull Edward's body halfway back to the cove, but during that time the sea had advanced and now her every step
was hampered by about three inches of water. Edward was
soaked and Amelia could feel the wet material of her skirts
dragging against her legs.

Despite all this, and despite her aching muscles, Amelia
never gave up. She was under no illusion that if she didn't
push on Edward would die. The tide would come in and
the water would cover his supine form and Edward would
drown just a couple of feet from the cliffs. On and on she
pulled him, covering the ground inch by inch, minute by
minute. Every time she paused to catch her breath Amelia
was aware of time ticking away and the ever-rising water.
Soon the water was above her ankles and then halfway up
to her knees, slowing their progress even further.

With her breath coming in short gasps Amelia paused
for just a moment and then with a loud roar born out of effort and fear Amelia dragged Edward's body up into the
cove and out of reach of the sea, at least for now. Immediately she collapsed down on to the sand, one arm flopping across Edward's chest to check he was still breathing.

Amelia lay there whilst her heart stopped pounding
and her muscles recovered. She didn't want to sit up, to
have to examine Edward's pale face again and wonder if
he would ever open those bewitching, kind eyes again.

All the time she had been dragging him along the beach she hadn't had any energy left to think, but now she could feel all the worry and the panic mounting up inside her.

He couldn't be dead, not Edward. Not the man who'd saved her and comforted her and allowed her to completely disrupt his entire life. Not before she told him how she truly felt about him.

Over the past few weeks as she had slowly got to know the man behind the grief and the gruff mask Amelia had often wondered if he would have preferred to have been taken in the fire with his family. She was sure on many occasions he probably thought he would, but recently she had glimpsed another side to him. Every so often she saw a glimmer of hope, a flicker of excitement about the future, something that told her that he would fight to stay on this earth.

'Fight for me,' she whispered.

Carefully Amelia leaned over and brushed his hair from his eyes, smiling as a wavy lock flopped back almost immediately. She lowered her head further before hesitating, knowing she should not kiss him, but already sure she would not be able to resist. Softly she pressed her lips against his, feeling the tears form in her eyes as she realised this might be the closest she ever got to a real kiss with the man she cared about so much. At first his mouth was cool and unresponsive, but as she began to pull away she felt just a flicker of movement.

'Edward?' Amelia whispered, sitting back and scrutinising his face.

Nothing. Amelia hesitated, knowing deep down that a kiss didn't make any difference to an unconscious man… that was just the stuff of fairytales.

What have you got to lose? she asked herself.

She kissed him again, squeezing her eyes shut, hoping and wishing for another flicker of a response.

This time there was no doubt. As she kissed him his lips began to move, drawing her in and taking some of her warmth.

Edward let out a prolonged groan and as Amelia sat back guiltily as his eyes flickered open. For a moment she could tell everything was unfocused and blurry, but after a few seconds his eyes locked on to hers and he frowned.

'What...?' he managed to murmur.

Amelia launched herself at him, reining herself in at the last moment so she embraced him gently. She felt Edward's hand on her back and had to choke back a cry of relief. He was alive, awake and he could move.

'What happened?'

'Part of the cliff collapsed. You were hit.'

Edward raised his hand to the cut on his forehead and grimaced.

'How long was I unconscious?' he asked, sitting up.

'About two hours. How are you feeling?'

'My head's pounding—' Edward broke off and looked around them. 'How did we get back here?'

'I dragged you.'

'You *dragged* me?'

'The sea was coming in, I didn't have a choice.'

'You managed to pull me all the way back here?'

Amelia nodded.

'Thank you,' Edward said, looking at her with renewed respect. 'You're stronger than I could have imagined.'

Amelia knew part of her success in pulling Edward to safety had been due to the knowledge that if she failed she would have to watch him die.

Slowly Edward sat up. He was still pale, but his eyes were focused and his expression determined.

'Did we…?' Edward started to say, looking at her thoughtfully, but then allowed the question to trail off with a shake of his head.

Amelia didn't press him, knowing he was probably remembering the kiss she had planted on his lips as he began to stir. He had never asked her to kiss him, never even indicated he ever would be interested in anyone romantically again.

'I see it started raining,' he observed drily after a minute.

Amelia laughed.

'I'm so glad you're awake,' she said, clutching on to his hand and hoping she'd never have to let go.

Edward was staring out to sea with a frown on his face. Suddenly he stood, stumbled a few steps before regaining his equilibrium and then ran forward.

'Edward,' Amelia shouted after him, wondering if the knock to the head had affected his brain.

He ran to the sea, wading into the shallow water for a few steps before stopping and turning to look to either side. The wind had picked up whilst Amelia was dragging him along the beach and now the waves were beginning to crash against the beach and the rain was pelting the sand. The clouds above had morphed into a menacing black blanket and Amelia knew another storm was on its way.

'What's wrong?' Amelia shouted from a few feet away, refusing to wade back out into the water without good reason.

'The tide's come in,' Edward said as he returned to her side.

'I know. That's why I had to pull you into the cove.'

'Look.'

Edward gestured back the way they had come, back towards where they'd left the horses and followed the narrow path down the cliff. As realisation dawned on Amelia she felt a wave of nausea and panic overcome her and she had to reach out and grip hold of Edward to steady herself.

'There's no way back,' she whispered.

Sure enough, the sea had already covered the narrow strip of sand they'd walked along to get to the cove.

Frantically Amelia ran up the beach towards the cliffs, looking for a path, a route up to the top. There was nothing. Down at beach level the cliff was smooth, all possible handholds and footholds eroded and flattened by the sea.

'Maybe it won't come in this far,' Amelia said as Edward joined her.

He didn't answer her and she followed his gaze to the very prominent water line about three feet above their heads.

'Amelia, I need you to keep calm,' Edward said, taking charge as usual.

'Keep calm? We're going to die. The sea's coming in and there's no way off the beach. Edward, we're going to die.' She could hear her voice rise in pitch with every word, but couldn't do anything to control it.

'No. We're not going to die. I will not let us.'

She wondered how he could remain so composed and assured in the face of certain death.

'Stop panicking and listen to me,' Edward said in his stern voice. 'We will survive this. I promise you.' Amelia felt him grip her by the arm and pull her to face him. When she was looking straight into his eyes he repeated himself. 'We will survive this, I promise.'

Slowly some of the panic seeped from her body and she nodded, wondering just how he meant to save them.

'I need you to take your dress off.'

Not quite what she'd had in mind.

'Why?'

Edward pointed to a spot in the cliff about eleven feet up from the ground. There, and leading up from it, were a series of grooves and ledges in the rock face that led up to the top of the chalky cliffs.

'I will boost you up and you will climb to the top of the cliffs. You can't do that with your bulky dress on.'

'What about you. Maybe I could pull you up.'

Edward shook his head. 'It's too far.'

'I'm not leaving you here,' Amelia protested.

He grabbed hold of her shoulders and held her tightly. 'When you get to the top run for the horses and then ride as fast as you can back to Beechwood Manor. Send a rescue party to fetch me, armed with ropes and horses, and I'll be back home with you in no time.'

'Is there time?' Amelia asked.

Edward glanced at the approaching sea and nodded. 'There's time.'

Quickly Amelia unfastened her dress and slipped out of it. Standing in just her long cotton chemise, she resisted the temptation to cover herself with her arms.

'I'll ride faster than I've ever ridden before,' she promised.

Amelia turned and faced the cliff, grimacing at the height and the thought of the long climb ahead of her. She felt Edward directly behind her and shivered as he placed a hand on her waist, turning her to face him.

A thousand unsaid words flowed between them and Amelia saw the concern and fear on Edward's face. She wanted to kiss him, to be enveloped in his arms and to draw her strength from him to sustain her on the long climb and journey home.

Gently Edward pushed the stray strands of hair that were whipping about her face in the wind behind her ears, not removing his hands from her face even once they were under control.

'Be careful, Amelia,' he said, gripping her tightly and for a moment Amelia knew he didn't want to let her go.

She watched as his eyes flickered over her face as if he were committing every detail to memory.

'Take your time on the climb, test each foothold before you transfer your weight,' he instructed, still not moving his hands from her face.

Amelia nodded, her heart pounding in her chest. Maybe he would kiss her, maybe he would hold her close and whisper that she was his hope, his reason for living.

Edward let his hands drop to his sides and nodded for her to begin the climb. Amelia's disappointment was almost overwhelming and she felt tears begin to form in her eyes as she turned and ran her hands over the cliff face. Of course he wouldn't kiss her and whisper what she wanted to hear in her ear—the idea was pure fantasy.

Just as she steadied herself for Edward to boost her up Amelia felt his strong hand on her waist, turning her back towards him. As they stood body to body Amelia saw the fire burning in his eyes and before she could dare to hope he pulled her close against him and covered her lips with his own.

He kissed her deeply and passionately, gripping her tightly as if he never wanted to let go. After her initial shock Amelia felt her heart soar and her body react to him as if she had been waiting her entire life for this moment.

Amelia was aware of his firm body against hers and wondered how she could have ever found any other man attractive. No one compared to Edward's wild appeal and sensuous charm.

Just as Amelia's lungs started burning and her brain started asking for air Edward broke away, his lips lingering gently on hers for a few seconds before he broke the contact completely.

'What...?' Amelia began to ask, all her hopes and dreams surging to the surface, chased closely by a very real fear of rejection.

Edward shook his head, 'There's no time,' he said quietly.

Amelia glanced over his shoulder and saw the sea creeping ever closer and decided not to argue. All her questions would be pointless if she didn't get help in time for Edward to be rescued.

'Goodbye, Amelia.'

His words sounded too final, too devoid of hope.

'I will be back,' Amelia said as she allowed him to boost her up the cliff face to grab hold of the first handhold.

At first it seemed too far for her to reach, but in the end, when she was standing on his shoulders, she could just about wrap her fingers round a jutting-out segment of the chalk. Slowly, with her muscles protesting, she pulled herself upwards until her other hand could reach above her.

Amelia's progress was painfully slow. She was already exhausted by the exertion involved in dragging Edward along the beach and the gusting wind and pelting rain weren't helping much either, but the memory of Edward's lips on her own, consuming her with a passion she'd never imagined possible, spurred her on. Inch by inch she hauled herself up the cliff face, trying to ignore the pain in her fingers as the skin was torn to shreds by the merciless rock face. Twice she slipped, her feet losing their precarious purchase on the ledges below her, and her body slammed against the chalk. Each time she had to wait for her heart to stop pounding and her vision to clear before she could continue the slow climb up.

Just as she wondered if she would ever make the top she

felt the grass under her fingers and let out a cry of relief. With shaking arms and burning lungs she was able to pull herself up on to the cliff top. She paused to glance back down to Edward's form below. He already looked despondent and for an awful few seconds Amelia wondered if he had given up, if this was the moment he'd decided to join his beloved late wife and son. Even the thought ripped at her heart. Surely his kiss had been more than a farewell, surely it had meant something more than that.

As she looked down Edward raised his head and waved. This small gesture pushed Amelia into action. It wouldn't matter if he had decided to live or die if she didn't return as quickly as possible with help. Later she could dissect exactly what their kiss had meant and exactly what Edward felt for her, but right now she had to run as fast as she'd ever run and ride faster than she ever had before. With a final glance at the man on the beach below Amelia turned and began her dash across the clifftop, praying she would make it back in time.

Edward had expected to feel at peace. As soon as he'd seen they were cut off from the route back along the beach he'd realised there was a possibility he wouldn't get out of this alive, but his panic had been largely for Amelia. He couldn't fail her now, not after all he'd done to protect her and keep her safe. Then he'd seen the route up the cliff, if only he could boost her high enough.

Although he'd told her she would have time to summon help, he doubted it was true. The sea was advancing quickly now and he'd only really said it to convince her to leave and get herself to safety.

He'd expected to feel a sense of relief. Many times over the past three years he'd contemplated taking his own life and joining his family, but something had tethered him to earth and a worldly existence. Now the decision was out of his hands he had thought he would welcome an escape from his grief, but he found his mind anything but peaceful.

Closing his eyes, Edward relived the kiss he'd just shared with Amelia. It had been spontaneous, totally unplanned and completely irresistible. As she'd stood in front of him just about to start up the cliff face Edward had known he couldn't let her leave without kissing her. The thought had taken over his entire body until there was no option but to spin her round and cover her lips with his own.

Now he had kissed her Edward could see the moment had been building for a long time, probably ever since they'd sat in the sitting room with him teaching her to draw. Deep down he'd been aware of his attraction for her, even been aware of the guilt that attraction had stirred up inside him. What was new was a curiosity of what might happen next. Visions of passionate kisses and tender embraces filled his mind and Edward was surprised not to be overcome with guilt. For the first time in three years he was considering his future and it did not look completely bleak.

He wanted to live, he realised. He wanted to escape from this cursed beach and return to his much-neglected home and fling open all the windows and doors, to let the light and the air into the darkest corners and whip off the dust sheets. Cautiously he wondered if maybe he wanted to start interacting with the world again, to embrace everything this life had to offer him and pull himself from the dark hole that had trapped him for the past few years.

Edward yelled in frustration. Why now? Why was it at the moment when he actually had something to live for and the urge to move forward with his life it was going to be cruelly taken away from him?

He ran at the cliff, launching himself up the smooth chalk, scrabbling for a handhold. Time and time again he slid back down, just to take another run at the towering white wall.

Eventually Edward sank to the floor with his back against the cliff and watched the approaching sea. It wouldn't be long now until it reached him, and then only a matter of time before the tide swept him out and pulled him under or dashed him against the cliffs.

Edward closed his eyes and thought about his life and about the past few weeks. What he regretted most was pushing Amelia away. He knew deep down he felt more for her than the friendship he pretended they shared. Every time he saw her his whole world lit up, every time she touched him his skin tingled and his heart pounded. Every time she smiled at him his heart squeezed. If only he'd seized his opportunity, if only he'd told her how he felt.

It wasn't fair. Any time in the past three years he would have welcomed the release from his guilt and sorrow, but now he finally could see a glimmer of hope in his life fate was going to give him what he had wished for.

Edward threw back his head and gave a primal roar, venting his frustration and his angst. He wanted to walk through his garden, to sketch and read, to hold Amelia in his arms and work out exactly what the future could hold. It was cruelly ironic that only now was he realising all that his life could be.

As the water rose to waist level Edward felt his hope fizzle and die so he focused on picturing his son and wondered if they would be reunited soon. He wanted to see his son's face, to kiss his hair and fold him in his arms, but still he wished he could have just a little longer on earth, a little longer to make up for all the time he'd wasted.

'Edward.' The voice floated down to him, and he for a moment he wondered if it were an angel from heaven. Then he recognised the tone and his eyes flew open. 'Edward.'

Quickly he stood, struggling to keep his balance as the waves pounded against him. Waving his arms above his head he opened his mouth and shouted as loudly as he could.

Amelia had managed it. She'd actually made it back in time. When he'd sent her up the cliff he'd never imagined she might return quickly enough to save him.

The rope fell just to his left and swung in to hit the cliff face a few times. Edward pushed through the seawater to reach it, grabbed hold with both hands and watched in amazement as slowly he rose from the sea.

Jerkily he was pulled higher and higher, inching away from the crashing waves below. As the distance between him and the sea increased Edward felt his heart soar. He was going to survive, he might be battered and bruised, but he would live. Now all of the things he had wished for more time to do would be within his grasp.

It took five minutes to pull him up on to the cliff. As Edward felt the strong hands grabbing his arms and swinging him on to firm ground his legs almost gave way beneath him. Amelia rushed forward, hesitating for just a minute before wrapping her arms around him and resting her forehead against his.

'You saved me,' Edward said quietly as he held her tightly.

Amelia didn't answer, instead burying her head in Edward's shoulder. He felt the shudder of her body before he heard the sobs and gently began to stroke her hair.

'I thought…' Amelia began, but couldn't finish the sentence.

'Shh,' Edward soothed. 'Don't think about it.'

He himself felt more than a little shaken by the experience and couldn't wait to get back to Beechwood Manor to get out of his wet clothes and warm up by a roaring fire. A good night's sleep would be very welcome and then maybe in the morning he might be able to start trying to work out exactly what he felt for the woman in his arms.

Chapter Nineteen

Edward paced backwards and forwards in the hallway, trying to stop himself looking at the clock every few seconds. Amelia was late, but that was her prerogative. He had rather sprung this surprise on her.

It had been a week since their disastrous trip to the beach and both Edward and Amelia had spent long periods in bed recovering from the cold and the physical exertion under doctor's orders. For Edward that had meant a lot of time to reflect on his realisations on the beach and a lot of time to plan.

He was very aware he needed to take things slowly. His growing desire to re-join the world of the living, his renewed excitement for the future, could just be a reaction to a near-death experience and he didn't want to rush into anything. What hadn't changed over the past week was his desire to spend more time with Amelia. He wasn't sure what his feelings for Amelia were and he couldn't quite put a name on them. He didn't feel that same comfortable feeling he had with Jane, but Amelia challenged him and riled him and lit a fire inside him.

Every day he still woke with a knot of guilt in his stomach and concerns that he should not be allowed to be happy, but instead of allowing these feelings to grow and fester Edward was taking a step back and distancing himself from them. Jane would never want him to be unhappy, so it was only he who had been holding himself back for the past three years. On the beach he had decided he'd wanted to live, so now he owed it to himself to give life a chance. And to give his feelings for Amelia a chance.

Whilst he'd been sitting in bed recuperating, filling his time with sketching and reading, Edward had decided he would approach Amelia as any man with an interest in a young woman would. He would attempt to court her. Not that he'd told her this yet, of course. Tonight he'd arranged for them to attend a small country dance, nothing too conspicuous, but an occasion where there would be dancing and high spirits and hopefully a few snatched moments alone. Maybe then he would be able to find the words to explain his cautious optimism about the future and gauge Amelia's reaction to his new level of interest in her.

Just as he glanced again at the clock he heard footsteps coming from the hallway above.

'Have I made you wait?' Amelia asked as she began to descend the stairs.

She looked beautiful. Dressed in a pale blue gown Edward had sent Mrs Henshaw to buy just for Amelia, she looked as though she belonged at the royal court, not accompanying him to a country dance. Her eyes sparkled with excitement and perhaps something more and she moved with such grace it looked as though she floated down the stairs.

'Yes.' He cursed his abruptness, but Amelia just smiled.

'Well, it's a good job I know you don't mind.'

'Oh, my goodness, don't you two look like royalty?' Mrs Henshaw said as she bustled out into the hallway and looked them both up and down.

Amelia twirled in her dress, letting Edward catch a glimpse of the bare skin of her upper back before placing her hand lightly on his forearm.

'You take care of her, Sir Edward,' Mrs Henshaw said. 'The young men will be flocking to her side.'

Edward didn't mean to let Amelia out of his sight. The young men of the village would not even get a chance to court Amelia. He had perfected his glare if any strayed too close or tarried too long.

'Goody, you look very lovely this evening,' Amelia said as she finished her twirl. 'Are you accompanying us to the dance?'

Edward looked his housekeeper up and down and re-alised Amelia was right, Mrs Henshaw was dressed in her finest. He wondered if she had taken it upon herself to chaperon them and his heart sank at the thought.

'Well, I *am* going to the dance,' Mrs Henshaw said, her ruddy cheeks colouring a little. 'But I wouldn't dream of inviting myself along with you two young things. Mr Guthry is calling for me in half an hour.'

'Mr Guthry?' Edward asked, bemused.

Amelia clapped her hands together in joy and Edward wondered if there was something he was missing.

'Well, you have a wonderful time, Goody, and give our regards to Mr Guthry. Perhaps you would be so kind as to ask him to visit tomorrow so we can discuss what his as-sistant found in London when he was seeking my cousin.'

'Of course, my dear.'

Edward could see the flicker of worry on Amelia's face at the thought of her cousin. They did not know the whole story yet, but Mr Guthry had sent a short note telling them his assistant had not been able to find Lizzie in London. There had been some sort of accident involving the house Lizzie had been staying in and Lizzie, along with

Amelia's aunt and other cousin, had travelled to Cambridgeshire whilst they recuperated. Amelia had been beside herself with worry, and Edward made a mental note to send someone to Cambridgeshire himself to track this errant cousin down.

Amelia placed her hand on his arm and together they walked outside.

'What was that all about?' Edward asked quietly, gesturing back towards Goody.

'I think Goody and Mr Guthry are courting.'

'Really?'

'Really. He's stopped by on a couple of occasions and always finds some excuse to head to the kitchens to seek Goody out.'

Edward supposed it made sense. Both had lost a spouse many years ago and now lived solitary lives, and both were kind and jolly people. When he thought about it they were a perfect match for each other.

'He'd better not steal my housekeeper,' Edward grumbled.

Amelia swatted him on the arm, 'I know you want them to be happy,' she said. 'Anyway, I don't think wild animals could drag Goody away from you and Beechwood Manor. No, if things go well I think you would be more likely to gain a live-in estate manager rather than lose a housekeeper.'

Edward grunted, but he rather liked the idea of Mrs Henshaw finding a bit of happiness of her own.

'Are you nervous?' he asked as he helped her up into the waiting carriage.

'I've never been to a country dance before,' Amelia answered.

'I'm sure it's not like the grand balls you're used to.'

Amelia shook her head. 'I've never been to a grand

ball. Sometimes my father would take my cousin and me to one of the regimental balls, but I've never been to anything special.'

Edward didn't say anything, wondering if she was regretting having to stay in the country with him rather than taking her rightful place in London society.

'I suppose if I hadn't run off to chase Captain McNair I'd be getting ready for some grand ball now,' Amelia said with a small smile.

'Do you wish you were?'

'There's nowhere I'd rather be,' she said, squeezing his arm.

Edward wondered if he should kiss her. Sitting next to her in the carriage with his thighs pushed up against hers and her hair occasionally tickling his neck, he felt almost intoxicated with desire. It would be so easy to lean over and kiss her. He knew she wouldn't object, he'd seen how she looked at him, how she shivered when he touched her. Amelia would welcome the kiss, but he knew he should hold back.

They both deserved more than a hurried kiss in a moving carriage. Edward deserved the time to work out what he was feeling for Amelia and Amelia deserved to be courted and wooed by a man who was sure of what he could offer. It would be the cruellest deed imaginable if he kissed her and led her on only to tell her he could never love her and they didn't have a future together. So with a gargantuan effort Edward sat back and listened to Amelia talk of the regimental balls in India and reminisce about the time before she'd met Captain McNair when she was happy.

As they pulled up to the village hall Edward jumped down from the carriage, turned and assisted Amelia out.

She looked nervous and quickly glanced right and left as if checking the coast was clear.

'He won't be here, Amelia,' Edward said softly. 'McNair will be far away by now.'

She nodded, relaxing a little as he led her into the hall. The dancing had already started. A group of lively musicians were playing a familiar tune on their assorted instruments and the hoard of people gathered in the village hall were twirling and stomping and sashaying in time. The room was hot from all the warm bodies crushed inside despite the large open windows and high barn-like ceiling.

As soon as they entered all eyes were on them and a murmur of surprise spread round the hall. He'd been a recluse for too long for his re-emergence into society to not cause a stir and now everyone would want a little piece of his story.

'Sir Edward,' a portly man called as he hustled over. Edward desperately tried to remember the man's name and summoned up a smile. 'What a pleasure to see you here. We are honoured you have graced our simple country dance with your presence.'

'May I introduce a dear friend, Miss Amelia?' Edward said, watching as Amelia curtsied.

'A pleasure to meet you. I hope you enjoy the dancing tonight, Miss Amelia.'

'I'm certain I shall. The music is so lively and the atmosphere wonderful.'

The portly man beamed at the compliment.

'Sir Edward, let me reintroduce you to some old faces who will be delighted to see you again.'

Edward was about to protest when the portly man beckoned over a rather handsome young man.

'This is my son, Mr Leonard Goone. Leonard, I'm sure

you remember Sir Edward? And this delightful young woman is Miss Amelia.'

Goone the Younger bowed over Amelia's hand. Edward felt his frown beginning to build as the younger man lingered just a few moments too long over her hand and flashed Amelia a charming smile.

'Maybe you could lead Miss Amelia in the next dance, Leonard, whilst I have a word with Sir Edward.'

'It would be my pleasure…if you would do me the honour, Miss Amelia?'

And just like that Amelia was whisked off in the company of an attractive young man whilst Edward could only watch. He wanted to run after them, snatch Amelia away and squirrel her back to Beechwood Manor where he didn't have to share her with anyone.

The next ten minutes dragged by, with reintroductions to all of the most important men of the area. Edward had known these men well before the fire and all were eager to renew their acquaintance, but he only had eyes for Amelia. Whilst the older men droned on about crop prices and finding a decent land agent, Edward nodded and agreed without paying much attention. His eyes were fixed on the dancing and in particular one very beautiful young woman in a light blue dress.

The young men were flocking to her and if he didn't step in soon she wouldn't have a single dance left for him.

'Please excuse me for a moment,' he murmured and stepped away.

Quickly he strode across the room, waited for the current dance to finish and then inserted himself in between Amelia and her partner.

'I say, old chap, I think it's my dance next,' a young man with a rather flamboyant taste in clothing said.

Edward restrained himself from growling at the man

and instead fixed him with a silent glare. The man backed away. Next to him Amelia giggled.

'There was no need for that,' she said as he took her into his arms for the next dance.

'There was every need.'

For the next five minutes it was as though they were the only two in the room. He held her close, probably closer than was socially appropriate, his hands pressing against the silky material of her dress. Amelia was light on her feet, a natural dancer, and she needed only the gentlest of guidance from him. For his part Edward actually enjoyed the dance. Never before could he remember wanting the music to continue for eternity, but tonight he didn't want the magical moment to end.

'Thank you,' Amelia said as the last note was played.

'Shall we step outside for a few minutes? It's rather warm.' Edward swept Amelia out of the path of an eager young man, glaring at the impromptu suitor until he cringed under the force of Edward's disapproval.

'That would be lovely.'

The doors to the hall had been thrown open in an attempt to cool the stifling room and many couples and groups had drifted outside. Edward guided Amelia to a spot under the great oak that stood in the village square a few hundred feet away. Here they were still visible to the rest of the guests in attendance, but they would have a modicum of privacy at least.

It was a clear night and for a few moments they stood looking up at the stars in the sky.

'When I was younger my father would spend hours pointing out constellations,' Amelia said. 'I never paid much attention, but I wish I had now.'

Edward smiled. He could imagine a younger Amelia restless and inattentive to her father's lessons.

'That one up there that looks a little like a plough, that's Ursa Minor. And this one over here that looks like a bear, that's Ursa Major.'

'You paid attention to your lessons.'

Edward smiled. 'My father was a bit of an enthusiast when it came to stargazing. Sometimes on clear nights he would take me up to the roof of Beechwood Manor and we would just lie back and spend hours looking at the stars.'

It made him feel peculiarly content to know that on one of those occasions somewhere half a world away Amelia might have been looking at the very same stars.

'Amelia, I've been wanting to talk to you ever since the incident on the beach,' Edward said, feeling as nervous as a schoolboy on his first day at school. 'That whole episode put a few things in perspective and…' He trailed off. Amelia wasn't listening.

He coughed, his heart sinking as he wondered if she just didn't want to hear what he had to say, then followed her gaze over his shoulder.

Strolling towards them down the village high street was Captain McNair. He had a cruel smile on his lips and twirled a walking cane as he approached.

Amelia was frozen in place and even as Edward grabbed hold of her arm she didn't respond. This wasn't the time or the place for a confrontation with McNair. If he could just get Amelia back to Beechwood Manor he would be able to protect her better.

Bodily he dragged Amelia a few steps before her head snapped round and her eyes met his. He'd never seen such an expression of despair or panic and he wished he could make her feel safe from this scoundrel and whatever else life had to throw at her for ever.

'Let's go,' Edward said quietly.

McNair was only two hundred feet away when Amelia jerked out of her trance and responded. Hand in hand they dashed down the high street and rounded the corner to where the short row of coaches were waiting to take the few people who lived outside the village home. Edward spotted their coach and Tom the groom who was acting as coachman for the evening in the middle of the row.

'Tom,' he roared, waking the slumbering man.

Tom sprang upright, rubbed the sleep from his eyes and guided the coach into the middle of the road just as Edward and Amelia reached it. Edward near enough threw Amelia inside and vaulted up after her. The coach was already moving by the time he'd settled on one of the seats, but he was just in time to see McNair jump out of the way of the moving carriage as they thundered past.

As the Captain disappeared into the distance Edward saw him point after the carriage with the walking cane and then slowly draw the handle across his neck. Next to him he heard Amelia choke back a sob. Quickly he gathered her in his arms and held her tight to his chest.

He would protect her, no matter what.

Chapter Twenty

Amelia was a nervous wreck. Every little sound made her jump and cower and every shadow made her heart beat just that little bit faster. She wasn't sure how McNair had traced her back to the village, but it didn't really matter. By now he would have worked out where she was staying and it was only a matter of time before he appeared to exact his revenge.

All night different scenarios had been charging through her mind. In one he arrived with an unforgiving magistrate who ruled she should hang for attacking a decorated Captain. In another he waited until she fell asleep and then slipped in and stabbed her whilst she slumbered. Needless to say Amelia hadn't slept at all.

Edward had stayed with her the entire night. On their return to Beechwood Manor he'd instructed a fire to be lit in his study, then he'd settled her down into one of the comfortable armchairs and taken up position in the other. All night he'd sat with her, talked to her in his calm, soothing voice, and when the first rays of light had filtered in through the window he'd escorted her to her room and promised to remain in a chair outside the door whilst she rested for a few hours.

A light tap at the door made Amelia sit up and a few seconds later Edward entered quietly.

'I heard you tossing and turning,' he said.

'I can't sleep, every time I close my eyes I think he's going to pounce on me.'

Edward approached the bed and after a moment's hesitation sat down next to her.

'I will protect you, Amelia. McNair won't get close to you.'

She looked up into his deep dark eyes and saw the sincerity burning there and felt herself relax a little.

'Why are you doing all this for me?' she asked quietly.

Edward frowned as if he didn't understand the question.

'All of this. I'm not your responsibility and I just keep bringing you trouble.'

Amelia found she was holding her breath whilst she waited for Edward's answer. She wanted him to declare his love for her, to tell her he would do anything for her, tell her she was his entire world. Deep down Amelia knew it couldn't be true, that it would be just too much to hope for, but she wished all the same.

'Come for a walk with me,' Edward said. 'It's a beautiful day and if we're outside then McNair truly won't know where to look. There's eight hundred acres of land out there for us to get lost in.'

She wondered if she should push him, repeat the question, but something told her he would answer in his own time. Maybe when they were away from the house and he'd had chance to clear his head a little.

Edward waited outside her door whilst she changed and escorted her downstairs to his study. Before leaving they picked up a blanket to lay on the grass if they fancied a rest and as usual Edward packed some paper and pencils into his bulging satchel.

Being in the fresh air did make Amelia feel better. All night she had tormented herself with McNair's face, but now with Edward's reassurance that he would protect her and a warm breeze clearing some of the cobwebs from her mind she felt a little more positive.

They walked in silence for a while, both lost in their own thoughts, and it was only as Amelia realised she didn't know where they were that she started to pay attention to their surroundings.

'Where are we?' she asked, looking around, trying to find some familiar landmark to orientate herself. In the time she had been at Beechwood Manor she had explored much of the estate, especially the parts close to the house, but she didn't recognise where they were now at all.

'I'm taking you somewhere very special,' Edward said with a small smile.

He led her down a grassy path, surrounded on both sides by overgrown, tangled bushes. Up ahead a mossy stone wall came into view, leading off in both directions for a few hundred yards.

'Come this way,' Edward said, pulling her off the path into a narrow gap between the bushes and into the long grass. Amelia could feel the skirts of her dress being dragged behind her by the undergrowth and at one point Edward had to stop to lift her over a particularly large fallen tree stump.

Eventually they met up with the mossy wall and Edward traced his hands along it as if searching for something. Amelia watched in amazement as he gripped an almost invisible knob, turned it and opened a concealed door.

Feeling as though she were stepping into some magical hidden kingdom, Amelia crossed the threshold into the secret garden and gasped in pleasure. Although it had obviously been neglected over the past few years the garden was beautiful, maybe even more so for the slightly wild air it had about it. The long grass was dotted with wild flowers, drawing the eye to a multi-coloured carpet stretching out before them. Tall trees were positioned around the edge of the garden and from one hung a wide rope swing. Amelia felt as though she wanted to sink into the long grass and never leave.

Edward closed the door behind them and caught up with her, taking her by the hand and leading her further into the garden.

'My grandfather built this for my grandmother,' he said quietly as he watched Amelia take in all the details.

A small white butterfly fluttered past and settled on a large daisy for a moment before continuing with its journey.

'How lovely.'

'They were very much in love. In a time when nearly all marriages were arranged they rebelled and married each other despite a big difference in social status.'

'Tell me their story,' Amelia said as they strolled arm in arm through the garden. She wanted to hear something positive now, something that would remind her of all the good in the world.

'My grandfather was titled and heir to the estate. When he was of an appropriate age his parents arranged a match with a local landowner's daughter. Their family were rich and her dowry would help to maintain the estate for years to come.'

'But your grandfather didn't agree to the marriage?'

'At first he protested quietly, refused to set a date for the wedding despite his parents' urging. And then he met my grandmother. She was a farmer's daughter, totally inappropriate for a man like him, of course, but they fell madly and irrevocably in love.'

Amelia felt herself smile at the thought of Edward's grandparents holding out for love despite societal pressures trying to force them apart. Maybe there was hope for everyone, if they were just strong enough.

'My grandfather informed his parents he was going to marry my grandmother. Of course they were livid, threatened to cut him off and disinherit him, but my grandfather stuck firm. For years he and my grandmother lived in exile from the family home. My grandfather worked as an estate manager for one of the local estates and they lived a simple but happy life.'

'What happened?'

'In the end his parents realised it was only them losing out. They wanted to see their son and their grandchildren and so they made an approach and slowly my grandparents were welcomed back into the family.'

'And your grandparents never regretted marrying for love?'

Edward shook his head.

'My grandfather built this garden for my grandmother when they were in their sixties, just a few years before they both passed away. I can remember being a small boy and watching them walk hand in hand as if they were courting. They loved each other for forty years.'

'That's a beautiful story,' Amelia said.

She wanted love like that. Amelia glanced at Edward and wondered if he was thinking of his late wife, wishing it were her he was bringing into the secret garden.

Edward laid out the blanket on the long grass in the sunshine and sat down beside Amelia.

'I need to tell you something,' he said in a serious tone.

Amelia turned her attention to him, pulling back from the self-pity she was wallowing in.

'You asked me why I was doing all this for you, protecting you and sheltering you,' he said quietly. 'You deserve an answer to that question, but I find it difficult to articulate sometimes.'

Amelia smiled encouragingly at him, her heart pounding in her chest. She could sense this was a monumental moment in their relationship and a small, excitable part of her dared to hope.

'Before you came into my life I was a husk of a man. I was overcome by grief, consumed by thoughts of the past. It wasn't healthy and it wasn't any way to live.' He looked at her as he spoke and Amelia could sense his sincerity and emotion. 'Many times in the past few years I've wondered if there was any point continuing with life, but last week on the beach when I was at a real risk of drowning I found myself desperate to be alive.'

He paused, staring off into the distance as if unsure how to continue. Amelia hesitantly reached out and placed her hand on top of his.

'I found myself wanting to restore the house and restore my life, to actually move forward instead of doing only the bare minimum to survive. I found myself wanting to spend more time with you.'

Amelia felt that small glimmer of hope start to swell and build inside her. She knew she cared for Edward, maybe more than she rightly should. He'd rescued her, kept her safe and welcomed her into his home and his life. In return Amelia had slowly and absolutely fallen in love with this gruff, gentle man, despite knowing she would never be the sort of woman he deserved. For weeks she'd been devastated by that realisation and the knowledge that he was still in mourning and might never love her back, but now maybe that was about to change.

'I miss my late wife and my son very much,' he said and Amelia saw the emotion on his face as he worked through the pain of remembering, 'And I don't think I will ever stop loving them.'

With those words Amelia felt all of her hopes crash to the ground. It must have shown on her face as Edward reached out for her hand and squeezed it tight.

'Listen to me, Amelia,' he said softly. 'Let me finish.'

She nodded, forcing herself to rein in all the negative thoughts and focus on what Edward was saying.

'I love my late wife and son just as I love my parents and my grandparents. They will always be part of my life, part of me. I will never forget and there will always be a place in my heart for them.'

Amelia nodded. In truth she couldn't expect anything less. Edward was a good man, of course he wouldn't abandon his love for his late wife and son just because someone new came along.

'For a long time I thought a man only got one chance in this life. One chance to live, one chance at caring for another.' He paused, looking deep into Amelia's eyes. 'I think now that I was wrong.'

She held her breath, hoping he would say the words, hoping he was going in the direction she thought he was.

'I care for you, Amelia, you've been the only person to stir me from my grief in the last three years and I find myself unable to stop thinking about you when you're not close. I think you were the reason I fought so hard on the beach to stay alive and I think you are the reason I have finally accepted I need to move forward with my life.'

It wasn't a declaration of love, but it was more than she had ever dreamed possible. He cared for her, the man she loved cared for her. Part of her cried out for love in return, but the sensible portion of her brain suppressed the thought. It shouldn't matter Edward hadn't declared his love, it was enough he wanted to see what might happen between them.

'I need you to know I can't forget my past,' he said, searching her face for a reaction.

'I wouldn't ever want you to,' Amelia said.

It was part of what she loved about him. He was a truly caring and loving man.

'I know I could never mean as much as Jane did to you, but—'

Edward shook his head, interrupting her as she spoke.

'Jane was a friend, a treasured friend, from childhood. We played together and grew up together and somewhere along the line the great regard I held her in turned into something more.'

'I think it is wonderful you grew to love each other,' Amelia said quietly.

Edward gripped her hand firmly, 'I'm not explaining myself very well,' he said. 'For a while I thought a man was only lucky enough to care for someone with every ounce of their being once, that I'd had my chance and I'd lost it. Now I see my thinking was completely wrong.'

Amelia felt her heart start hammering in her chest. Was this when he told her he loved her, that theirs would be an everlasting love?

'I cared for Jane the way I cared for my parents. She was kind and warm-hearted and had always been part of my life. But you, Amelia, you light this fire inside me. You make me want to shout and laugh all at the same time. I've never felt this depth of emotion before, this sort of connection.'

Amelia found herself grinning like a mad woman and threw her arms around Edward's neck. He might not have said the words, but Amelia could see the sincerity and

emotion in his eyes. He loved her, even if he hadn't realised it himself yet.

'But I need you to remember I can't promise you anything right now, we need to take things slowly,' he said
softly.

Amelia ran her fingers over his jawline and smiled. 'Just
knowing you're giving us a chance is enough.'

She knew he was trying to temper the excitement that
he must be able to see burning in her eyes. Edward was a
good man, he wouldn't ever dream of building her hopes
only to dash them on purpose, but he would be worried
about his grief and guilt returning and sabotaging anything
they built between them. All the more reason to take things
slowly and allow him time to adjust, but already Amelia
could feel herself getting carried away with dreams of a
happy ending for herself and Edward.

Slowly he shifted position, sitting up so his body was
close to hers. Amelia felt herself shudder with anticipation,
knowing it was only a matter of time before he kissed her
and losing herself in the desire she could see in his eyes.

'I think we should see if we're compatible,' Edward
murmured, inching closer.

Amelia couldn't answer, but eventually managed a
small, jerky, nod. Already her heart was racing and her
body begging to be touched.

'Our kiss on the beach was very enjoyable,' Edward
said, his voice low and seductive, 'but I think we need to
repeat it to ensure nothing has changed.'

Slowly he raised a hand and traced his fingers over her
cheek, before lacing them through her hair. Gently but
firmly he pulled her towards him, claiming her lips with
his own. Amelia felt herself lose control of her body as
Edward expertly teased and tickled her with his lips and
tongue.

She couldn't suppress a groan as he pulled away, but the loss of contact was for a mere few seconds as he regarded her with lust-filled eyes. It was almost inconceivable for Amelia that she was the source of such desire from the man she loved, but had never even dreamed could want her back, and she felt truly happy for the first time in years.

He whispered her name into her ear as he caught the lobe between his teeth and nibbled gently. Amelia gasped as he darted his tongue out to taste her skin, murmuring how sweet she was, how he wanted to kiss her all over. Amelia had been kissed before, but never like this. Never had her body responded so instinctively, never had she felt so out of control, so overwhelmed.

Something inside her was swelling and building, an uncontrollable desire for the man in front of her. She wanted him to lay her down and kiss every inch of her skin, she wanted to touch every part of him, to explore his body for hours on end.

Slowly, Edward pulled away.

'We're compatible,' he said gruffly, shifting a little uncomfortably.

Amelia immediately tensed, wondering if she had done something wrong. Edward must have caught her worried expression and reached out to pull her closer to him.

'You deserve more than a hurried fumble in the grass,' Edward said with a pained smile. 'If I kiss you for another second then I may not be able to control myself.'

With her heart soaring Amelia dipped her head and kissed the man she loved, giggling as he groaned as she pressed her body against his.

Chapter Twenty-One

Edward felt the warm glow of contentment as he lay in the long grass with Amelia in his arms. Lazily he traced a pattern on her back, stopping to pepper the silky skin with kisses every now and then.

After a few minutes Amelia rolled over so they were face to face. He couldn't help but smile. In this moment everything felt right in the world. He couldn't believe just two months ago he'd never wanted to see another human again. He'd been shut away in Beechwood Manor, spiralling into a never-ending whirlpool of grief and sadness and guilt.

'Lay right there,' he instructed Amelia as he sat up. The sunlight was bathing her in a warm glow and, with her hair cascading over her shoulders and her skin still pink and warm from their intimacy, Edward knew he had to draw her.

She looked at him questioningly as he took out his pencils and paper, but he gave her a smile of reassurance.

'Edward?'

'You've never looked more beautiful than you do right now,' he said. 'Let me draw you. I want to capture this moment for ever.'

He wondered if she might protest. Most women would laugh nervously and then refuse, but after a moment's contemplation Amelia rested her head back on her hand and relaxed.

'I just need to alter one or two things,' Edward said.

Gently he gripped the neckline of her dress and tugged until the material was off her shoulders, leaving the caramel-coloured skin exposed. She looked irresistible.

With long pencil strokes he sketched, tracing her contours and capturing her essence. As he drew he found his eyes roaming over her body, taking in her gentle curves and her perfectly proportioned features. He couldn't quite believe a woman like Amelia could want to be with him. She was young and beautiful, and if she were introduced into society she would surely be the belle of the debutantes, but here she was with him, a man with a complicated past and more unresolved emotion than most of her possible suitors would have put together.

'What happens now, Edward?' Amelia asked as he began to add the finer details to his drawing.

'Now? Now I think I need to kiss you again.'

She giggled as he pounced on top of her, kissing her long and hard. Leisurely they explored each other with hands and lips, and Edward felt as though they had all the time in the world. He wanted this afternoon never to end. Here in the secret garden it felt like a little slice of paradise just for them.

'You never answered my question,' Amelia said, resting her head on his chest.

'For now we need to focus on keeping you safe,' Edward said, brushing her hair back from her face and tucking it behind an ear. 'I will not let McNair harm a single hair on your head or inch of your skin.'

Amelia nodded, but Edward could see already the fear was back in her eyes.

'I don't know what he wants,' she said eventually.

'He wants revenge. You've hurt his pride.'

'Will he report me to the magistrate? Is that how he will punish me?'

Edward wished it might be as simple as all that. Given McNair's less-than-pure reputation he had no doubt he could convince a magistrate to drop any charges against Amelia. No, he thought McNair would want to exact a more personal revenge on her.

'From what you have said, and from Mr Guthry's report, I think he will prefer to take matters into his own hands,' Edward said slowly. He didn't want to scare Amelia, but he knew she had been through every option, every outcome, a hundred times in her head.

'He wants to hurt me.'

Edward nodded.

'I can't see how this will end. What will make him stop?'

It had been a question Edward had been asking himself over the past twenty-four hours. He wondered if maybe he could pay the scoundrel off, bribe him to forget the whole matter. It seemed McNair was pretty money-orientated and maybe a large enough amount would convince the man to leave Amelia alone. The only downside to the plan was they could never be sure he wouldn't come back once he'd spent the payoff and demand more.

That left a show of strength. Edward wasn't a violent man, but some people only seemed to understand power and violence. He rather feared the only way to make McNair leave Amelia alone would be to make the man see she was protected by someone stronger than he was. Edward might not have had the army training that the Captain had benefitted from, but he had something worth fighting for, and that was why he was sure he would beat McNair if it came to that.

'We'll figure it out,' Edward said, 'but for now just remember he can't get anywhere near you, not whilst you're here with me.'

Amelia leaned across and kissed him, squeezing her eyes shut as she did so.

Amelia felt as though she were walking through the air, bouncing easily from fluffy cloud to fluffy cloud. The memory of Edward's kisses were imprinted in her mind and she could see by the look in his eye that he cared for her. Amelia couldn't quite believe it was true. Ever since discovering McNair's betrayal she knew her confidence had been dented. Nevertheless, all of her worries and insecurities seemed to melt away when Edward was by her side and even if the future was a little uncertain, she knew that as long as she was with Edward everything would work out just fine.

Still, there was that occasional hesitation in his eyes, the fleeting expressions of guilt that Amelia thought might always be there in the background. His near-death encounter had shown him he wanted to live, but that didn't mean he would be able to leave his guilt and memories behind him easily. And of course he'd never said that he loved her. Having Edward care for her should be enough, but already Amelia was craving more.

They walked back to the house in the late afternoon sunshine hand in hand, stopping before they entered the courtyard to straighten their clothes and brush the last pieces of grass from their bodies.

'Can we check on Milly?' Amelia asked as they passed the barn.

Inside it took a few moments for their eyes to adjust to the gloom before they could make out Milly and her foal curled together in the hay. For a long while they stood side by side, watching mother and baby, and Amelia felt an unfamiliar maternal tug on her heart. She realised that she wanted this, this instinctive and natural bond between mother and baby. She wanted to cradle her and Edward's child in her arms and know she would love the baby she held for eternity. With a small smile she warned herself not to get too carried away. They'd shared a few kisses, nothing more at present, and there had been no mention of marriage.

Glancing sideways at Edward's profile, Amelia felt a surge of hope. There had been no mention of love or marriage, but perhaps one day there might be. A girl was allowed to dream.

'Tom,' Edward called out to the groom as they crossed the courtyard. 'Gather the servants. I want to speak to everyone in my study in ten minutes.'

They went inside and straight to Edward's study. Amelia recognised the determined look on his face as he sat her down in one of the chairs and began pacing up and down, murmuring to himself as he did so.

'Thank you for coming,' he said to the assembled servants ten minutes later. 'We have a problem and we need your help.'

Amelia thought she saw the servants standing slightly taller as Edward called them to action.

'Miss Amelia is in trouble. A dangerous man from her past has tracked her down and is intent on causing her harm. He knows where she is and he is determined to find a way to hurt her.'

The servants glanced at her, but nobody said anything, turning their attention back to Edward as he continued speaking.

'Now I know there are not many of us and I don't pro-pose this is a job for such a small band, but I wanted you to know exactly what was going on. Tom, once we've finished here I want you to ride into the village and round up as many young men as you can. Tell them what's going on and tell them I will pay the first eight men who turn up to help guard the house.'

Tom nodded, looking eager to set off on his mission.

'Everyone else, I need you to be vigilant at all times. If you notice a window open that wasn't open before, raise the alarm. If you hear a noise in a room that should be empty, raise the alarm. Anything out of the ordinary, raise the alarm. This man is dangerous and we need to apprehend him.'

All the servants nodded seriously and Mrs Henshaw moved closer to Amelia and squeezed her arm.

'Don't you worry, ducky, we'll find this scoundrel and keep you safe. I will send a message to Mr Guthry, I'm sure he will want to be on hand to help.'

Amelia nodded. She just wanted this to be over. For weeks she had lived in purgatory, at first convinced she was a murderer and then scared beyond belief about what McNair might do to her if he found her. She still wasn't sleeping properly, and whenever she did close her eyes she imagined the letter opener slipping into McNair's soft flesh and the blood seeping through his clothing. Now the images had evolved and often it was Amelia's abdomen the small blade was plunged into and her blood oozing from the wound.

Edward waited for the servants to leave and then gave her a reassuring squeeze on the shoulder. 'We'll find him,' he said softly. 'And then we can get on with our lives.'

Chapter Twenty-Two

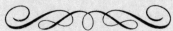

For three days men from the village had been positioned around the outside of the house and Mr Guthry had more or less moved in to one of the larger servants' rooms up in the attic, adding his calming presence to the household. Edward had accompanied Amelia nearly everywhere. Even when she had asked to take a bath he'd sat dutifully on the other side of the screen, much to Mrs Henshaw's absolute indignation. Amelia had caught his frown of displeasure as the housekeeper had taken up position firmly between him and the screen and couldn't help but giggle.

She had never been very good at being alone and spending time with Edward was never tedious, but Amelia was beginning to feel as though there were eyes watching her everywhere she went. Part of her wished McNair would just appear now so they could have their confrontation and the men of the village could see him off.

Edward seemed strangely calm. He was sitting across from her in his comfortable armchair, happily reading a thick book. Every so often he'd glance up, check the room and smile. She wished she could be so content to sit and read.

A light tap on the door made Amelia and Edward look

up in unison and Amelia felt her heart racing, but it was just Betty one of the maids who slipped into the room.

'There's a Mr Pollard here to see you, sir,' Betty said with a deferential curtsy.

Amelia immediately sat up straighter. Mr Pollard was the young man Mr Guthry had sent to London to warn Lizzie about McNair.

'Good afternoon,' Edward said as the tall young man entered the room.

'Good afternoon, Sir Edward... Miss Amelia.'

Edward motioned for him to sit down and Pollard awkwardly manoeuvred his lanky form into one of the free armchairs.

'Tell us,' Edward said simply. 'What did you find out?'

'Well, sir, I travelled to London as instructed and headed straight to the address Miss Amelia had provided. I could see as soon as I arrived that there had been a fire and the building looked to be damaged beyond repair.'

Amelia held her breath as he continued, wondering if McNair had decided to target Lizzie, to injure the woman Amelia thought of as a sister.

'I talked to some of the servants and it seems as though the fire was started by a candle being left burning by the curtains in one of the bedrooms. Luckily no one was hurt and there was no question of there being an intruder involved. What's more there had been no sightings of anyone fitting Captain McNair's description.'

Amelia felt herself begin to relax a little, 'And Lizzie, did you find her?'

Mr Pollard shook his head. 'The servants informed me she, along with the two women she had been staying with, had been taken to the countryside to recuperate from mild smoke inhalation by a gentleman, the Earl of Burwell.'

'Do you know him, Amelia?' Edward asked.

She shook her head. 'Maybe he is a friend of Aunt Mathilda.'

'I travelled to Cambridgeshire after satisfying myself Captain McNair was not involved in the house fire and approached a member of Lord Burwell's household. By the time I got there it seemed Miss Lizzie had left.'

Amelia frowned, wondering where Lizzie would have gone to next. Her cousin didn't know anyone else in England so she didn't have many choices.

'I bought one of the grooms a few cups of ale and he told me he thought there had been a lovers' row between Miss Eastway and Lord Burwell.'

'Lizzie, involved with an earl?' Amelia found herself smiling. If anyone deserved to find love it was her cousin, but she just hoped this Lord Burwell was good enough for her kind and generous cousin.

'I could not pick up her trail after that, miss, but I got the impression Lord Burwell is not the sort of man to leave your cousin stranded without anyone to turn to.'

Amelia felt some of the worry she had been carrying over the last few weeks begin to dissipate. At least it looked as though McNair hadn't decided to target her cousin, but she would feel much better if she could just lay eyes on Lizzie and reassure herself she was well.

'Thank you, Mr Pollard,' Edward said, standing and shaking the young man's hand. 'I am sure you understand what a matter for concern this is for Miss Amelia and you have done a wonderful job in reassuring us so far. I wonder if you would be against returning to Cambridgeshire and approaching Lord Burwell on our behalf.'

The young man's eyes widened and he looked from Edward and Amelia and back again.

'I would give you a letter explaining our predicament

and I feel confident you will be able to impress the importance of our queries on this Lord Burwell.'

Amelia held her breath, hoping Mr Pollard would agree.

'I am sure you understand how important it is that we find Miss Eastway. And you will be remunerated for your time and effort, of course.'

'I am honoured that you trust me with a matter of such importance, Sir Edward,' Mr Pollard said.

'Go to the kitchens and ask Mrs Henshaw for some refreshment and I will write the letter for Lord Burwell whilst you wait.'

'Thank you,' Amelia said as Mr Pollard left the room.

'We'll find your cousin, Amelia, even if we have to scour the whole of Cambridgeshire ourselves.'

He sounded so sincere, so concerned for the safety of a woman he hadn't ever met, that Amelia wanted to wrap her arms around him and kiss him. She took a step towards him, and then another, but before she could turn her face up to meet his the door burst open and Tom the groom came rushing in.

'We've caught him, sir,' he said, bending forward slightly and resting his hands on his thighs as he caught his breath.

Edward stiffened and immediately put a protective arm around Amelia.

'Where?'

'Sneaking through the gardens by the old gazebo.'

'Have you restrained him?'

'William and Big Peter are holding him, and I sent some of the other men to join them on my way over here. What do you want us to do?'

'I'll come at once.'

Amelia made to follow, but Edward placed a firm hand on her shoulder, pressing her back into the chair.

'I should be there,' she said quietly, knowing she needed to face her tormentor, but not really wanting to.

'There's no need. I'll have a quiet word with him and send him on his way,' Edward said with a stony expression on his face.

Amelia doubted it would be just 'a quiet word', but she saw the determination behind Edward's eyes and stopped fighting to stand up. Maybe it would be better if she never had to see McNair ever again.

'I'll be back soon.' He kissed the top of her head and strode out of the room, closely followed by Tom.

Amelia stood up and stretched, feeling suddenly free. In no time at all Edward would be back by her side and they would no longer have the threat of McNair hanging over them. They would be able to plan for the future and enjoy a proper life, not one just confined to the walls of Beechwood Manor.

'Hello, Amelia, my sweet.'

Amelia screamed, but the sound was cut off by a firm hand being clamped over her nose and mouth.

'There's no need for that. I thought you'd be pleased to see me.'

Amelia felt herself being dragged backwards towards the middle of the room, her feet tangling in the heavy rug on the floor.

'Now, if I release my hand, do you promise to be a good girl and stay nice and quiet?'

She nodded her head. At this precise moment in time she would agree to anything to get the oxygen her lungs were screaming out for.

McNair slowly released his hand and Amelia sucked in a few deep breaths.

'How lovely for us to be together again,' McNair murmured into her hair. 'Now, let me be very clear. I have a pistol and I'm holding it against your back. If you make any sudden moves, or if you do anything to displease me, then I will shoot you.' There was a cold, dead tone to his voice and Amelia wondered how she had ever fancied herself in love with this man. He might be conventionally handsome, but there was no warmth inside him, no capacity to love.

'You sent in a decoy,' Amelia said flatly, realising how McNair had outsmarted them.

'Of course. Your new beau had the house guarded round the clock, I needed some way to get you alone.'

Amelia wondered just how long they had before Edward reached the gazebo and realised the man they had captured was not McNair.

'I assumed your gentleman would have given a description of me, but it's not too difficult to find someone who looks vaguely similar in need of a little money.'

'What do you want?' Amelia asked, not sure she wanted to know the answer.

'What do I want?' McNair mused. 'Well, my sweet, I want you to realise quite how much you hurt me.'

'I'm sorry,' Amelia whispered.

'I'm sure you are, but that doesn't change the fact you stabbed me and left me for dead. That broke my heart, Amelia, and so soon after our reunion.'

Suddenly Amelia felt a flare of anger inside. 'You *used* me. I fell for you and you used me. If you hadn't been sent back to England, I would have run away with you and been ruined for ever.'

'That doesn't give you the right to stab me.'

He had a point, but that hadn't been why she'd stabbed him.

'I thought you were going to kill me,' Amelia said quietly. 'That was why I stabbed you.'

'How did that work out for you? Feel any safer for it now?'

'What do you plan to do?'

McNair chuckled. 'Do you know, I've no idea? I've thought of a thousand different things, of course. Maybe scar your pretty face, or plunge a knife into you at random and give you the same chance you did me. Or maybe I'll take you away with me and get your father to pay for your return, just as I'd planned all that time ago.'

Amelia wondered if he was a little deranged. She understood he was cruel and she understood he was angry that she'd bested him and left him bleeding, but there was a slight note of hysteria in his voice as he talked through the options.

'Amelia!' Edward shouted as the door burst open.

'Ah, your knight in shining armour. Keep back, Sir Edward, or I might have to harm Amelia.'

Edward froze and took a moment to assess the scene. Amelia could see the second he noticed the pistol. Carefully he stepped into the room, giving both Amelia and McNair a wide berth.

'What do you want?' Edward asked bluntly.

'No niceties? No formal introductions?'

'No. What do you want?'

'Has Amelia told you what she did to me?'

'She stabbed you.'

Amelia felt McNair stiffen a little behind her at Edward's bluntness, but the Captain soon rallied and continued.

'We had been involved, of course, which was why her actions were the ultimate betrayal.'

'You seduced her, planned to ruin her and blackmail her father to avoid any scandal. Then your commanding officer found out and sent you back to England quietly to pre-empt any trouble. When Amelia followed you here you hit her and she stabbed you in self-defence. Have I left anything out?' Edward asked.

He spoke slowly, and seemed cool and detached, but Amelia could see what was going on under the surface and realised Edward was petrified for her.

McNair shook his head. 'Quite accurate. At least we can't accuse Amelia of holding anything back.'

'What do you want?' Edward asked again.

'Why are you here, Amelia?' McNair asked, completely ignoring Edward's question again.

'Hiding from you,' Amelia mumbled.

'But why here? Tell me the truth. I'll know if you're lying.'

'I took shelter here from the storm when I was fleeing Brighton.'

'So you didn't know Sir Edward beforehand? Don't take another step, Sir Edward, or we'll find out just what shade of red Amelia's blood is.'

Edward had been edging forward, step by tiny step, but it seemed McNair still had his sharp powers of observation, even when distracted by the person he was holding at gunpoint.

'No, I met him two months ago for the first time.'

'So why did you stay here?'

'It was safe and I didn't have anywhere else to go.' She didn't see any point in lying to McNair. Besides, he'd known her for so long he'd probably be able to tell if she was speaking the truth or not.

'Why did you let Amelia stay, Sir Edward?'

'To protect her from you.'

'She was a complete stranger, yet you welcomed her into your home and have gone to a lot of trouble to protect her. Do I detect some deeper feelings here? Have you fallen for Amelia's considerable charms?'

Edward remained silent, but behind her Amelia heard McNair chuckle.

'Of course! Two little love birds cooped up in this dusty old house.'

'I suggest you tell us what you want and then leave,' Edward said. 'This is beginning to feel like the ramblings of a senile old man.'

McNair pulled Amelia a little closer to him.

'Careful, Sir Edward, or you might lose someone you care for. I hear it wouldn't be the first time.'

Amelia watched the flicker of pain cross Edward's face before his expression turned inscrutable again.

'But you're right, we haven't got all day. I have decided how we should settle this.' McNair sounded positively cheerful. 'Amelia injured me greatly and I demand recompense.'

For a moment Amelia's heart soared as she thought he was about to ask for money.

'I propose a duel. Tomorrow morning. Me and you, Sir Edward. Pistols. And only one of us will leave alive.'

Amelia felt her heart skip a beat and then another. An acute pain ripped through her chest as she saw Edward consider the proposal and nod slowly.

'That seems fair,' he said eventually.

'No!' she screamed.

'Shh, Amelia, everything is settled,' McNair said, releasing her and pushing her into Edward's arms. 'I'll see you at dawn tomorrow, Sir Edward, past the lake and on the rise near the northern edge of your estate.'

'Tomorrow.' Edward nodded.

McNair walked calmly out of the room without looking back.

Chapter Twenty-Three

'You can't go,' Amelia said, a note of hysteria in her voice. 'He'll kill you.'

Edward grimaced. It was quite possible. McNair had served in the army for a long time and had no doubt been trained to fire a pistol accurately. Whilst Edward owned a gun, and had learnt to shoot as a boy, he hadn't picked up his pistol for many years.

'It's settled, Amelia.'

'It's not settled. We can find another way.'

She reached out to him and Edward hated the look of pain and confusion that crossed her face as he let her hand hang in the air. He couldn't touch her, not now. He'd sworn to protect her, to keep her safe no matter what, and he'd failed at the very first test.

'Edward?' Amelia said, trying to catch his eye.

'I need to go and prepare. I'll see you later,' he said shortly.

Quickly, before she could react, he strode out the door and made for his rooms in the West Wing. He needed to think, to puzzle things through, and that wasn't possible with Amelia right there distracting him.

He closed the door to his bedchamber behind him and

sank down on to the bed. Edward couldn't believe he'd let himself be fooled by McNair's trick. The wily scoundrel had paid a man to sneak into the grounds and be caught in his place, then used the distraction to get to Amelia. He should have seen it coming, should have stayed with her no matter what. Instead he'd rushed off to confront McNair and left Amelia vulnerable. When he'd burst into the room and found her with a gun to her back he'd almost expired on the spot.

'You can't just run away from me,' Amelia said, flinging open the door to his bedroom and stepping inside. She was fired up, recovered from her ordeal only minutes earlier, and ready to do battle.

'Amelia, I need some peace.'

'What for? What's going on, Edward? You need to talk to me. You can't keep trying to solve everything by yourself.'

Edward remained silent. Amelia sighed dramatically and flopped down on the bed next to him.

'Do you know I've just been held at gunpoint by a man who would like to hurt me very much?'

'Of course I do, Amelia.' And he felt like such a cur for not being more supportive.

'I thought I might die. He threatened to cut me, you know. And to shoot me.'

Edward felt the nausea rise inside him as he pictured all the awful things McNair would likely want to do to Amelia. It was his job to protect her and so far he'd failed miserably.

'I was scared—in fact, I was petrified—but nothing scared me as much as hearing you accept his challenge to a duel.'

He was just about to open his mouth to reply when

her words hit him and he stopped to consider them for a moment.

'I don't know what I'd do if you were harmed…' She paused for a moment and took his hand. 'Please don't push me away.'

Her plea was so heartfelt and so sincere Edward knew that for once in his life he would have to share his innermost thoughts.

'I promised to protect you, Amelia,' he said quietly. 'And I failed.'

He watched as she opened her mouth and then closed it again as she digested his words.

'I swore I wouldn't let anything happen to you and three days later a man is holding a pistol to your back.'

'You couldn't have done any more,' Amelia protested quietly.

'You deserve someone who can take care of you, Amelia, a man who will protect and shelter you.'

'I deserve a man who cares for me,' Amelia said, 'Nothing more and nothing less. Everyone deserves to be cared for, but I can't ask someone else to be responsible for the consequences of my actions.'

He studied her face, saw her earnest expression and knew she believed what she was saying. She'd changed so much in the couple of months she'd been staying with him. The energetic, mischievous little minx was still there, but Amelia was more thoughtful, more considerate now. He supposed she'd had to do a lot of growing up in the last few months.

Amelia leaned forward and kissed him softly, conveying all of her compassion and understanding through the meeting of their lips. Edward wanted to give in, to let himself accept her forgiveness, but some small part of him held back.

'Kiss me, Edward,' Amelia whispered. 'Kiss me and show me you care for me.'

With a groan he surrendered and kissed her, pulling her body close against his and running his hands down her back. He wanted to stay in this moment for ever, just the two of them with no McNair and no duel and no threats.

His position hadn't changed. Tomorrow he was still going to ride out and meet McNair in a duel. Edward had no doubts that by early morning he would either be dead or a killer, but maybe that was all the more reason to enjoy today.

Amelia let her head drop back and felt her hair tickle her skin as it fell down her back. Edward was kissing her neck, making her shudder with anticipation as he slowly moved his lips across her skin. Alongside the almost overwhelming desire she felt elated. For once in her life she'd made a difference. Edward had come up to his room withdrawn and brooding, but she'd managed to coax the truth from him, and make him see he wasn't responsible for every little consequence when something went wrong.

True, they still had the dilemma of what to do about McNair, but Amelia was sure together they could come up with a solution. As long as Edward agreed not to go and face him in a duel, especially with pistols. McNair had years of army training and a familiarity with the weapon he'd chosen. Although Edward was more powerful than McNair, and surprising agile for a man of his size, Amelia knew he wouldn't have a chance in this sort of duel.

She knew Edward was just trying to protect her, trying to take McNair's wrath towards Amelia and direct it towards him instead, but in a way McNair had chosen the right way to wound Amelia when suggesting the duel. Right now physical pain would not be worse than the thought of losing Edward. For so long she'd felt alone and now she had someone who cared for her, all her faults and quirks included. And she rather thought she loved him more than she'd ever imagined was possible. If McNair killed Edward, then Amelia would be destroyed.

Pausing for a moment and pulling back, Edward looked at her face as if to check she really wanted him to go further. Amelia felt light-headed, swept away, but she knew if Edward pulled away now she would be devastated.

Amelia gasped as Edward pushed the neckline of her dress down to expose the skin of her chest. She shivered as the cool air hit her sensitive skin, but immediately Edward's hands were on her, warming and teasing. Never had she been touched like this before, never had she imagined a fingertip could cause such a delicious sensitivity.

Suddenly she wanted to see him as he saw her and with agile fingers Amelia lifted Edward's shirt up over his head and threw it on to the bed behind them, placing her own hands on his chest. For a moment they both paused, looking into each other's eyes and just enjoying the feel of the other's hands on their bodies. Then Edward was on his feet, lifting Amelia and pushing her dress down past her waist and over her hips so it fell and pooled around her ankles.

Amelia felt his eyes on her, roaming over her body under the thin chemise. She'd always imagined she would be self-conscious when a man saw her naked, but with Edward it just felt right.

Slowly he stripped her of the rest of her clothes, allowing her to savour the feel of the cotton chemise as it glided over her skin, baring her body as he pulled it up over her head. Five seconds passed, and then ten, with Edward's eyes darting over her body. Amelia felt a delicious anticipation as slowly he kicked off his boots and divested himself of his trousers. For a moment they both just stood there, then Edward took her in his arms and they tumbled back on to the bed.

There was something frenzied, almost wild, about their movements, as if both of them knew something had changed. Amelia told herself it was the brush with death, the residual feelings of danger and relief to be alive, but as Edward pushed against her she lost all coherent thought.

Amelia felt her body tense, but instead of the pain she'd been told to expect she just felt Edward's fingers stroking her gently. Rhythmically he teased and tantalised until Amelia felt as though her entire body was going to melt into the bedsheets. A warm sensation began building deep inside her and she felt her hips begin to rise to meet Edward's touch.

As he withdrew his fingers and positioned himself on top of her he searched her face as if checking she wanted to continue. Amelia moved her body up towards him, drawing him in, and groaned as he pressed into her.

Faster and faster he moved until Amelia felt something burst inside her and a warm wave of pleasure washed over her. Above her Edward stiffened and groaned before collapsing on to the bed beside her.

Afterwards she lay with her head resting on Edward's shoulder, his arm looped around her body and holding her close. She felt contented and safe, despite the events of earlier that day. As she traced her fingers over Edward's chest she wondered what this meant for them, whether it meant Edward would ask her to marry him. Of course she knew plenty of people were intimate and didn't marry, but she could dare to hope this might mean he definitely wanted a future with her.

They were no closer to finding a solution to their problem, no closer to working out what to do about McNair and his thirst for revenge, but Amelia felt strangely calm. Throughout this entire episode she had felt as if events had been taken out of her control. At first, when she'd been convinced she was a murderer she had been petrified and unstable. Then when she'd discovered McNair was alive and seeking her out she had been scared of what he might want and what he would do. Now, even though the threat was very real, even though he'd held a gun to her back earlier that day, Amelia felt as if for the first time in ages she had some say in what happened next.

Of course Edward couldn't go to meet McNair in the duel, so instead they would have to decide whether to involve the local magistrate or deal with him in another way themselves. Whatever they decided, Amelia was determined they would do it together. Edward might want to protect her from McNair and she was never going to discourage him from looking out for her, but this was her mess and for once she was going to face the consequences of her actions and help come up with the solution.

With this firmly resolved in her mind Amelia allowed her mind and body to relax into Edward. He held her close against him, every so often bending down to plant kisses on the top of her head.

The late evening sun was streaming through the bedroom window, warming up Amelia's naked body making her eyes droop. Edward's hand stroking her upper arm was lulling her off to sleep and Amelia felt her entire body relax. Right here, right now she felt safe. Later they could talk some more and decide what path they would take, but now she was going to enjoy resting in the arms of the man she loved.

Chapter Twenty-Four

Edward felt like a cur as he slipped out of the bed an hour before dawn. Amelia had slept soundly since their intimacy the evening before and hadn't stirred when he had gently rolled her off his arm. He knew he should wake her, he should give her the option of accompanying him to the duel site, but he just couldn't bring himself to do it. As she'd fallen asleep in his arms he'd watched her contented smile and peaceful expression and he felt awful for misleading her.

Edward knew Amelia had taken their intimacy the night before as a sign he wouldn't go and meet McNair and he hadn't disillusioned her. In a way it would be much easier to walk out with a pistol in his hand, facing down the seasoned army Captain, without Amelia watching.

Quickly he dressed, throwing on a clean shirt and breeches, and grabbed his boots to put on outside the bedroom. Before he left he bent over and kissed Amelia on the forehead, smoothing away her hair and taking a moment to take in her serene expression, how her eyelashes rested on her rosy cheeks and the gentle curve of her lips. He knew he might never see her again and he wanted to imprint her face on his memory to have something to hold on to if he was shot and his life blood was ebbing away.

Forcing himself out of the room, Edward strode down the stairs and out into the fresh pre-dawn air, pausing only to pull on his boots and pick up his pistol from the study. He didn't have a second. Over the years of his seclusion he'd lost contact with his friends and he had no desire to pull any of them into this mess anyway. No, if he was shot then he would just have to accept his fate without anyone to fuss over him.

As he began the process of readying his horse, securing the saddle and talking softly to the restless beast, he wondered if he was being a little self-indulgent going off to meet McNair in this manner. He knew the guilt he felt over his late wife and son's death had nearly consumed him, nearly destroyed him. He'd promised to love and protect them, and whilst he'd fulfilled the first part of his vow, he'd failed miserably on the second. Now, with Amelia filling his thoughts and his heart, he had someone else to protect. And this was the only way he could think about doing it.

Pushing all doubts aside, Edward mounted his horse. The fact remained that if he didn't go and meet McNair then Amelia would be at risk and he couldn't have any harm to her on his conscience.

It was peaceful riding out over the estate as the first rays of sunlight filtered up over the horizon. It was going to be a beautiful day and already the birds were chirping and singing.

He arrived at the duel site first, dismounted and secured his horse. Quietly he sat down with his back against a tree and waited for McNair to arrive.

'I see you honoured our agreement,' McNair sneered as he approached about ten minutes later.

'Of course.'

'You didn't bring a second.'

'Nor did you.'

The two men looked at each other warily.

'There's nothing to stop me shooting you where you sit,' McNair said eventually.

'Nothing but honour.'

'You think I'm an honourable man?'

Edward snorted. 'No. But I think you have some sense of justice, even if it is a little twisted. You won't shoot me until the duel is under way.'

McNair looked at him curiously and for a moment Edward wondered if he'd read the man wrong. Eventually the Captain threw his head back and laughed.

'So you left the little lady at home?' McNair asked, looking around as if checking Amelia wasn't hiding behind a tree or under a bush.

It was Edward's turn to laugh. He'd never heard such an inaccurate description of Amelia. She might be petite in size, but she was large in spirit and courage and soul. McNair would never understand just what he'd missed out on by not embracing Amelia.

'That is none of your concern. Shall we stop gossiping like old women and get this over with?'

Edward stood, drawing his pistol. McNair nodded, took two tarnished swords from where they were sticking out of a saddlebag and began to mark out the parameters.

When the two swords were a good distance apart McNair made his way back to Edward.

'Seeing as there's no independent witness we'll start at the swords. I'll shout advance and we shall begin walking towards each other. You may fire at any point.'

Edward had never been in a duel before, but it sounded fair enough. Of course McNair might decide to shoot him as he was walking out to the starting point, but he didn't think so. The army officer might be a scoundrel, but he seemed to have his own warped sense of honour.

Checking his pistol one last time, Edward began walking out towards the sword, occasionally glancing over his shoulder to check McNair's progress. Just before he reached the starting point he heard a faint thundering of hooves and turned sharply. Galloping up the gentle slope was Amelia, her hair flying out behind her and her expression frenzied.

Amelia had woken slowly, revelling in the warmth of the bed and the glow of the memory of the night before. As she allowed her eyes to flutter open she expected to see Edward's form lying beside her, but instead there was an empty bed.

Immediately she was wide awake, her eyes roaming the room for possible clues as to where he'd gone. The inevitable realisation that he'd sneaked out to meet McNair kept trying to push its way into her mind, but Amelia desperately sought for more pleasant alternatives. Maybe he'd gone to bring her breakfast in bed, or maybe he'd just woken early and had decided to go for a morning stroll.

Jumping out of bed, Amelia knew none of these things were true. Last night she'd been foolish thinking Edward had agreed to stay clear of McNair and the ridiculous duel. She had wanted him to see sense and accept her point of view on the matter and she had fooled herself into thinking that he had.

The anger she felt at him slipping out to meet McNair was overshadowed by a much greater feeling of worry. There was no way Edward could win this duel. She had seen McNair shoot—in fact, he'd been the one to teach her and her cousin to fire a pistol, setting up targets for them to practise on. McNair was good, better than good. She'd never seen him miss. And she doubted he would fire wide to preserve Edward's life.

It felt as though an icy hand of dread was gripping her heart, the pain shooting all through her chest. She couldn't lose Edward, not so soon after she'd realised how much he meant to her. Not when he had finally allowed himself to move on from his grief and start living again.

Amelia pulled on her dress, not bothering to do up all the fastenings, just ensuring it wouldn't fall down as she rode. Her hair was still loose from the night before and she probably looked a fright, but for once she didn't care. If she didn't get to the duel site before the men began pacing, then she would lose Edward for ever. She wasn't sure if McNair would then come after her also, but that point was moot. If she lost Edward, she would be destroyed.

Running out to the barn, Amelia began the time-consuming process of saddling her horse. Eventually everything was secure and she used a wooden crate to climb up and mount the restless animal, before urging it forward. Before she was even out of the courtyard she'd pushed the horse into a gallop, leaning low over its neck. Her eyes darted backwards and forward, trying to pick up a clue as to where Edward and McNair were. She knew she was heading in the right general direction, but the estate was vast and she could easily miss them. Right now every second counted and she knew just a few moments' delay might be the difference between life and death for Edward.

Finally she caught sight of the two men, standing a little way apart. As she watched, getting closer by the second, Edward and McNair began to walk away from each other. Amelia screamed as loud as she could.

'Stop,' she shouted. 'Stop.'

Both men paused and looked around. Amelia could see neither had reached the swords that were sticking out of the ground as markers for the start of the duel. Maybe she wasn't too late.

'Please, stop!' she shouted as she pulled on the reins and drew to a halt in between the two men.

'Get out of here, Amelia,' Edward said and Amelia could see the fear for her safety written all over his face.

'No.'

'Oh, no, Sir Edward, let Amelia stay. This way will be much more fun.'

'Come back with me, Edward,' Amelia begged, ignoring McNair behind her.

'I don't think so, Amelia, we have a deal,' McNair said. 'Get out of the way and let us get on with our duel.'

'Please.' She looked deep into Edward's eyes and saw the look of resignation. Quickly she slipped from the horse, letting go of the reins and allowing the animal to walk over to where Edward's horse was munching on the grass under a tree. 'Please don't do this. I can't risk losing you.'

'I have no choice, Amelia.'

'Of course you have a choice. Stop punishing yourself.'

'Hurry up. I've got a lunch engagement,' McNair called.

'I was meant to protect you. This is the only way McNair will leave you alone.'

'And what about when you're gone?' Amelia asked, the tears running down her cheeks. 'Then who will protect me? What's to stop McNair from coming after me when he's killed you?'

'He wouldn't do that.'

'You really think McNair is a man of his word? A man of honour?'

Edward glanced doubtfully over Amelia's shoulder and she felt a surge of hope. She was actually getting through to Edward.

'He will shoot you and then he will come for me.'

Edward shook his head slowly, but she could see the worry in his eyes.

'I'm getting impatient,' McNair called. 'If you don't hurry up, I'll just shoot the two of you.'

'What will happen when the duel is over?' Edward shouted.

'You mean once you're dead? Then the debt of honour is satisfied and I will leave Amelia alone.'

Taking Amelia firmly by the upper arms, he kissed her, pulling her body close to his.

'I love you,' she whispered as he stepped away.

Edward froze for a moment, a look of panic in his eyes at her declaration, then steadied himself before gently pushing her away from him. She stumbled backwards, only just managing to remain upright, the tears filling her eyes and blurring her vision. She felt paralysed, rooted to the spot, as she watched the man she loved slowly approaching the sword sticking out of the ground.

At the other end of the duelling ground McNair had reached his start point and was tapping his pistol impatiently against his thigh. Amelia knew the Captain was a good shot even at a long distance, but she calculated the two men would have to come a little closer together before they stood a good chance of hitting one another.

'Advance!' McNair shouted.

Both men began walking towards each other. For Amelia it was as if the entire world had slowed. Each step seemed to take an eternity, each movement was drawn out over long seconds. Her eyes darted backwards and forward between the man she loved and the man she'd thought she had killed. The pain in her chest was acute and almost overwhelming and her breathing had become shallow and ineffective.

Amelia saw the moment McNair decided he was close enough to fire, saw him begin to raise his pistol. Edward was still moving forward, his gun at his side. McNair paused, aimed and fired.

In that moment Amelia knew she couldn't lose Edward. He was her entire world and if he died her life wouldn't be worth living. She loved him with an all-consuming passion and wanted to spend the rest of her life helping him to heal and find happiness again.

Without thinking of the consequences, Amelia leapt forward, throwing herself between the two men. For a moment, as she hit the ground, she thought she must have been too late, that the bullet must have sailed past her before she had jumped, but then a strange burning pain just below her collarbone flared and all conscious thought fled her mind.

Chapter Twenty-Five

Edward saw McNair raise the pistol and knew he wasn't close enough to return the fire yet. He just had to hope the Captain was firing prematurely and would waste his shot.

The second the crack of the pistol sounded Edward saw the movement from the corner of his eye. Amelia was diving forward, right into the path of danger.

Edward sprang into action, running towards her, hoping to push her back. As he reached her side and saw her collapse to the ground he knew he was too late, even before the blossom of blood began seeping through her dress.

'Amelia,' he whispered, gathering her up into his arms.

A bubble of blood came out between her lips and Edward knew there was no hope. She'd been hit in the chest—people didn't survive wounds like that. He felt his entire world collapsing and his heart ripping in two.

'Stupid woman!' he heard McNair exclaim from somewhere beside him. 'Why did she jump?'

Edward didn't have time for McNair's callous remarks. The woman he loved was dying in front of him and there was nothing he could do about it.

Quickly he ripped the sleeve from his shirt and pressed the balled-up material against her wound, trying to stem the blood flow. As he knelt beside her he realised what he had just thought. *The woman he loved.* Pushing it aside, he focused on the oozing wound and gently pulled Amelia into his lap.

'I didn't think she would jump,' McNair mumbled.

Edward glanced at him and realised he was in shock. Far from the confident, callous scoundrel he had seen before, McNair looked genuinely worried.

'Get help,' Edward ordered.

'I'll be arrested.'

'If you don't get help then Amelia will die. If that happens, I will kill you myself. Slowly.'

Edward knew there probably wasn't much a doctor could do, but he had to try. He would move heaven and earth to give Amelia even the smallest chance of surviving this.

'Go!' he bellowed, and watched as McNair scrambled to his feet and ran to his horse. 'Send the doctor to the house,' he shouted after McNair.

There was no guarantee McNair would fetch a doctor. He might well just flee the county, probably even the country, but there was a small chance his conscience might stop him. Edward had to hope that was the case.

'Edward,' Amelia whispered, her eyes flickering open.

'Shh,' he said, leaning down and planting a kiss on her forehead. 'I'm here.'

'I love you, Edward.'

It sounded too much like a final farewell and Edward felt the tears rolling down his cheeks. He couldn't lose her, he loved her too much. She had helped him to heal, helped him to realise his life was worth living and now she was saying goodbye.

'Hang on for me, Amelia,' he whispered in her ear, 'Everything will be all right. I promise.'

It was a promise he shouldn't make, but as he scooped her up into his arms he knew it was one he had to keep. If Amelia died then his life would be over. He knew he wasn't strong enough to withstand the grief of losing the woman he loved for a second time.

Carefully he stood, then picked her up and draped her unconscious body over the front of his horse before mounting it. He was aware the movement of the horse could hasten her death, cause the bullet to dislodge or the blood to flow more quickly, but he also knew he didn't have a choice. Amelia was bleeding and struggling to breathe, that wasn't something he was going to be able to sort out in the middle of nowhere on his own. If he could just get her home and find the doctor, then maybe she might have a chance.

'Hang on for me, my love,' he said as he pushed his horse into a gallop, cradling her body in his lap.

The ride home had been the longest ten minutes of his life and as Edward thundered into the courtyard he felt a great sense of relief. Amelia was still breathing, he could see the rise and fall of her chest, but there were more bloodstained bubbles appearing between her lips. As he slid from the horse, lifting Amelia carefully down after him, he shouted for help, loud enough to wake the entire household. Before he had entered the front door Mrs Henshaw was hurrying out of the kitchen, the other servants trailing behind her.

'Amelia's hurt. Send someone to fetch the doctor immediately,' Edward ordered, knowing he couldn't rely on McNair to do as he had asked.

For a moment all the servants froze as they took in Amelia's deathly pale face, the bloodstained dress and her shallow, noisy breathing. Then Mrs Henshaw rallied and began issuing orders.

'Tom, ride and get Dr Bolton from the village. Daniel, ride and get Dr Peacewell from South Heighton. Girls, we need fresh water and clean sheets.'

Edward didn't hear any more as he was already halfway up the stairs, but he felt some relief that Mrs Henshaw was in charge of the practical matters. Now he just had to focus on Amelia.

He carried her straight to his bedroom, laying her down on the bed they had shared the night before. Carefully he peeled away the blood-soaked material of his shirt sleeve, pulled down the neckline of her dress and ripped open her chemise underneath.

With the wound exposed Edward felt himself sway slightly at the shock of how serious her injury was. A large circular hole gaped just below her collarbone, the edges ragged and seeping blood. As Mrs Henshaw entered with the water and sheets he took some of the clean material and pressed it firmly against the wound.

He felt an immense relief when Amelia grimaced. Of course he didn't want her to be in pain, but pain meant she was still alive and whilst she was still alive there was hope.

'Please don't die,' he whispered as he sat down next to her.

There was no response, just the shallow, raspy breaths that told him she was still holding on for now.

A commotion outside the doorway roused him from his vigil and he was relieved when the tall, thin frame of Dr Bolton walked into the room.

'Thank you for coming, Doctor.'

'I didn't have much choice,' Dr Bolton said. 'A young man raised such a fuss I couldn't exactly refuse.'

So McNair *had* gone to fetch the doctor. There was no

way Tom would have been back with the elderly physician yet, so McNair must have felt some remorse.

'What happened here?'

'She was shot, at a range of about twenty feet. She's lost a lot of blood.'

The doctor moved close to Amelia's side and carefully removed the wadding Edward had used to try to stem the blood from her wound. He drew a sharp intake of breath as he examined the damage.

'Can you do anything for her?' Edward asked, hearing the faint pleading note to his voice.

'The bullet has penetrated through to her chest cavity and hit part of her lung…' The doctor paused, frowning.

'What is it?'

'I can't quite work out why she isn't dead yet.'

Edward felt his whole world start to collapse.

'If the bullet penetrates the lung then normally the damaged tissue bleeds profusely into the rest of the lung, effectively drowning the patient. Or sometimes the lung itself will collapse. Either way the patient normally dies within a matter of minutes.'

Edward glanced at Amelia's pale face and the laboured rise and fall of her chest. He hated the detached, clinical way Dr Bolton was talking about Amelia. She was a beautiful, caring, vibrant woman, not some dead flesh on a slab.

'Can you help her?'

'Well, she's unconscious so she's not in any pain…' The doctor trailed off as he saw Edward's expression.

'This woman means everything to me,' he said quietly. 'You will do everything in your power to try to save her life.'

'I don't know…'

'Everything in your power, Doctor.'

Edward spoke softly, but the force of his emotion was obvious in his tone.

'Ah, I see you arrived before me,' a friendly voice came from the doorway.

'Dr Peacewell,' Edward greeted the young man dressed all in black.

'Everything is under control, Dr Peacewell, there is no need for *your* breed of medicine,' Dr Bolton said icily.

Dr Peacewell breezed into the room as if he hadn't heard the older doctor. Gently he pushed his way to Amelia's bedside, his eyes darting across her body, assessing the damage. Edward watched as the younger doctor felt for Amelia's pulse, laid a hand on her chest to check her breathing and then carefully examined the wound.

'She's been very lucky,' he said finally.

'Yes, thank you, Dr Peacewell. I established that almost ten minutes ago.'

Dr Peacewell ignored his colleague and turned to Edward. 'If she is to have any chance of surviving we need to remove the bullet, but that is not without risks—'

'I disagree,' Dr Bolton interrupted.

'Let the man speak,' Edward warned firmly.

'As we remove the bullet the lung could collapse, or there could be further bleeding.'

'And if we don't remove the bullet?' Edward asked.

'Then she will die.'

It wasn't as though there was much of a decision to make. Amelia was a fighter and she deserved the chance to fight for her life. Doing nothing would be cruel and stupid.

'Do it,' Edward said, grasping Amelia's hand to give him strength.

'I object,' Dr Bolton said.

'Do you have an alternative plan?' Edward asked.

'This is cruel and unnecessary. We should ensure the young lady's passing is as peaceful as possible.'

'Either you help or you get out,' Edward said.

Dr Peacewell was already rolling up his sleeves and unpacking row after row of surgical instruments from his bag.

Edward watched as Dr Bolton hesitated, but then pushed up his own sleeves and began to prepare the wound.

'The bullet looks as though it has gone in at an angle and chipped against the clavicle,' Dr Bolton said as Dr Peacewell stretched open the already gaping hole. 'It will be difficult to grab hold of, especially as there might be bone fragments loose in there, too.'

'I propose you stabilise the area externally. I will try and hook the bullet forward and then, once it is visible, you grasp hold of it with the forceps.'

Both doctors set to work and Edward watched with a worried fascination. Dr Bolton held the skin back for his colleague and waited whilst Dr Peacewell fished around in the wound with a long, thin instrument. Edward grimaced as he struck bone and a dull scraping sound followed. Amelia's breathing was shallow but steady throughout and Edward was just beginning to wonder if maybe she might survive when she uttered a low, animalistic groan. It was a primal sound, like that of a wounded animal, and it made both doctors stop momentarily.

'She's in pain,' Edward said, grasping her hand even tighter.

'We need to continue,' Dr Peacewell said, his expression worried.

Edward wanted to stop them, wanted to ease Amelia's discomfort, but he knew if he did then she would certainly die. Hearing her moan in pain and doing nothing was the hardest thing that he'd ever had to do, but he didn't interfere any more.

'I've got it,' Dr Peacewell said five minutes later.

Dr Bolton reached into the wound with the forceps and plucked out the small bullet Dr Peacewell was pushing forward. Once the bullet was out all three men watched Amelia carefully. If she was going to bleed or her lung was going to collapse, it would be now.

'I'll dress the wound,' Dr Peacewell said. 'It is too soon to say if she will survive or not, but there's not much more we can do.'

Edward nodded, his eyes fixed on the rise and fall of Amelia's chest. For now, at least, she was still breathing.

Chapter Twenty-Six

'Why don't you go and get some rest, Master Edward?' Mrs Henshaw suggested, addressing him as she used to when he was a boy.

'I can't leave her.'

'I'll sit with her a while. You must be exhausted.'

He was exhausted. It had been nearly two days since the duel, two excruciating, tortuous days. In that time the doctors had been to check Amelia over four times, but not much had changed. Still she was breathing, still her heart beat, but her eyes never flickered open and there was no sign Amelia was behind her closed lids. A few hours after the impromptu surgery to remove the bullet Amelia had grown hot with fever, and over the past two days both doctors hadn't dared speculate whether she would survive this latest development, but were clear she would only wake once the fever was under control.

'I can't leave her,' Edward repeated. If he left her then he had this peculiar fear that she might die whilst he was away. If he could just sit it out, remain by her side, then maybe everything would work out.

'Then let me sit with you for a few minutes.'

It was comforting to have Mrs Henshaw's presence by

his side. For a while he could imagine they were just waiting for Amelia to wake from a normal sleep, ready to jump up and enjoy the new day.

'What happened?' Mrs Henshaw asked softly.

'I was a stupid fool,' Edward replied, keeping his voice low. 'I didn't realise what I had until I lost it.'

'You pushed her away?'

Edward nodded, for in a way he had. Oh, he had held Amelia tenderly, whispered he cared for her, even made love to her, but he hadn't given himself to her fully, that he could see now. If only he'd let go of that final piece of himself, if only he'd shared the decision about McNair with her, then maybe it would be him lying in her place as it should have been.

He regretted not telling her he loved her. He hadn't realised it before the duel, he'd been too afraid he wasn't good enough, wasn't the man to protect her and cherish her. He'd been too preoccupied with regrets about failing to keep her safe from McNair that he hadn't realised what she truly had needed from him. Now he'd give anything to see her face light up as he whispered a declaration of love into her ear.

'I thought it was my duty to protect her,' he said eventually, 'but I didn't realise the thing that would hurt her the most would be pushing her away.'

Mrs Henshaw remained silent by his side, stroking the back of Amelia's hand.

'I wish I could tell her I'm sorry,' he said. 'I wish I could tell her how much I regret my actions.'

'You can, dear,' Mrs Henshaw said. 'She's listening, even if her eyes aren't open. Talk to her, let her know you're here and let her know she's got something to wake up for.'

The older woman stood and kissed him lovingly on the top of his head, then made her way from the room.

Edward sat in silence for a few minutes, wondering if Mrs Henshaw was right or if he would be stupid to sit here talking to an unconscious Amelia. Realising he had nothing to lose, he took a deep breath and gathered his thoughts.

'I'm sorry, Amelia,' he whispered quietly, holding on to her hand as though it were an unbreakable connection between them. 'I got so caught up in my own head...so caught up in the idea that I had to protect you I didn't even think about what you really needed.' He paused and then pushed on, knowing the words had to be said. 'I thought I'd failed you. I promised to keep you safe and protect you from McNair. When I couldn't do that I felt an absolute failure. I thought that you deserved better.'

Gently he shook his head. If only he hadn't tried to punish himself by agreeing to the duel. It had been self-indulgent and selfish, and if he'd just thought things through a little better then Amelia might never have got hurt.

'I know you saw that, I know you saw I was going to meet McNair for the duel to punish myself, but I was too caught up in the moment to realise it.'

He wished he could turn back the clock...that he was still in bed with Amelia tucked into the crook of his arm and instead of misleading her he had actually discussed the situation and came up with a better solution than meeting McNair with pistols at dawn.

'Please don't leave me, Amelia. I need your strength, your resolve. I love you.'

He watched her eyes, hoping for some flicker of acknowledgement, some sign that she might have heard what he was saying. Edward knew there was a good chance she might never wake up. Both doctors had been pretty clear on the subject. Right now Edward couldn't think about how he would survive if she died. At first he had wondered if he would shrivel and die, too, but as he had spent the hours by her side he knew no matter what he would keep on fighting his demons for Amelia.

Another thing that scared him was the thought of her walking away from him. He knew if she ever did wake up there was a good chance he had ruined any possibility of having a future together. He'd misled her and even if he hadn't lied to her outright, he'd certainly lied by omission.

Edward stood, stretched and carefully got on to the bed beside Amelia. Gently he wrapped an arm around her and held her as he had the first night they'd met.

Amelia struggled to open her eyes. She'd never been a morning person, but today it felt particularly difficult to lift her lids. As she became more aware of her body she realised there was a dull ache in her shoulder and a sharp, shooting pain every time she breathed in. The events on the duelling field came rushing back and Amelia felt her pulse quicken as she remembered the searing pain as she'd dived in front of Edward.

'Edward,' she murmured, her voice coming out as a dry croak and her lips cracking painfully.

She felt his warm presence beside her, his arm draped over her midsection protectively. He looked exhausted, even in sleep, with deep dark circles around his eyes and a few days' growth on his jawline.

As she tried to sit up in bed the pain ripped through her chest and she let out a loud squeal. Immediately Edward was awake, looking at her with a mixture of disbelief and hope.

'Amelia,' he said, gently taking hold of her and propping the pillows behind her so she was comfortable. 'I thought I'd lost you.'

'Water,' she managed to croak and sipped gratefully at the glass he held to her lips. The water was warm, but as it soothed her parched throat she thought it was the most delicious drink in the world.

'Are you in pain?' Edward asked. 'The doctor left some laudanum.'

Amelia shook her head. Maybe soon the pain would get too much, but for now she wanted to think without the heavy haze laudanum brought on.

'What happened?' she asked.

'What do you remember?'

Amelia closed her eyes for a moment. Trying to think was like putting together a puzzle where half the pieces were missing.

'I remember waking up and finding you gone and dashing out to the stables.' She paused, frowning, 'And I remember reaching you just as you were walking out to the markers to start the duel.'

'Do you remember what happened next?'

Amelia bit her lip, trying to focus. The memories were all there, but they were fragmented and distorted, as if she were looking at them through curved glass. Then all of a sudden things came into focus and she remembered the sound of the shot being fired and her jumping out in front of Edward, followed by nothing but pain.

'You saved my life,' Edward said softly. 'You jumped into the path of a bullet for me.'

'How silly of me,' Amelia said, trying to keep her voice light.

'Downright reckless,' Edward agreed. 'The bullet hit you in the chest, just below your collarbone.'

Amelia glanced down at the bulky white bandage covering her entire shoulder.

'It penetrated your lung and glanced off the bone. The doctors said you're very lucky to be alive.' Edward's voice held just a hint of a tremble. 'We weren't sure if you would ever wake up.'

'Is the bullet still in there?' Amelia asked, running her fingers over the bandage gently.

'No, they fished it out. Apparently you are more likely to die of the wound putrefying if the bullet is left in.'

'It sounds as though you've become quite an expert.'

'I've never been so worried in my entire life.'

'Edward, we need to talk,' Amelia said softly.

She saw the panic in his eyes and wanted to reach out and soothe him, but quickly he stood up, distancing himself from her.

'I know,' he said. 'But first you must rest. We'll talk later, I promise.'

Gently he leaned over and kissed her on the forehead, brushing his lips against her skin as though she were made of porcelain.

Amelia didn't protest as he left the room. In truth, she did feel exhausted and to manage the emotional intensity of the talk they needed to have she wanted to be in a better condition. Closing her eyes, she listened to Edward's retreating footsteps and wondered just what the future held for them.

Chapter Twenty-Seven

A week and a half later Amelia was feeling much stronger and now she was beginning to get restless. She'd never been good at sitting still and now she'd spent the longest time ever confined to her bedroom. Edward had sat with her most of the time, reading passages from his book aloud, or discussing the renovations he planned on the house, and that had helped to pass the time, but now Amelia was desperate to get out of this room and feel the sun on her face.

'You have to be very careful,' Dr Peacewell warned. 'The wound could still open up and your lung needs time to heal.'

'But maybe I could just take a short trip outside,' Amelia suggested.

She'd even settle for sitting in a different room for an hour or two.

Dr Peacewell looked at her appraisingly. 'Very well,' he said, 'but just a short trip. And then it's back to bed to recuperate.'

'Yes, Doctor,' Amelia said meekly, catching Edward's eye and grinning once the doctor had turned his back.

'A short trip,' Edward reinforced after the doctor had

left, 'And if you begin to look tired I'll bring you straight back to bed.'

Amelia nodded, not bothering to argue. She'd got what she wanted. Soon she would be sitting with the sun warming her face and the breeze in her hair.

'And then maybe we should have that talk.'

Amelia looked at Edward in surprise. Every time she had brought up their need to discuss the future since she'd woken up he'd shaken his head and said she wasn't strong enough. Now he was agreeing to talk Amelia felt nervous about what he might say. She was very conscious that she had declared her love just before the duel had started and not received any words of love in return. Edward cared for her, he looked after her more than anyone had in her entire life, but she craved another sign that would tell her he felt something deeper.

An hour later Edward reappeared and looked her over carefully.

'Are you sure you want to do this?' he asked, concern etched on his features.

'Edward, if you don't take me outside now I might scream.'

Carefully he scooped her up into his arms and ensured she was comfortable before making his way through the house.

'Be careful, ducky,' Goody called after them as Edward pushed out through the front door and into the sunshine.

Amelia sighed with contentment. Finally she had escaped her sick chamber. Even just a few minutes out here in the daylight would do her the world of good.

'I heard from Mr Pollard,' Edward said as he carried her carefully across the lawn.

Amelia stiffened and found herself struggling to breathe.

'There's no need to worry,' he soothed her. 'Your cousin is back with the Earl of Burwell. Mr Pollard has delivered your letters and I am sure you will hear from Lizzie soon.'

Amelia let go of the breath she had been holding and smiled. Finally she could stop worrying about Lizzie and instead await the news on what was happening between her beloved cousin and this Earl. Maybe Lizzie had found the man she wanted to spend her life with, too.

'Can you bear to be carried a bit longer?' Edward asked.

'If you're not tiring,' Amelia said, 'I could spend all day up here.'

He carried her through the gardens, treading carefully so as not to disturb her wound. After a few minutes Amelia realised where they were going and couldn't help but smile. He was taking her to the secret walled garden, the first place they had allowed themselves a long, leisurely kiss. It was very apt for the serious conversation they were going to have to have.

Once inside the garden Edward set her down in a chair he must have brought over from the house earlier and spent a moment ensuring she was quite comfortable.

'Stop fussing,' Amelia said, swatting him away, 'I'm not an old invalid.'

'You were shot in the chest less than a fortnight ago. I'm allowed to fuss.'

Amelia smiled, closing her eyes and lifting her face to the sun. For a few minutes she just sat there, enjoying the feeling of being alive, listening to the buzzing of the bees and the hum of the insects.

'What has happened to McNair?' Amelia asked as the thought popped into her head.

She heard Edward grimace and opened her eyes.

'He's fled the country. I should imagine he was scared of retribution for shooting you.'

'He's actually left the country?'

Edward nodded. 'I think he realised I would have killed him if you died.'

'Do you think he'll come back?'

'Maybe once he's heard you're alive, but I don't think he will bother us again.'

'I suppose he exacted his revenge. I was injured just as he was.'

'Let's not talk of McNair any longer,' Edward said and Amelia sensed the conversation was about to get serious.

'We need to talk about the future,' she said after a minute.

Edward looked nervous, she realised, as if he had been dreading this conversation. Her heart began to sink as she wondered if he wanted to pull away from her, whether this brush with death had been enough to make him realise he didn't love her.

'Before we make any decisions I need to apologise,' Edward said, 'for many things.'

Amelia frowned. Yes, he had been a bit stubborn racing off to the duel with McNair, but his heart had been in the right place.

'I wanted to protect you.'

'There's no need to apologise for that.'

'Let me finish. I wanted to protect you and when I failed I felt as though I didn't deserve you. That clouded my judgement'

Amelia leant forward, grimacing as the pain shot through her shoulder, and took hold of Edward's hand. She didn't interrupt, sensing he needed to get whatever he wanted to say off his chest.

'After the incident on the beach I felt as though I'd been

given another chance at happiness. Even with the threat of McNair's revenge hanging over us I thought if I could protect the woman that I loved then all would be well.'

Amelia felt her heart leap in her chest and struggled to concentrate on what Edward said next.

'When McNair broke in and I wasn't there to protect you, it felt as though I'd failed all over again. I didn't think I deserved you, not if I couldn't protect you from a man who wished you harm.' Edward paused, looking into Amelia's eyes. 'But I shouldn't have deceived you. I should have told you I was going to meet McNair, not let you wake to an empty bed. For that I am truly sorry.'

'I know you acted out of consideration for my well-being,' Amelia said quietly. 'It might have been the wrong thing to do, but I can't question your motives.

'I think there was also a little bit of me that wanted to punish myself for not protecting you.'

Amelia shrugged. 'We're all human, we're all flawed.'

'I should have realised we needed to make that decision together. It was wrong of me to push you out and I know it was what got you shot.'

She studied his expression, trying to read his thoughts. For a while she had wondered if Edward blamed himself for her injury. It had been McNair who had aimed the pistol, McNair who had pulled the trigger, but it would be just like Edward to blame himself.

'You need to let go of this guilt and this sense of responsibility for everything. I made my own decision when I followed you to the duel site, I made my own decision when I jumped in between you and McNair. That wasn't you.'

'I know,' Edward said quietly.

'We both made mistakes, but you can't live your life in a perpetual cycle of guilt and regret.'

'You're right,' Edward said. 'But I refuse to give up my sense of responsibility for you,' he added with a smile.

Amelia leant forward, ignoring the pain shooting through her chest, and pulled Edward towards her until his lips rested on hers.

'You saved me, Edward,' she said after a long, deep kiss. 'You saved my life.'

Amelia felt her heart soar as he kissed her back. For ten long days, ever since waking up after being shot, she had wondered what the future might hold, but sitting here kissing Edward she was in no doubt. His kiss contained love and hope and passion. He couldn't kiss her like that and then tell her they couldn't be together.

'What's next?' she asked as she pulled away, looking up into Edward's dark eyes.

'Well, I thought I'd kiss you again,' Edward said, a teasing note to his voice.

Amelia swatted him on the arm, but before she could exert herself any further Edward slipped from his chair and knelt in front of her.

'Before you came bursting into my home I thought my life was over,' he said. 'I couldn't see a way through the grief and the guilt. I'd built this cocoon of solitude and I was slowly suffocating in it.'

Amelia thought back to the man she'd first encountered on that stormy night when she had stumbled into Beechwood Manor. He *had* been slowly suffocating in his self-imposed solitary confinement.

'It's not just your life that's changed,' Amelia said, her heart beginning to beat faster as she realised what Edward was building up to.

'Well, you're no longer a murderer,' Edward said with a grin.

'I'm no longer a lot of things.'

She'd been bored and lonely before coming to England, a spoiled young woman who was acting outrageously to try to relieve the tedium. No wonder her father had been eager for her to find a husband and settle down.

'I know exactly what you are, Amelia.' Edward paused, looking into her eyes before continuing, 'The woman I love.'

Amelia felt the tears spring to her eyes. He loved her. There was nothing more that she desired in the world.

'And I love you, too.'

'I would very much like you to be my wife.'

Amelia grasped Edward by the shoulders and pulled him in for a passionate kiss. His wife. That would mean they would spend every blissful day together for years and years to come.

'And I would very much like for you to be my husband,' she said as they broke apart.

'I can't promise it will be easy. I know I have a lot of issues to work through.'

'Stop trying to put me off.' Amelia laughed, kissing him again. 'You won't succeed.'

'But I will promise to love you for eternity.'

'Eternity is a very long time.'

'You'd better behave yourself then,' Edward said, dodging Amelia's hand as she swatted at him.

Amelia took his hand and squeezed her eyes closed. When she had first stumbled on Beechwood Manor in the middle of the storm she'd never imagined things would end like this. Fear and regret had been turned into love and compassion and it was all thanks to the man she would spend the rest of her life with.

Epilogue

Amelia darted forward and dabbed a blob of paint on Edward's nose. For a moment he looked disapproving and stern, making Amelia pause, before he grinned and caught her by surprise with a paint attack of his own.

'So this is why you wanted to help decorate,' Edward said as he drew Amelia in closer to him.

The workmen from Turnball and Son, the decorating company who had transformed much of Beechwood Manor over the past few months, largely ignored Edward and Amelia now. Although it wasn't normal for clients to want to pick up a paintbrush, Sir and Lady Gray seemed to live in their own little world, one where they didn't much care for the customs of normal society.

'What do you think of the colour?' Amelia asked, standing back and admiring the progress.

'I think it looks very fetching on you,' Edward said, daubing another blob of paint on her cheek. 'Although it does clash with your dress a little.' He came in closer and whispered in her ear, 'Maybe we should take the dress off.'

Amelia felt the familiar surge of desire as Edward's breath tickled her neck and she knew it wouldn't be long until he scooped her up into his arms and carried her up to the bedroom.

'Focus, Sir Edward,' Amelia said, trying out her best strict voice.

'Yes, darling, now what was the question?'

Amelia struggled to maintain her composure as Edward moved in closer and peppered kisses across the back of her neck.

'What do you think of the colour?' she managed to stutter.

'It's grey.'

Amelia sighed. It wasn't grey—well, not exactly. Mr Turnball the younger had explained it was called celestial blue and was a calming, delicate shade that worked perfectly for a nursery.

'It's a very nice grey,' Edward added as he caught her sigh. 'I'm sure young Mistress Gray will appreciate it.'

Amelia felt her hands move instinctively to her round belly, her fingers trailing over the hard bump that held their first son or daughter. Edward was convinced she was carrying a girl, a daughter for him to dote on and indulge. Amelia secretly thought the child inside her was a boy, but she was content to wait another month to find out.

'Do you think they'll be finished in time?' she asked, smiling as she felt a kick from inside her.

'As long as little Mistress Gray stays put for another few weeks, the nursery will be perfect.'

Rather than rebuild the nursery in the East Wing they had decided to transform one of the rooms in the main section of the house into a space for their children. Edward had suggested the idea, stating he wanted a fresh start for their growing family. The East Wing had been largely demolished and in its place they had planted a rose garden together, somewhere Edward could go and sit, surrounded by the beautiful flowers, and remember his son and his late wife if ever he needed to. Often of an evening they would walk through the rose garden together, hand in hand, talking of the past and planning for the future.

'I think she's perfectly comfortable where she is,' Amelia said, placing Edward's hand on her belly so he could feel their child's kick. 'I doubt whether she's going to grace us with her presence any time soon.'

Edward smiled as he felt the strong kick of their baby and after a few moments he took the paintbrush from Amelia's hand.

'She'd better wait for your father to arrive,' Edward grumbled. 'He is adamant he wants to be here for the birth of his first grandchild.'

It was the first time Amelia would have seen her father since leaving India almost eighteen months ago, and although she knew he would reprimand her for all that had happened with Captain McNair, Amelia couldn't wait to see him.

'That's enough exertion for one day,' Edward said, taking hold of her paintbrush, 'Now you must rest.'

Amelia pulled a face. Even at eight months pregnant she wasn't good at sitting still.

'Your cousin will be here later this afternoon and I'm sure you'll want to have some energy to greet her properly.'

Amelia let Edward lead her from the nursery, but when he tried to guide her upstairs she pulled gently on his arm and directed him outside. They walked through the garden in the crisp mid-morning air and Amelia enjoyed the crunch of the lingering frost under her feet.

She couldn't wait to see her cousin Lizzie later and show her all the changes they'd made on the house. Lizzie was coming to stay, with her husband Daniel, the Earl of Bur-

well, and their six-month-old baby, Oliver, for the foreseeable future. She'd promised to be there for the birth of
Amelia's baby even though she had a little one of her own.
When Amelia had protested Lizzie had laughed her off,
saying it was unthinkable that she could miss the birth.
It was typical of her cousin, always putting everyone else
before herself, but Amelia wanted her there so much that
she hadn't protested too much.

'Do you think everything will change once the baby is
born?' Amelia asked.

'Are you worried?'

She shook her head. Ever since their wedding just over
a year ago Amelia had known she'd wanted to be a mother.
Before Edward she hadn't really thought of having a family of her own, but as soon as they'd said their marriage
vows Amelia had known she wanted to make a family with
the man she loved. He would be a brilliant father and she
couldn't wait to hold their baby in her arms and share some
of the love she already felt for the little person inside of her.

'I think a lot will change, but much will stay the same.
I will still love you.'

'I can't imagine having someone completely reliant on
me, someone who needs to be cared for every minute of
the day.'

'You'll be a brilliant mother, Amelia, you've got nothing to worry about.'

She supposed maybe she was a little worried if she was
honest. She loved the baby inside her already, but she just
hoped she was good enough to be its mother.

'And I'll be by your side every moment of every day.'

Amelia felt some of her worries melt away as Edward
squeezed her hand and then pulled her along the path that
led to their secret garden. Once they were inside he di-

rected her to the rope swing and ensured she was comfortable.

'Are you sure this will take my weight?' Amelia asked, testing it carefully.

'You're still tiny,' Edward said. 'And remember in the summer it took the weight of both of us.'

Amelia felt the blood rushing to her cheeks as she remembered the balmy evening they had spent entwined on the swing. Of course she wasn't still tiny. Her pregnant belly was huge compared to many women in the same stage as her, but Edward always brushed it off, saying she would just have a healthy, bonny baby.

'Sit back and relax, my lady,' Edward instructed. Gently he began pushing her backwards and forwards, every so often darting in to place a kiss on the nape of her neck.

Amelia was just starting to relax back when she felt something warm and wet soaking through her skirts. For a moment she was paralysed, unable to speak, unable to comprehend what was happening.

'Edward,' she managed to whisper eventually, 'I think my waters have just broken.'

Edward paced up and down the corridor, growling at anyone who came near him.

'Relax, old chap,' said Daniel, Lizzie's husband, as he prowled past him. 'Women have been giving birth successfully for thousands of years.'

He knew it was true, but surely it shouldn't take this long. She had been labouring for nearly twenty hours and the cries of pain coming from the room were no less intense, even if Edward could hear the exhaustion in Amelia's voice.

'Don't fret, Sir Edward,' Mr Guthry said in his perpetually cheerful voice. 'I've never known a stronger or more determined young woman than Miss Amelia.'

All three men were positioned in the corridor outside Amelia's bedchamber, with Mrs Henshaw dashing backwards and forwards with cups of tea and plates of biscuits to sustain them as they waited. Every so often she would stop and let Mr Guthry squeeze her hand in reassurance, before busying herself again.

The muffled voice of Lizzie came through the door. 'Come on, Amelia darling, push!'

Edward couldn't bear it any longer. He threw open the door to their bedroom and dashed inside. The midwife turned to him with indignation, but Edward pushed past her to Amelia's side.

'You can do it, my sweet,' he said, grasping her hand.

For a second their eyes met, then Amelia squeezed her eyelids shut and put every ounce of her being into pushing. Edward couldn't see what was happening down below, but he heard a slippery little gush and Lizzie's intake of breath.

After a couple of seconds an insistent tiny cry started and Edward found himself holding his breath as the midwife carefully wrapped their child in a bundle and handed it to Amelia.

'Your son,' she said.

Edward felt himself stumble a little and had to sit down on the edge of the bed. He had a son…another son to dote on and cherish. Throughout Amelia's pregnancy he hadn't known how he would feel if their child was a son. He knew no one could replace Thomas in his heart, but now, looking down at the small, perfect little baby boy in Amelia's arms, Edward knew he had been silly to worry. This was his child, his son, and he would love him with all his heart, just as he loved Amelia.

He watched as Amelia kissed their son on the tip of his tiny nose and then grimaced.

'It hurts,' she said, groaning again.

Quickly Edward took the baby from her as she clutched at the bedsheets and moaned in pain.

'It's just the afterbirth, Amelia,' Lizzie said, coming to her cousin's side.

'It hurts,' Amelia repeated, her face pale.

The midwife fussed around for a few minutes whilst Amelia grew increasingly agitated, placing her hands on Amelia's belly and then disappearing to the foot of the bed.

'I'm not quite sure,' the midwife said eventually, 'but I think there's another baby in there.'

Edward and Amelia froze and looked at each other, before another spasm of pain took all of Amelia's attention.

'We need the doctor,' the midwife said.

Immediately Lizzie left the room, returning a couple of minutes later.

'One of the servants will ride to fetch Dr Peacewell,' she said, coming back to her cousin's side.

'I can't wait,' Amelia groaned.

Edward saw all the tension and pain on her face as she focused on pushing. He wished he could take some of the agony and suffer it for her. She was so brave, his wonderful wife, and he vowed to cherish her every single day of their lives, just as long as she made it through the next little while. He couldn't bear the prospect of a future without her. Together they were strong, but as Edward looked down at the baby in his arms he knew no matter what he would survive for his son.

Thirty agonising minutes later a second cry filled the room and Edward watched as the midwife handed his wife their daughter.

'One of each,' she said, looking up at him, 'We were both right.'

Edward perched on the bed next to her, helping her hold both their children in her arms, and found himself wondering at how close he had come to giving up on life. If he had given in to his grief and his guilt then he would never be sitting here right now, holding the woman that he loved and his two children. Two years ago Edward would have dismissed this sort of happy family scenario, but now it was his reality.

He smiled as Amelia tried to push herself up in the bed, wriggling her backside and kicking off some of the bedsheets.

'For once in your life sit still, woman,' he said gruffly. 'You've just given birth twice.'

Amelia flashed him a tired but mischievous grin. 'You'll have three of us to run after now.'

'What have I let myself in for?' Edward murmured, bending forward and kissing Amelia gently on the forehead.

* * * * *

*If you enjoyed this story, you won't want
to miss these other great reads
from Laura Martin*

*THE PIRATE HUNTER
SECRETS BEHIND LOCKED DOORS
UNDER A DESERT MOON
AN EARL IN WANT OF A WIFE
GOVERNESS TO THE SHEIKH*